Murder in the Masterpiece

A Teacher's Deadly Lesson

Kathy Hendley, PhD

Savannah House
Covington, Kentucky

Visit Savannah House publishing at www.kathyhendleyphd.org
Visit Dr. Kathy Hendley at www.kathyhendley.com

Murder in the Masterpiece: A Teacher's Deadly Lesson
Book one in the Teacher's Lounge Series

Printed in the United States of America

ISBN 979-8-9921631-0-0

DEDICATION

To Daddio - Here is the book I promised you I would write.
I'm only sorry you won't get to read it.

One

Three teens rode through the streets like criminals escaping the scene of the crime. They had just entered the canopy of trees near the ravine when their phones chimed.

"I guess we gotta go," the girl shouted.

One of the boys held up his hand. "Did you guys hear that?"

"Hear what?"

A twig snapped followed by a deep growl.

"Yeah, I think it's coming from over there." He motioned to the trees.

They stood quietly and waited. Another deep growl. This time drawn out and louder.

"Guys, I think there's somebody over there."

Nobody moved.

Parents never allowed their children down to the ravine alone. Situated beyond the trees, the ravine served as a watershed for the homes, and provided the perfect place to hide. They had all watched the police investigate the area last year. The danger of it all made it a great place for the teens to ride.

"HEY! IS THERE SOMEBODY THERE?!" One of them shouted slowly as though his words would injure any would-be predator.

They heard groans from the bushes. The girl inched her way over. "Guys, call for help! There's a person over here!"

Both of the boys rushed over. They could tell that it was a man, but he had been badly beaten. Bruises and blood covered his face and arms.

"Are you ok, mister?"

"Gus." The man said through groans. He was attempting to get up, but he couldn't seem to move his legs.

"Do I know you?"

"It's me." The man struggled to catch his breath. "Don Ambrose," he managed just before he fell unconscious.

Parents and neighbors rushed to the scene. One of the dads pushed through the crowd. "I'm a doctor. Let me pass."

"It's Mr. Ambrose!" Gus announced. "I don't think he is awake right now."

"Don. Don! Can you hear me?" The doctor asked.

Don opened his eyes and tried to speak.

"We have an ambulance coming. Don't worry."

"F…Fa…" Don coughed. He rolled to his side and groaned loudly.

"Don't try to say anything right now. Save your energy."

"Faye!" He coughed again. "You have to find her."

"You can tell us about it later, Don. Don't worry. It's going to be ok."

Don reached out and grabbed the doctor, "she's in trouble."

***

Faye looked up from her coffee as the sun peeked through the city skyline. A warm breeze blew across her face, and she squinted at the shadows of buildings in front of her. For a moment she closed her eyes and allowed the sun to warm her. She inhaled the last few moments of summer on her balcony and refused to think about tomorrow. Faye set the cup on a table and grabbed her paintbrush. The black canvas welcomed strokes of yellows and pinks. She worked vigorously to shape the skyline before the sun reached its peak.

The heavens declare the glory of God; the skies proclaim the work of his hands. The verse echoed through her mind as the sun continued to rise above the buildings and illuminate the city below. Faye paused to watch the community of Arlington below. Lined with trees and shrubs, the town appeared to originate in the forest. From her balcony, Faye could see the tree tops and the outlines of children

3

zipping by on bicycles. The trees hid the swings and picnic tables of the small park. Beyond the trees, a ravine served as a watershed for the homes and a natural boundary for the school. Faye shifted her gaze from the school back to her painting. She added some purple and blue to create the perfect portrait of her favorite part of town.

Faye relished the remaining moments of summer on her balcony. The alarm on her phone startled her at first. She quickly packed up her paintbrushes and paints. *Better get going. Don always shows up early.*

Faye slid on her oversized sunglasses and scanned the street for shady characters, a habit she developed early in life. Main Street businesses bustled with people shopping and walking. Nothing unusual, so she left the security of her lobby and matched the pace of the crowd. At the corner, she stopped to check for traffic before crossing.

A shady character on the opposite side of the street caught her attention. *I don't remember seeing him around town. Why is he wearing long sleeves? It's gotta be a hundred degrees out here.* She rolled her eyes and kept walking.

Faye loved to stop at the flower stand. The fresh-cut flowers had the most beautiful aroma. *I need to stop by on my way home. These lilies are gorgeous.* From the mirrored reflection of her sunglasses, she noticed the shady character from before a little closer to her now.

She pretended to smell the flowers to see where he went. The tall stranger was an attractive guy even if he did have poor fashion sense.

He pulled out his phone. *Is he taking photos of me?* Faye smiled at the vendor and moved toward the coffee shop. *I need to lose this creep.* Faye checked her watch and picked up her pace. She waited until she needed cross the street to look back. Still there. *What is his deal?* Faye crossed the street to put distance between them.

He followed. She walked faster. He walked faster. *Don't panic. Slip into the jewelry store. You can lose him in there.*

The smell of incense made her dizzy. Not jewelry. CBD. *"Great! That's all I need."* Faye imagined the comments she would receive from concerned parents as they dropped off their children in the morning. She had already endured a year of parents questioning her fashion choices. Her refusal to walk around with embroidered sweaters or dangling apple earrings invited numerous conferences and meetings with her principal.

Faye looked out the window for the stranger. She tried to talk herself into feeling calm, "I'm sure it's just a coincidence. I'll be fine. I can make it to the coffee shop. It's two doors down."

"Are you Ok, miss?" The lady at the counter called out.

Was I speaking out loud? She swallowed before addressing the sales clerk. "Sure. I'm getting ready to meet someone down the street. I'm a little early, so I thought I'd shop."

"Is there something I can help you find?"

Pepper spray. "I don't think I've ever been in here before," Faye said, "What is the most popular thing you sell?"

The sales clerk proceeded to identify a series of oils. Faye allowed the clerk to describe it all in detail. *I'm sure that guy's long gone by now. Taking photos of me?* Faye shuddered at the thought of it. It didn't take long before she learned too much about CBD. She couldn't see that creep outside anymore, so she purchased a small vial with a lemon scent before she left.

Faye made it to the coffee shop without incident. She took off her sunglasses and scanned the room. Don usually arrived early, but she didn't see him at their table near the window. As she walked to her seat, she looked over her shoulder. No Don.

Six o'clock came and went, no Don. Faye grabbed a sandwich and gave him the benefit of the doubt. At 8:30, she stood to leave, but stopped suddenly when the door flew open.

Jodi burst into the coffee shop with arms stretched out. "Ahhhh! Hey, girl!" Faye forced a smile and gave her an awkward hug. Jodi continued, "I need a coffee. Do you want anything?"

"Um, sure. Just whatever you get."

When she returned, Jodi picked up where she left off. "That party last night was a-mazing! I had no idea so many eligible bachelors lived in Arlington."

"It's a great place to live." Faye had considered moving to Chicago to get away from her parents, but she loved Arlington. The charm of the town went beyond the nosy neighbors.

"Are you coming to the exhibit this weekend?" Jodi continued talking, but Faye focused her attention on the creepy stranger entering the coffee shop.

"Jeffrey could probably enter some of your pieces. Are you interested?"

"Yeah, sure. Whatever." Words exited Faye's mouth, but her her eyes watched the stranger advancing toward her.

Two

"Are you even listening to me?"

"Of course." Faye, spotted the exits behind the stranger.

"Then, it's settled. I'll let Jeffrey know that you're in."

"Wait. What?"

"I knew you weren't listening. There's an exhibit Friday night. Jeffrey can get your paintings on display. So, you're in, right?"

The stranger, only a few steps away, looked directly at Faye.

"He's here!" She gasped.

"Who? Jeffrey?" Jodi started to turn around, but Faye stopped her.

"Don't look." Faye said with closed lips and gritted teeth. "I don't want him to notice me."

"What's going on?" Jodi said in a whisper.

"That guy. He followed me here. I saw him outside my building, too."

"What? Are you sure?" Jodi slowly turned to get a good look at the stranger.

"Yes, I'm sure."

"What should we do?"

"Chloe!" The barista from behind the counter shouted.

Faye took a deep breath and braced herself. Jodi appeared completely unconcerned as the stranger walked toward them.

"CHLOE," the barista called again.

"That's me. Don't worry, Faye. I've got this." Jodi stood between Faye and the stranger.   She gave a smile and a wink to the stranger as she made her way to the barista. The man bypassed Faye and met Jodi at the counter.

Jodi grabbed her drinks and turned to the stranger. She slid close to him and whispered something as she passed. He looked at her and smiled. Then, he moved over to let her pass.

"Chloe?"

"Yeah. It's my fake name. I always have a fake name for public places. You never know." Jodi nodded in the direction of the stranger.

"What did you say to him?"

Jodi smiled, "A little something I learned in Chicago. Men love it, and it totally distracts them."

Faye grabbed the drink and held it up for a toast, "Well done." She took a sip of the coffee and noticed something that didn't quite taste like coffee.

"What is this?"

"Well, you said to get you whatever I got. I got a little something extra."

Faye held up a hand. "I don't want to know."

"Let's just say, it will help you calm down. You need a little something to get you over your heart attack." Jodi said with a giggle.

"You don't believe me, but I know he was following me!"

Jodi laughed even harder. "Don't worry. I'll walk you home."

The "little something" seemed to do the trick. Faye left the coffee shop unconcerned about strangers following her home. They had a great time loitering outside before walking to her building. Jodi said goodbye when she reached the lobby. Faye nodded to the doorman then surveyed the unusually crowded lobby.

"Fancy party on the mezzanine?" Faye walked up to the doorman.

"No. Why do you ask?"

"No reason." Faye looked in the direction of several men wearing fancy suits talking in hushed tones.

The doorman shrugged, and Faye didn't push it. She pictured Jodi laughing at her.

"Any messages for me?"

"Not tonight. Were you expecting someone? Maybe your new friend?" The doorman added a little grin for effect. He never missed a beat. He knew everything that went on in that building.

"Not tonight." Faye smiled as she made her way to the elevator. *She might call Jeffrey.* The thought quickly left her mind when she noticed the stranger enter her lobby. She gasped as the elevator doors closed.

***

The early morning did not find Faye bright or wide-eyed. After seeing the stranger enter her lobby, Faye locked herself in her apartment and prayed. No one had followed, but Faye stayed awake most of the night, aware of the possibility. However, she needed to be awake this morning. The school board reorganized the whole district for some new education model. Administrators rearranged classrooms and shuffled teachers across the district into different schools. Faye knew to report to Arlington Community, but didn't know who else might be there.

Don could have told me something. Where was he last night?

Upon her arrival at the school, Faye zipped past the front office toward the Media Center. The modern library, served as the information hub for everything in the school, especially gossip. A small office inside housed the copy machine and an earful of the latest "tea." Faye walked in on Richard and Susan, mid-conversation.

"Well, they don't know who it was." Susan said over the sound of the copier.

"Then, how do you know it even happened?" Richard replied while arranging the copies.

Neither of them noticed Faye enter the room. Donna and Jesse sat with coffee and donuts listening to the exchange.

"What's going on?" Faye whispered.

"Get some coffee, first. You look like you need it." Donna answered.

"I live next door to the Browns. I watched that woman run out of the house like it was on fire." Susan looked up at Richard for emphasis.

"Did you go down there to see for yourself?" Richard added his own emphasis on the word 'go.'

"Everybody did. Which means, nobody saw nothin', but I'm telling you. I know it's him." Susan continued her copies as she spoke.

"They found somebody last night in the ravine." Jesse whispered to Faye.

"Really? Anyone we know?" Faye attempted to ask quietly.

Susan turned to Faye, "It was Don Ambrose." Then, she focused on Richard, "I'm sure of it."

Faye's eyes grew wide as her mouth fell open.

"She doesn't know for sure." Richard said to the three of them shaking his head back and forth. Then, he turned to Susan, "You gotta stop telling people this is the truth until we know for sure."

Outside the small office, tables began to fill with other teachers and school personnel.

"They're about to get started," Richard said. "We need to get out there."

Faye added more coffee to her mug before heading out with the others.

The Principal entered accompanied by a man in a cheap suit and a police officer. Then, he stepped forward to get everyone's attention. "Good morning, everyone."

People sat around tables and whispered greetings to one another.

The principal raised his hand to get their attention. "I hope you all had a good summer. Before we get into our training, I want to introduce a special guest."

The room grew quiet and still.

"This is Detective George. He has a few things to tell you before we get on with our day."

"Good morning everyone," the Detective started. "Yesterday evening, one of your fellow faculty members was assaulted in

Arlington Park." A hush fell on the crowd as they waited to hear more. "Don Ambrose is currently recovering at the hospital."

The room exploded with gasps and murmurs.

"I told you." Susan whisper-yelled at Richard.

"Quiet, please." The detective raised his hand to say more. "I will be here this morning to talk with you and answer any questions."

"That's right," the Principal added. "They will be using my office. We'll call you to the office if they need you. There is no need to bombard the detectives right now. I promise that we will get information to you as we know it."

The room rumbled with noise of speculations.

***

Faye familiarized herself to the principal's office years ago. As a student, she practically lived there. A familiar feeling of trouble came over her. *I'm not in trouble. I didn't do anything wrong.* She told herself as she took her seat opposite the detective.

"State your name." The detective said motioning to the cell phone on the desk.

"What will you do with the recording?" Faye asked.

"Someone will type it up later. It's faster to record the interviews and listen back than to try to take notes in the middle."

Faye stared ahead blankly. Years ago, she'd learned how to calm herself as the principal asked questions.

"Let's begin," the detective reset his phone recording, "state your full name, please."

"Faye Unger."

"Ms. Unger, how did you know Don Ambrose?"

"Did? Is he dead?" Her voice cracked.

"Sorry m'am. He's alive. Let me try that again. How do you know Don Ambrose?"

"We're colleagues. He's my mentor."

"Your mentor?"

"Yes. The school district assigns mentors for all of the new teachers. This is my second year."

"I see. Do you know anyone that might want to hurt him?"

"No. Everyone liked Don. He is friendly and kind."

The rest of the detective's questions blurred as Faye pictured Don laying in the ravine. She considered him a veteran teacher, but he wasn't much older than herself. *Was it theft? Why would he be walking in the ravine? Nobody goes down there except a random homeless camp or teenagers looking to hide.*

"Thank you, Miss. That'll be all." The detective had to repeat himself.

"Sure." Faye said as she stood to leave.

She opened the door to the office only to come face to face with the stranger from last night. Her stomach dropped as she stood frozen in the doorway.

"Hi there. Brandon Foster. I don't think we've met." He held his hand out for Faye, as she stood there, staring at him. "I'm a new Math teacher here."

Three

A police officer stood outside the hospital door marking the room where Don Ambrose recovered from his injuries. Brandon approached the officer and whispered something. The officer nodded and made a phone call while Brandon entered the room.

"So, what's the word?" Brandon asked offering Don a fresh cup of coffee.

Don, already sitting up, wrote feverishly on a notepad. "Did you bring my laptop?"

Brandon patted the bag slung over his shoulder. "What have you got there?"

"Just some notes. Trying to write down details before I forget."

"Did you see the attacker?"

"No. Came out of nowhere." Don shook his head. "I should've seen 'em coming."

"They? More than one?" Brandon took a sip of coffee.

"Had to be. Maybe from two different directions."

Brandon placed the other cup on the bedside table, "Do you think she had something to do with it?"

"She's definitely involved, but I don't know how much she knows."

Brandon nodded and pulled the laptop out of the bag.

"Did you have eyes on her?" Don grabbed the coffee and took a sip.

"As soon as I got your message." Brandon walked over to the window and opened the blinds. "I know she wasn't near the park."

"Did you make contact?"

"I started to approach her at the coffee shop, but she wasn't alone."

"Oh?"

"Don't worry. I'm a new teacher at Arlington Community School." Brandon said with a little bow.

"Nice!" Don smiled.

"Yeah, I came over during the morning break."

"This morning? The orientation! I gotta get out of here. Do they all know?"

Brandon chuckled and nodded. "You couldn't drop a pen in that place without everyone knowing. I don't know how you survived all this time. They have officers in the building." Don started to get up, but Brandon put out his hand to stop him. "Don't worry. I made sure that I was one of the first few interviewed."

"And?"

"They have moved their investigation elsewhere."

Don sat back relieved.

"The uniform outside the door is a bit much. Don't you think? You might attract more attention than necessary."

"It's the parents," Don shook his head, "Their kids found me. The neighborhood's up in arms. They insisted that I have police protection. It's more for show than protection." He groaned as he adjusted himself in the bed. "No. This will not happen again. I can assure you."

"Either way, we're close. You must have stumbled onto something."

"That I did. Stay close to Faye." Don leaned forward and whispered, "She is good. She talks like she has no idea what's going on, but trust me. She is the key to unlocking this whole operation."

Four

Faye accepted Donna and J.J.'s offer for a ride over to the hospital. She wanted to see Don for herself but hated to drive. The drive seemed to take longer than it should have. Faye's mind scrolled through millions of scenarios, and the silence only made it worse.

"I wish I knew what happened," Donna said, as they exited the SUV.

A volunteer met them in the lobby. "He's on the third floor."

"Thank you, Ms. Brown." Donna stopped to talk with the volunteer. "Have you been up to see him yet?"

Of course, Donna knows the hospital volunteers. Faye smiled at the volunteer and followed J.J. to the elevator. Donna joined them inside the elevator.

When the door closed, J.J. asked, "Were you able to get information from the detective, Faye? I went to the office, but he left before I got there. "

The elevator stopped.

"Um…". Faye couldn't recall anything the detective had said to her.

The doors opened, and Faye's stomach dropped. Brandon Foster stood waiting for the elevator. The feeling of dread washed over Faye. Her stomach may have been in knots, but her face didn't show it. She inched by him, pretending not to remember him.

"Ms. Unger, is it?" Brandon said to her as she passed.

"I'm sorry. Do I know you?" Faye attempted to be aloof.

"Brandon Foster. We met this morning in the office." He looked around at the other teachers. "I'm the new math teacher."

"Why hello," J.J. reached out to shake his hand. "We missed you in the department meeting today."

"Have you been to see Don Ambrose?" Donna asked.

"Yes, I was just there."

"How do you know Don?" Faye asked.

"I'm sorry, but I've really got to get going." Brandon didn't answer their questions. "See you tomorrow." He waved behind him as he walked toward the exit.

The three of them made their way to Don's room. A cold chill ran up Faye's spine when she noticed the officer outside of Don's room. He scanned them with a metal detector before allowing them to enter. Don greeted them from a chair opposite the bed. Aside from a few bruises and cuts, he appeared unharmed.

"You look good, considering," J.J. said as they entered.

"I've been better. That's for sure." Don responded with a smile.

Faye smiled and gave a small wave. Visiting people in hospital rooms always made her uncomfortable.

"Faye. I'm sorry about the coffee shop last night." Don said.

"It's no problem, really. I'm just glad you are ok." Faye bit her lip nervously. "What happened?"

"He probably doesn't want to talk about it." Donna said through clenched jaws.

"No, it's fine, really. I was taking a walk. Well, on my way to meet up with Faye," Don gestured toward Faye. "Some guys came out of nowhere and knocked me out. They said I landed in a ravine, but I don't remember that part."

"They must have hit you pretty hard," Donna said.

"I didn't even see it coming."

"I thought I saw someone following me last night, too." Faye said in a joking-but-not-joking kind of way. "Turns out it was nothing." She chuckled. "I guess I was a little paranoid."

The others joined her in nervous laughter, except for Don. He looked at her seriously, "You should be careful. The city can be a dangerous place for a single woman." Then, he added, "Look what can happen," and pointed to his bruises.

They stayed for a little while catching up on the summer vacation stories and the day's training at the school. Don mentioned that he would go home that afternoon. The others tried to get him to take another day off, but he insisted he would attend tomorrow. They started to leave, but he asked to speak with Faye.

"Give me a minute. I'll catch up with you guys," Faye waved them off.

"How are you? Is everything ok?" Don asked her.

"Yeah, sure."

"Are you still seeing that guy from the art guild?"

"Jeffrey?"

Don nodded.

"Yeah, he's from the art collective. I've seen him a few times over the summer."

"Be careful."

"You worry too much, Don. Seriously, you're a brother I never had." Faye chuckled to make light of the situation.

"Are you painting or just hanging out?" Don pressed her for more information.

"I painted a few things. Jeffrey says that I show promise." Faye said with a smile. "He wants to put a couple of my pieces in the exhibit this weekend," she added to make her point.

"I'd like to see them."

Faye let out a giggle. "Focus on getting better. Maybe, I'll have a party in a few weeks. Give you some time to heal," she said with a wink. Then she gave him a hug and headed out the door.

Five

The next morning, Faye's legs carried her to her classroom, while her mind scrolled through thoughts of Don's return and Brandon following her. Faye bypassed the main office and the media center. She veered right toward the eighth grade hallway and moved along at a fast clip toward her organized, happy place. She breezed past the sign posted above the hallway that read "Science." Faye turned left toward what used to be her tranquil, symmetrical classroom. Instead, she ran into a woman rearranging science tables.

"Oh!" Faye stood in the doorway, shocked.

"Oh my!" A woman jumped at the sound of Faye's voice. "Bless your heart! I'm Gina Mazzi. New Science teacher."

"But. Isn't this the…"

Donna walked up and interrupted the confusion. "Faye! You're here."

"Donna, what's going on?"

"This is the Science Wing, now," Donna said rolling her eyes. "You need to find the Math wing. They split us all up this year."

"That's right," the memory of yesterday's department meeting came to Faye's mind, "I'm sorry. I guess, I'm distracted this morning."

"Seriously, though, are you ok? You seemed a little distracted yesterday at the hospital."

"I'm not good around hospitals, and seeing Don like that…" Faye shook her head. "I'll be ok. This is a lot," Faye pointed to the signs in the hallways, "but I'll get used to it." She turned to Gina, "Sorry."

Faye located the Math wing only to find a disorganized mess of desks and computers all in one room.

"Don't freak out," J.J. said. "This will be better for collaboration."

"What?"

"They combined these two rooms for our math office. They said that they want to improve collaboration."

Faye spied her old desk in a corner. Chairs and filing cabinets blocked her path toward it.

"Let me introduce you to one of our new teachers," J.J. walked over to a man in a suit.

The stood to introduce himself, "John Mazzi,." Mazzi towered over J.J. and Faye for that matter. His broad frame carried an expensive jacket. Faye recognized the style as the kind her father wore.

Faye shook his hand, "Do I know you?"

"I don't think so."

The tinge in his voice held a familiar accent. *He has to be a friend of my father's.* "Are you sure? Maybe you know my parents, Jack and Judy Unger?"

"Sorry," Mazzi shrugged.

Alright, Jack, who did you send to spy on me this time? Faye forced a smile and made an excuse to exit the room.

She searched for a classroom, and found an empty one filled with a mess of desks and posters. Faye closed the door behind her and took her time arranging the desks in symmetrical rows. Then, she shuffled through the posters until she found one with examples of algebraic properties. Faye took a deep breath and exhaled slowly. She always enjoyed the order and structure of Math. Solutions presented themselves in time, step by step.

Faye tried to view the events over the last few days as math problems, puzzles to be solved. The puzzle of Don's attack occurred at the same time as her being followed by the stranger. *Coincidence?* The stranger, she now knew as Brandon Foster, held his own set of equations. He could just be one of the new teachers in the new school model. *He could be connected to Don's attack.* Gina and John

Mazzi also came as new, oddly familiar, teachers. *Did my parents send them as spies? Are they connected to Don or Brandon?*

Instead of trying to figure it all out, Faye decided to let it go. Usually, these things sorted themselves out. Faye survived the ordeal last night. As though God sent her, Jodi had appeared at the right moment. God would provide another way out, a solution for the chaos of the school change, Don's attack, and her stalker. She left the unobstructed classroom, and headed toward the the math office.

Inside the office, J.J. and Mazzi had sorted the desks and filing cabinets. Faye searched the room for her desk from last year. She found Brandon Foster sitting at it. All of her belongings had been placed into a box in the corner of the room. He stood and smiled at her.

Faye took a deep breath and unloaded her frustration. "Why are you following me?"

"What?"

"I know it was you outside my building yesterday. You followed me to the coffee shop. Then, you were at the principal's office and the hospital. I want to know why."

Brandon didn't say anything. Faye waited for a response. The two of them engaged one another in an epic staring match. Neither of them spoke until Don walked through the door.

"What's going on here?" Don asked, breaking their concentration.

"Good morning, Don, Faye seems to think that I am following her."

"You are," Faye responded without taking her eyes off of Brandon.

"She is beautiful. I can see why you might like to go after her," Don smiled at Faye as he spoke.

"I'm not following you. I just happen to live in the neighborhood," Brandon defended himself.

"And teach in my school, and know my friends, and sit at my desk!" Faye fumed.

"You have good taste in friends and employment and desks," Brandon looked over at Don helplessly.

"Stop it. I don't want you to follow me any more. I'm tired of running into you. Every. Where. I. go. If you are so attracted to me, you can ask me out," Faye looked at Don and winked.

"Would you like to go out some time?"

"What?! No. And this is my desk," Faye picked up the box of her belongings and placed them on the desk. She grabbed an empty box and handed it to him. "As the newest member of our team, you take the new desk, right J.J.?"

J.J. stepped into the room and looked around, "Yes, of course. Looks like everyone's getting settled in. Faye, would you mind showing Brandon around on the computer systems?"

Brandon smiled and laughed while Faye expelled a long sigh.

"Can you catch me up, too?" Don asked.

Faye looked over at him with a grin, "of course."

***

On her drive home, Faye attempted to empty her mind of the day's frustrations. She enjoyed teaching, but the paperwork and record keeping brought unwelcome stress. She looked forward to pulling out the paintbrush and canvas. Painting always helped her relieve stress in the past. Faye took a deep breath and tried to envision the next scene for her canvas.

The image of a man lying in the ravine came to her mind. She gasped at the gruesome image. Behind her, a horn sounded launching her back to reality. She pulled into the garage to avoid the lobby. Ready to put the day behind her, Faye made her way to the elevator in the garage. She noticed someone approaching and prepared herself to confront Brandon. *Is he still following me?*

"It's Faye, right?"

The voice startled her.

"John Mazzi. Math teacher at school. We met earlier."

"Oh, yeah. Do you live here?"

"My wife has a friend in the building. Do you live here?"

Faye gave a polite smile. *He is her father's spy after all.*

Mazzi had a friend join him. They mumbled some sort of greeting, and Mazzi took off. His friend, however, joined Faye in the elevator. He looked at her and raised his chin in greeting.

"Are you a friend of John's?" She asked.

"Johnny and I go back a ways." His gruff voice held the same, familiar accent.

"Where are you headed?" Faye looked at the buttons and waited for his answer before she pressed her floor.

"Five."

She pressed the five for his floor and then pressed the eight. Faye lived on the 12th floor, but she didn't want him to know that. She might have trusted Mazzi, but this guy looked like he walked out of the Godfather.

"You teach?" He asked.

Faye nodded, "You?"

"Nah. Exports."

Six

Don waited for Brandon to get into the vehicle before he spoke, "It's important that Faye learn to trust you."

"You told me to follow her."

"Watching her is not the same as creeping up on her."

"She's easily spooked, alright?"

"Did she see you at the hospital?"

"Yeah," Brandon looked out the window and back at Don, "but I didn't say anything about you. As far as she knows, we just met."

Don started driving as he spoke."I have reliable information that puts Elaine Andrews in Arlington."

"Andrews? I thought they were based out of Chicago. What are they doing here?"

"We know they ran Arlington for years before going to Chicago."

"How does that involve us?" Brandon asked as the car pulled into the lot. "I'm not sure we want to get involved in that kind of operation anyway."

Don reached into his jacket and pulled out a newspaper article. He unfolded it and handed it to Brandon. The headline read: *The Auction House Opens in Arlington.* Brandon opened the paper to read the article.

> Chicago-based company brings Arlington into the next century. The Auction House formally opened its doors in Arlington today after years of searching for their newest market. "Arlington has a beautiful Main Street with dozens of small businesses," Auction House spokesperson, Jodi Daschle told *The Post*, "we are delighted to add another dimension to this up-and-coming town."
> The Auction House has been a staple to Chicago art lovers for over a decade. They offer unique, hand-crafted furniture and unique works of art. Their selection of art comes from countries all over the world., but we take particular interest in local artists. "We are excited about bringing in a new element of folk art to the auction," Ms. Daschle adds, "local artisans will soon have a voice."

"I'm not sure what to think about this Auction House," Brandon summarized, "it looks like a good thing."

"It opens the doors for all kinds of goods," Don said, "imports and exports with minimal oversight. If Elaine Andrews is involved, it means trouble."

Seven

The keys shook with Faye's hand as she attempted to unlock her apartment. Something about the man in the elevator triggered an earthquake of emotion in her mind. Memories resurfaced like a violent volcano. Some came into her throat along with the contents of her stomach. Faye stumbled to the bathroom. The eruption did not end there. Droplets of sweat framed her forehead as her cold, sweaty hands attempted to wash her face.

Deep breaths. You can do this. You are safe. Breathe.

The phone chimed and she jumped. *Breathe.* Her hands shook as she stooped to sit on the edge of the tub. Jeffrey. A sigh of relief. He wanted to come over and hang out. Faye felt like collapsing into a puddle. She was in no condition to entertain, especially Jeffrey.

Jeffrey embodied charm and sophistication. Faye became an art lover and critic with Jeffrey. He didn't know anything about her past. He didn't really know her at all. Faye went out with him to spite her parents and gain access to the art community. She needed to remain cautious while spending time with him, so she could remain in control.

Her phone chimed again. Faye's hands shook as she looked at her phone. It was her mom.

"Hey, Sweetie. Can you talk?"

Tears began to fill in her eyes. *I can't do this right now.* Faye typed a response, "Not now."

Mom replied, "Ok. I heard about Don. Are you ok?"

Faye responded, "I'm fine."

She wasn't fine. It took a few minutes for Faye to get herself together enough to walk out of the bathroom. Faye made her way to the kitchen, but stopped at the stereo on her way. Instrumental music and fresh coffee set the tone for the painting and healing. The coffee might keep her up, but it also forced her to slow down at every sip.

"God, help me sort this out."

She reached for her phone and typed a message to Jeffrey, "Busy day, today. Can we meet up tomorrow instead?"

Faye turned off the notifications on her phone and placed it on the table. *I wish I could turn off the whole world.* Instead, she opted for hot coffee and painting.

Memories from the day swept over Faye like a tidal wave. Unlike the eruption earlier, these emotions rolled off of her. All at once, she felt pain over Don's attack and not being there for him. The image of someone in the ravine flooded her mind, and tears began to flow. She picked up the paint brush and covered the canvas with thick layers of paint. Colors mixed and collided. The brush continued its work until the image of the person in the ravine faded into the recesses of her mind.

A chill came over her, along with intense terror at the memories of being followed in the city. The brush dipped into icy whites and blues. Every startling encounter with Brandon held its own stroke. Faye added purples and blacks, mixing them on the palette with touches of white. She placed brush to canvas and unleashed every fear from the last two days.

Deep groans came from within her as she recalled her friend sitting in the hospital. She didn't know where the emotions came from, but they flowed onto the canvas in brilliant displays. Each stroke of the brush released a weight, and each dip into the paint brought healing. It was a deeply, spiritual exchange that she would never be able to explain with anything other than the painting in front of her.

"Thank you," Faye whispered as she sat in peace.

Eight

The teacher training dragged on and on as Faye looked forward to the evening. Her mind scanned her closet for cocktail dresses. She wanted to impress Jeffrey and Jodi at dinner. Jeffrey personified the romance of Chicago, and Faye fell for it, hard.

Jeffrey arrived shortly after Faye completed her finishing touches.

"Jodi told me that some guy was following you. Are you ok?"

"Yeah, I'm fine," Faye smiled and gave him a peck on the cheek as he walked through the door, "I think it was just a coincidence or something. I guess he moved to the neighborhood to work at the school."

"Well, then, I don't blame him. I would probably follow you, too," he passed her a flirty grin.

Faye didn't need to tell him that Jodi was coming. She walked in as if she owned the place. Someone else walked in behind her.

"I hope you don't mind, Faye. I brought a friend."

Brandon.

"Of course you did." Faye gave Brandon a half smile and whispered under her breath, "How did this happen?"

Jodi smiled sheepishly, "I gave him my number at the coffee shop. What can I say? I'm a sucker for the tall handsome type."

Faye rolled her eyes and whispered, "more like tall, creepy type."

"Look at that view!" Brandon said in surprise.

"It's great, isn't it? Faye has the best apartment for parties," Jodi sidled up to Brandon and leaned into him.

Jeffrey busied himself in the kitchen preparing drinks for everyone. He handed one to Faye, "I guess this is the new teacher?"

Faye nodded.

"It's breathtaking. I'm surprised you can afford it on a teacher's salary."

"I'm Jeffrey, and you are?" Jeffrey held out his hand.

"Brandon Foster, nice to meet you." Brandon gave a hearty handshake.

Faye smiled to herself. Brandon and Jeffrey couldn't be more different. Jeffrey, full of grace and dignity, could not allow Brandon's rude comment. He stepped into the space to redeem the social graces of the evening.

"So, Brandon, are you from around here?" Jeffrey handed him a glass a wine.

"I'm new to the neighborhood. Moved in from up north."

"Really?" Jodi eyed him. "Me too."

"How long have you been a teacher?" Faye asked.

"I'm new to that too."

"Ooooh," Jodi snuggled up to him. "what did you do before?"

"I was on active duty in the army."

"Did you do anything dangerous?" Jodi swooned.

"I'd rather not talk about it."

"Let's eat while the pasta's still hot," Faye passed around bowls of pasta and bread. She looked forward to changing the subject.

"How did you all meet?" Brandon stuffed his face with bread.

"We stumbled into one another at a cocktail party in Chicago," Jeffrey smiled at Faye.

Faye could feel Brandon's gaze, "I have family in Chicago."

"Really?" Brandon leaned in to hear her details.

"They invite me up every summer. This year, I took them up on it. I found a course on Art and Math at the Institute," Faye looked at Jeffrey, "and I'm so glad I did."

"And how did you meet Jodi?" Brandon looked at Faye but leaned toward Jodi.

"Jeffrey and I work together. I met Faye a few years back," Jodi snuggled into Brandon.

"Faye's family supports a lot of charitable organizations," Jeffrey spoke up, "I'm surprised we didn't meet sooner."

Faye attempted a smile, but the awkward evening seemed to drag on and on. *What is the deal with Brandon? Why so many questions?* The memory of him snapping photos of her kept popping up.

Jeffrey held up his glass for a toast, "Tonight, we celebrate."

"What are we celebrating?" Faye looked confused.

"Faye's first art exhibit."

They all joined Jeffrey in the toast. He gave a small speech with a lot of adjectives that made little sense to Faye. Then, Brandon started in on her again.

"Art? I didn't know you were an artist, Faye?"

Faye nodded she dabbed her mouth with a napkin. She made every effort not to roll her eyes.

"Well, can I see your work?"

Faye stood and moved toward the living room. "I hung them on the walls. This one might still be wet."

"Gasp!" Jodi's dramatic reaction stirred the attention in the room, "Breathtaking, Faye. Simply breathtaking!"

Brandon walked over to view the painting Jodi fawned over.

"My favorite is the cityscape," Jeffrey smiled at Faye and winked. "Don't be shy, Brandon, tell us your thoughts. It will help us prepare for the exhibit."

"It's nice."

Faye looked at Brandon, "You sound surprised."

"How long have been an artist? If you don't mind me asking."

"I've always enjoyed art. When I was young. my parents took me to classes in the city," Faye paused for a moment, "It feels like coming home."

"Well spoken, my dear," Jeffrey beamed.

"You have a lot of talent here. I guess I just expected them to be more symmetrical, mathematical…" Brandon motioned toward the paintings.

"This one has squares and shapes in it," Jodi brushed past Brandon to get his attention.

"… but it's whimsical," Brandon finished his statement without taking his gaze from Faye.

"What can I say? I'm unpredictable."

Nine

Don pulled stacks of file folders out of the hall closet. He set them on the dining table next to the Chinese take-out.

"So, what did you learn about Chloe?"

"Well, her name's not Chloe," Brandon opened a package of soy sauce and dumped it into a container of fried rice, "at least, that's not what Faye and Jeffrey call her."

Don smiled. "What's her name?"

"She goes by Jodi."

"What about the boyfriend? I've been curious about him for a while. Faye doesn't say much," Don shoved an egg roll into his mouth.

"He's charming and attractive. I expected them to be all over each other, but she keeps her distance. Unlike her friend, Jodi."

"Do you think Jodi knows anything?"

Brandon shook his head, "She's flirty and attractive, but also pretty shallow. I doubt she knows anything."

"Did the boyfriend say anything about his job? People always talk about work."

"No," Brandon grabbed a napkin and an egg roll, "they both work at the Auction House, but he kept talking about Faye, really stroking her ego."

"Jodi works at the Auction House? Is she the woman from the article?"

Brandon raised his eyebrows, "Yes, she is."

"Did you see her paintings? Are they any good?"

Brandon nodded, "Oh yeah. Maybe, it's the colors that she uses or the type of paint. I don't know, but I couldn't stop looking at them."

"I need to go see them."

"Go to the exhibit?" Brandon nearly choked.

"Maybe. I don't want to blow my cover, but I would like to see her work. Compare them to the others we found."

"Speaking of the others, do you have anything for me?"

Don handed him a file. "I took these two days before Julie's attack."

Brandon pulled out photos and began to sort them, "These guys look rough. Do any of them look familiar to you?" He handed Don several photos that contained three men in expensive suits smoking cigars.

"No. I don't recognize them, but I do recognize that building behind them."

Brandon looked closer. "That's Faye's building! Is this why you think she is connected?"

Don shrugged, "Check this out."

He handed Brandon a photo of a young woman standing next to a limousine talking with an older couple.

"These are Faye's parents. And she…" Don pointed to the young woman, "is a member of the Andrews family."

Brandon nodded, "Now, it's starting to make sense." Brandon paused and cleared his throat. "Don, there's something I need to tell you."

Don continued thumbing through the photos.

"You're being reassigned."

"What?" Don looked up at him,

"They sent me to bring you out."

"No. I'm getting close. I know it!" Don stood up and walked across the room. "It's because of what happened to Julie, isn't it."

Brandon nodded.

When he closed his eyes, Don heard the gun going off. A chill ran up his spine as the memory played. *Why didn't I wake up sooner? I should have moved faster.*

"I know there's something bigger here, Brandon. They knew her. The man came to take her out. I want to know why," Don paused, eyebrows creased in concern.

"Don, you need to step back. Let someone else take it from here."

"But we're so close. We uncovered the Schmidts' involvement last year. Julie found something."

"Whatever it was, it got her killed, Don. She was your wife. You guys were great together. Take some time off."

"It's been a year, Brandon. I mourned."

"Don, I'm here to help you transition out. They want you to take a leave."

"What? I'm fine."

"You kept going full strength, even after the funeral."

"Working helped me through it."

The days following the funeral had been rough. He had wanted to stay in bed. Not be awake without her. He didn't sleep either. Work kept him going. Gave him purpose. He had a reason to get up. *Am I distracted? Is that how they got me?*

"No. Thanks for the offer, Brandon, but I need to keep going."

"I don't think you have a choice in this. Look, Don, you've got a reason, now. No one will blame you for taking a leave after the attack."

"I know, but I'm good. They didn't take me out." Don took a deep breath before he continued, "I can't stop now. Last year, it was Julie. What if Faye's next? I can't let them take out anyone else."

"The Schmidts are out of the picture. You got Diane last year, and they arrested her husband for Julie's attack."

That was low, even for Brandon. They had been friends as long as Don could remember, and they both knew that Robert Schmidt had nothing to do with Julie's murder. *Something else must be at play here.* Don paced the room while he mulled it over.

"The Bureau hasn't sent me any message about taking time off." Don stopped pacing and stared at Brandon. "You came the day of the attack. Was it you?"

"What? No!" Brandon stood up to face him, "Don, what do you take me for? I'm not going to leave you to die in a ravine!"

"Someone did. Was it Jacobs? Scott?" Don stood over Brandon.

"No. None of us. Calm down."

"Is there someone in the Bureau that wants me out of the picture? Who sent you?"

"Rogers gave me the ok to come."

"Did he confirm with you that I was off the case?"

"He didn't say anything about that. He offered the evidence from the shooting, though."

Don backed off and sat down shaking his head. The room grew quiet. Don had been in the Bureau long enough to know how orders were given. If they wanted him off the case, Rogers would have told him. He came to the funeral. He even stayed with Don the week after to collect evidence and make the arrests.

"Brandon, where do you stand on this? Do you think the order was legit?"

"I'm not so sure, anymore," Brandon's voice trailed off. He leaned forward and put his face in his hands. He mumbled something, then he sat up. "I can't believe it. I can't believe that I was so stupid!"

"What?"

"That order can't be legit, Don. They played me. Rogers didn't know what I was talking about in coming here. I surprised him when I showed up. I don't even know why he agreed to let me come."

"It's ok," Don said reassuringly. "At least Rogers is aware that we are here. We can fill him in later. He may have additional information we need."

"That's probably why he gave me the evidence from the shooting."

"Yeah. I'm sure there's something there. We'll have to look at that later. In the meantime, don't trust anyone, Brandon. We need to keep up our cover. Are you any good at Math?"

"They have me teaching remedial classes. I should be fine."

"It's not as easy as you think."

Ten

Faye met Jeffrey and Jodi in the lobby of her building to ride to the art exhibit. The exhibits she'd gone to over the summer paled in comparison to this. This exhibit featured her work. Faye tried to distance herself from possible criticism. *Art is subjective, someone will like it. Just smile and look pretty. Or maybe, slightly frown to look thoughtful.*

"You look amazing!" Jodi shouted when Faye stepped out of the elevator.

Faye's evening attire came straight out of her mom's handbook. Her parents attended a lot of fancy dinner parties. She secretly played dress up in her mother's closet all the time. Faye enjoyed the jeweled necklaces and sequin dresses.

Today, Faye wore a ruby necklace to compliment her black, satin dress. The exquisite, gown had ruching on the left side to an asymmetrical hem. The neck line scooped in the front and dipped lower in the back. Faye accessorized with stiletto heels, ruby earrings, and red, satin gloves that came to her elbow. She had borrowed her mom's derby hat, a black and red, feathery fascinator. The bold move seemed to complete the look.

"I bought it yesterday. You like it?" Faye directed the question more to Jeffrey than Jodi, but that didn't stop Jodi from answering.

"I love it!" Jodi answered.

"It's perfect." Jeffrey said as he walked closer.

Jodi stopped him before he got too close. "That's enough, you two. We need to go. Our car is here."

The Auction House hosted tonight's event, which meant they got to ride in a limousine. Faye climbed into the back of the luxurious vehicle. Jodi poured them all a glass of champagne. Faye didn't care for champagne, so she held the glass and pretended to sip. Memories of her parents trotting off for evenings out returned and she smiled.

This event held the highest status for The Auction House as it provided benefactors an opportunity to meet the artists in person. Both groups aimed to impress the other. Faye's ensemble, while not the typical teacher appliqué, suited the event perfectly. The artists displayed their art through their attire. Some artists complimented their art in ways that made it difficult to separate artist from painting. Others appeared as though they had walked through a painting before arrival.

Faye had given the paintings to Jeffrey for preparation before the event. She and Jodi grabbed a couple of hors d'oeuvres on their way to view his handy-work. Jeffrey transformed her paintings from a simple canvas using exquisite frames and auspicious lighting. They looked completely different.

"Jeffrey, you have outdone yourself."

He smiled at the compliment. "Every work of art deserves careful consideration,"

"I knew you said you were good at framing, but this…" Faye stepped back to admire it. "This looks…"

"Captivating." A voice from behind interrupted her.

Faye turned.

"Ms. Andrews." Jeffrey spoke the name with an element of surprise. "Faye, this is Elaine Andrews."

The name sounded familiar to Faye, but she couldn't remember how.

"This is your work?" Elaine spoke softly in hushed tones as though the noise would spoil the art and ruin the moment.

"Yes, it is." Faye copied the refined, elegant manner that Elaine projected. Something about Elaine exuded importance and mystery. Faye didn't want to say anything that would expose her own insecurities.

"Divine." Elaine spoke the word and left.

The three of them just stood there.

"Who is Elaine Andrews?" Faye whispered.

Jodi looked at her with wide eyes. She glanced around the room before she mouthed, "I'll tell you later."

Jodi and Faye wandered off to mingle while Jeffrey networked with benefactors.

"So, you didn't invite Brandon tonight?" Faye asked sarcastically.

Jodi gave her the side eye. "He asks a lot of questions. Talks too much. He didn't even make a move on me last night."

"Sorry?" Faye spotted a waiter, and placed her empty plate on his tray before picking up a glass of something bubbly, "Didn't you just meet him?"

Jodi shrugged, "Yeah, well…"

"He said he was in the military. Maybe, he's being respectful of you." *Wait. This is Brandon you're talking about.* "Or maybe, he's just some creep you met at a coffee shop."

"We'll see if he calls."

"You'd give him another try?"

"Well, it's like you said. I did just meet him," Jodi shrugged.

They grabbed more appetizers from the waiter. Faye scanned the room for Jeffrey or Elaine. She didn't see either of them anywhere. She did see a familiar tall figure along the wall.

"Brandon?"

"What? Where?" Jodi flipped her hair to look.

"Along the wall. I'm probably wrong. Remember, my little heart attack?"

"No, you're right. I'm gonna go talk to him." Jodi handed her glass to Faye and glided across the room.

Faye passed Jodi's drink to a waiter and made her way the opposite direction. She wondered over to an exhibit to listen to the artist describe his motivation.

"I can only paint what I feel. The canvas chooses the colors and so on and so forth."

"Sometimes, these guys just don't make any sense at all," Jeffrey whispered in her ear.

Faye smiled.

"I think someone is interested in your painting."

"Mine?"

"Come on, let's talk to them."

"What do I say?"

"Just answer their questions," he glanced at the abstract artist, "The words will come to you when you need them."

Faye moved in the direction of the artwork. Insecurity crept into her mind as she walked across the room. The flaws highlighted before her eyes. Objects appeared wobbled and abstract. The cityscape tilted to the right 30 degrees. Imperfections sounded through her mind like a record player through a stadium.

Stop.

Faye paused. She sipped her drink and allowed the bubbles to cascade down her throat. Then, she smiled and looked over in the direction of her work to see a small crowd gathering.

"This one speaks to me," a tall gentleman spoke to several friends.

"I can feel it," his friend responded.

"This one is different than the others." Elaine walked up to the painting inspired by the ravine. Then, she looked at Faye, "Wouldn't you agree?"

"Yes. It is." Faye acknowledged.

"What was your inspiration?"

"Prayer."

A slight gasp escaped the small crowd around her.

Faye sipped her drink and waited for further questions.

Elaine gave her a small nod before exiting the crowd.

***

They waited until they were in the car to recap the event.

"Success!" Jodi announced. "I think you had some real interest in your art, Faye."

"Absolutely," Jeffrey agreed.

"It's all thanks to you." Faye motioned toward Jeffrey.

"Even Elaine seemed interested!"

"Ok. So, who is Elaine?" Faye had been dying to ask them that question all night.

"Elaine Andrews is the premier art collector and distributor in the Midwest." Jodi started.

"and the South," Jeffrey added. "She owns auction houses all over Kentucky, Ohio, Illinois, and probably more."

"Was she in charge of the exhibit tonight?" Faye asked.

"She doesn't organize the exhibits. She works in sales and distribution. Everyone goes through her at some point in the sales process." Jeffrey added.

"Has she ever bought any of your work?" Faye asked him.

"Of course. I've worked with her people on numerous occasions. Though, I've never spoken with Elaine. Usually, her people contact me."

"How do you know that she liked my paintings?"

"She spoke to you." Jodi said.

"Elaine doesn't speak to everyone." Jeffrey added. "If she wishes to purchase your art, she will be in touch."

"How will she know where to contact me?"

"Don't worry." Jodi said, "She will be in touch."

Eleven

The first day of school resembled Black Friday shopping. Students arrived early accompanied by parents. The halls buzzed with students, parents, and teachers. Parents met with teachers in classrooms, while neighbors discussed summer vacations and upcoming projects over coffee in the media center. This morning, conversations centered around the attack on Don. Faye pushed her way through the crowds toward the Math office to find Don Ambrose giving a press conference.

"Thank you all for your concern. I am happy to be back," Don talked to them as he would an old friend.

"Have they found the attackers?" Someone shouted from the crowd.

"I'm not sure where the police are in the investigation." Don paused to sip his coffee. "I have confidence that they will be able to apprehend the men responsible."

"Will you be taking leave?"

"I am fit for duty so to speak," he smiled in an attempt to lighten the mood. "I'm not supposed to lift over 25 pounds, but I think the students will help me with that."

"I think we need to give Mr. Ambrose a break. Could you please make your way to other hallways in the building," Faye recognized Brandon's voice over the tightly packed crowd. "We want to be sure that everyone is able to meet their teachers and learn the building."

"I agree with Mr. Foster," Don spoke over the rumble of voices. "I'll be here all day. You can stop by later."

The crowd lingered until word got out that Don was doing well and planned to stay for the remainder of the day. Faye managed to get to her desk and position herself to meet with families.

"Ms. Unger," Stephanie Brown called from the end of the hallway, "we're happy to see you here today. Megan had wanted to move on to the new high school this year."

"But I'm happy to be in your class again, Ms. Unger," Megan interrupted her mother and rushed over to give Faye a hug.

"Me too, Megan. How have you been?" Faye heard that Megan had been one of the teens that found Don.

Megan shrugged.

Faye looked into Megan's eyes. "You saved his life, you know. You're so brave."

Megan nodded and looked at the floor. "It was hard to see Mr. Ambrose like that. I'm glad he's going to be ok."

The image of the person lying in the ravine came into Faye's mind. The person covered in blood and leaves didn't move or make a sound. *Leaves? Don wasn't covered in leaves, not in August.*

"Ms. Unger?"

"I'm sorry. I guess I'm a little distracted this morning."

"It's understandable. We'll go ahead and leave you to it. Megan and I need to find the English hall next."

"Thank you. I'll see you later, Megan."

The Browns made their way out of the hallway. Faye met several other families from last year. The halls remained crowded through lunch.

"I know you!" A voice called over the crowd. Several people stopped talking and looked around.

"I know you!" It spoke again.

A woman began to walk toward Faye with two children behind her. The crowd parted for her to pass. Her sharp brow matched her determined gait as she walked straight up to Faye.

"Do I know you?" Faye addressed her directly.

"I know your family."

"You might know my parents." Faye attempted a smile. "We've lived in Arlington for quite some time."

"I know what you did." The woman moved into Faye's personal space.

Faye froze. She opened her mouth, but words did not come. She tried to walk away, but her legs refused to carry her. Tiny beads of sweat formed on her forehead. She felt cold. *Oh no. Please don't. Not here.*

Then, her legs gave up. The rest of her dropped into a pile on the floor.

***

Faye woke up on a couch in the Media Center Office. She had a blanket around her, and someone brought her a cup of coffee.

"What happened?"

"You blacked out for a minute, there," Don said. "It's a good thing Brandon was nearby."

Faye looked up at Brandon.

"I made my way over there when I saw Ms. Schmidt heading toward you. She looked like she was up to something," Brandon started, "I caught you before you hit the floor. Are you hurt?"

"You caught me?" Faye looked up at Brandon. "Wait, did you say Schmidt?"

"Yeah. I think she's related to our friend from last year," Don said. "Did she say anything to you?"

"She kept saying that she knew me. Something about knowing my family. I don't know why it bothered me so much."

"She's scary," Brandon said. "I'm not just sayin' that."

"I'll look at your schedule and make sure that her children are not in your classes. You don't need that. I can also check with the police to see if she has threatened any other teachers."

"Thanks, Don. I'm sorry for being so high maintenance."

"You're worth it."

Twelve

The Browns had an open-door policy, as far as Don was concerned. The incident with Julie taught them all what it truly meant to be good neighbors. They had an unspoken rule that neighbors needed no invitation to bring food or just come by to check in. Don walked through the front door straight into Taco night. The house smelled of grilled steak and garlic. Hints of lime wafted through the air.

"Hey, everybody! I brought the salad!" Don shouted over the festive music that accompanied Taco night.

"We're in the kitchen!" Stephanie called from the other room.

"Hey, Mr. Ambrose." Megan waved from the dining table.

"Time to clean up, Sweetie," Stephanie brought placemats to the table.

Megan closed her books and picked up her things. Stephanie waited until she left the room to speak, "That was some first day!"

Don nodded his head.

"Are they all as eventful?" Brandon looked up from the onions and blinked.

"Some people have a way with drama." Don placed the salad on the island next to a bowl of cheese.

"They always have." Stephanie rolled her eyes.

Brandon slid the onions into a bowl. "I thought you and the Schmidts were close."

Stephanie shook her head, "We use to be."

Jason walked in and washed his hands. "I'm sure these guys aren't interested in all that, Steph." He pulled plates out of the cabinet and placed them on the table.

"I don't think I remember seeing that lady last year."

"That's cause her daughter is too young, Don." Megan entered the room and smiled, "she's just now in 6th grade."

"That makes sense. Have they always lived here?"

"I don't remember those people around here before." Jason handed Don a plate. "Go ahead and make a plate. It'll get cold soon."

"Of course you do. Tricia Schmidt," Stephanie spat the words like sour milk. "She was that creepy little tattletale, remember?"

Jason squinted to remember the details.

"You remember, senior year." Her eyes grew big as she glanced over at Megan. "The ravine." The last part, she whispered between clenched teeth.

"Oh," Jason drew out the word for several seconds. "I remember now. Yeah, today makes a lot more sense. Now."

"You know, Brandon, you remind me of that kid we hung around with in high school. What was his name?" Stephanie looked at Jason for help.

Jason shrugged.

"You know, the tall kid. Was he related to Mazzi?"

Jason smiled, "Yeah. He graduated before us, though."

"What was his name?"

"Jack? Jamie?" Jason tried to guess the guy's name.

"Jo!" Stephanie squealed with excitement, "Jo Mazzi!"

"Yeah, that's it!" Jason looked over at Brandon, "I don't see it. I mean you guys were similar in size, but nah."

"I totally see it," Stephanie patted Brandon on the shoulder.

"Ok, whatever. Back to that ravine business." Brandon sprinkled cheese over his mound of taco and headed to the table.

Don didn't need Stephanie's encounter of the ravine to put two and two together. High schoolers weren't the only folks to use the ravine. He read reports of everything from bribes to prostitution exchanged in the ravine. *They really need to get better surveillance cameras over there.*

Dinner conversation covered the other events of the school day. Megan signed up for the Math Tournament team and the cross-country team. She told them all about the new kids and her plans for ruling the school as one of the only 9th graders. Stephanie and Jason asked questions about the organization of the new model and how it affected classes.

Megan excused herself to finish homework, and Brandon wasted no time asking about the ravine.

"Ok, spill it. What happened in the ravine senior year?"

"Let's just say, the ravine provides excellent cover." Jason looked over at Stephanie and smiled.

"Surely, you weren't the only couple to sneak off to the ravine," Don picked up plates to the clear the table.

"More like Seniors skipping class." Megan brought coffee to the table.

"Just the two of you? Scandalous."

"No, uh there was a group of us. John Mazzi brought his girl," Jason looked to Stephanie for the name.

"Wait a minute, it's coming to me," Stephanie sipped her coffee, "Elaine."

"Elaine. Not Gina?" Brandon set down his cup.

"Trust me, Gina had a crush on him." Stephanie rolled her eyes. "But he never saw her."

"Where did the 'tattletale' come in?" Don smiled at the juvenile reference.

"Probably, Gina," Stephanie groaned, "well, she had a thing for John. So, she sent Trish to spy on us."

"Steph, really? Do you still hold a grudge?"

"We missed the homecoming dance because of her,Jason." Stephanie took a deep breath in order to keep her voice down.

"Brilliant story, but I don't see how this has anything to do with Faye," Brandon leaned back in his chair.

"It doesn't really. Her beef with Faye is probably something else," Jason said.

Stephanie stood to clear the rest of the dishes from the table. "Drama always followed Trish and Gina."

"Were they in the same class?" Don needed more to establish the connection.

"No, they're cousins," Stephanie spoke on her way to the dishwasher.

Jason stood and patted Don on the shoulder, "Trish has walked around with a chip on her shoulder ever since her brother's murder."

"Murder?!" Brandon spit coffee across the table.

"That's right," Stephanie spoke calmly, "everybody expects it now. Honestly, I'm surprised Faye responded the way she did. She grew up with Trish's nonsense too."

"Were they in school together?" Don wished he'd brought his notebook to keep track. The Browns went through names quickly.

"No, but yes." Stephanie dried her hands and looked at them, "everyone in this town knows each other."

"You don't have to be in the same grade to be irritated by somebody." Jason walked over and high-fived his wife.

"Did they ever catch the guy that murdered her brother?" Don asked completely serious.

Jason returned the serious expression, "That is a story for another night, my friend. Let's just say, the jury's still out."

Thirteen

Faye's school day ended earlier than planned, but she didn't complain. That episode with Schmidt took a lot out of her. She could use a hot bath to wash it all away. She gave a wave to the doorman as she headed toward the elevator.

It took too long to reach the 12th floor. Faye started her decompression in the elevator. She closed her eyes and took a deep breath. Then, she began to stretch her head from side to side. She rolled her shoulders back to relieve the stress. She almost didn't notice the elevator doors open.

With her eyes still closed, Faye stepped off the elevator and turned left. A noise startled her, and she opened her eyes. *Someone's in my apartment.* The door opened slightly. She pulled out her phone.

Male voices echoed through the slightly open door. *Someone really was in her apartment. And he brought friends.* Keeping her eyes focused on the door, she spoke into her phone, "call help."

Faye scanned the hallway for exits and inched slowly toward the door. *I really need to invest in pepper spray.* One of the men stepped out of the apartment dressed in navy coveralls and work boots.

"Ma'am? This your place?"

Faye nodded.

"We're almost all set here. We can move them around if you want."

Faye paused.

"You can go in and see what you think." The man stood aside so she could get inside.

She found another man inside hanging a painting on the wall. With her mouth slightly opened, she looked around the room to find three other paintings hanging there.

"What do ya think? Is this good?"

"That's fine. Thank you." Relieved, Faye let out her breath and watched the men leave.

"You're home early." Jeffrey walked in from the hallway and gave her a hug.

"What are you doing here?"

"I brought your paintings back. Those guys helped me with the heavy frames."

"Did you tell me that you were coming?"

"I wanted to surprise you. Looks like I succeeded." Jeffrey smiled and put his arm around her.

"I've had a few too many surprises for one day," Faye said.

"Well then, come, have a seat. Let me put on a pot of tea and you can tell me all about it," Faye's plan for a hot bath transformed into a tea by the fire. She slipped off her heels and settled into the sofa.

Jeffrey handed her a glass and cozied up beside her. "Have you ever thought about doing this full-time?"

Faye took the cup from Jeffrey and looked around the room. Jeffrey's question got lost in the beauty of it all. The paintings brought a new life to her apartment. The frames brought elegance to the space and the paintings told a beautiful story. Faye could hardly believe she had painted them. She knew that God had helped her. A divine peace fell on her like a warm blanket. The worries of the day and the terrors that it held had gone.

"Thank you." Faye often responded in prayer aloud.

"Oh, it was my pleasure," Jeffrey's response reminded Faye that he was still there.

"You did a beautiful job on them, Jeffrey. The frames are gorgeous. And I love the way you have them arranged in the room."

"I'm glad you like it." Jeffrey took a tray of tea and set it on the table. Then, he took Faye's face in his hands and leaned in for a kiss.

Suddenly, the apartment door sprung open. Don charged in holding a gun. Faye and Jeffrey jumped in surprise.

"Faye!"

"Don?!"

"Step away from her," Don said to Jeffrey and motioned with his gun. Then, he looked at Faye, "Are you ok? I'm sorry it took me so long."

"Yes, Don. Put the gun away!"

"Do you know him?" Don asked still pointing the gun.

"This is my boyfriend."

"Oh."

"What are you doing here?" Faye asked.

"I was in the car when you called me, but you didn't say anything. I heard what sounded like men's voices in the background, so I drove here first. "

Faye grimaced. "Oh. I saw the door opened when I got off the elevator. I thought I called 9-1-1. I must have dialed your number by mistake. I'm sorry for the misunderstanding. Please." Faye motioned to the gun.

Don put the gun away.

"I surprised her by hanging her paintings on the wall while she was at school," Jeffrey reached out his hand to Don. "I'm Jeffrey, by the way."

"Sorry for the mix-up, but I'm glad to finally meet you. I'm Don. I work with Faye." Don returned the handshake, then looked at the walls. "These are your paintings?" Don walked toward the artwork.

"Um hmm," Faye smiled.

"The colors are so vibrant in this one, but completely different in the next," Don spoke about her paintings with enthusiasm. "What's your inspiration?"

"Prayer," Jeffrey responded and Faye looked at him in shock. "That's what she told the collectors at the exhibit over the weekend." He looked over at Faye and grinned. "I thought it to be a brilliant response."

"I pray while I paint," Faye glanced at Jeffrey unsure of his sincerity, "that makes all the difference to me."

Don looked at her and nodded. "I understand the power of prayer. That must be what it is, because I've never seen paintings like these before."

"Faye, do you think you'll be alright here?" Jeffrey attempted to excuse himself. "I really must get going."

Don looked at them both, "Oh, no, you don't have to go on account me. Clearly, I interrupted something. I'm so sorry." Don scrambled to leave also.

Faye grabbed his arm. "No. It's ok. I had something to ask you about school anyway."

"Right, then, I'll get going." Jeffrey leaned in to give Faye a peck on the cheek. "We can get together this weekend."

"Thank you again for the paintings. I appreciate it." Faye walked him to the door.

After he left, she turned to Don. "Thanks for coming by. This…" Faye pointed to the door, "isn't very serious, so don't feel bad."

Don nodded.

"Since when do you carry a gun?"

"Since, Julie."

Don walked over to the paintings to change the subject, "What happened with this one?"

"Hmm," Faye walked over to get a closer look. "I didn't paint that one." Faye's surprise was evident in her voice. She looked around the room and counted four paintings. She had only given Jeffrey three. "I'm not sure where that came from. Jeffrey must have grabbed it by mistake. Is it signed?"

Don searched the painting and couldn't locate a signature, "I can't tell. Can you?"

Faye leaned closer to inspect the painting.

"Faye, do you mind if I take a picture of it? I can ask around to see where it originates"

"Go ahead. Wait," Faye ran her fingers across the bottom left corner, "Here it is… EA."

***

Faye did her best to sleep in Saturday morning. While her body remained in the bed, her mind began the work of lesson planning the next week. Before her feet hit the floor, she had made plans to organize lessons and set up her classroom. *Susan and Richard are probably already at the school. If I make copies today, it'll save me time on Monday.*

She checked her phone before making breakfast plans. Nothing from Jeffrey. She quickly gathered her things and made her way to the lobby. The crisp morning air beckoned crowds of neighbors to outdoor cafes. Faye had her pick of breakfast options. She would definitely run into people at breakfast. The question remained, *Who do I want to see during breakfast?* Arlington knew no strangers. Quiet breakfast spots quickly became family-style meals.

Faye exited her building and stood on the sidewalk taking in the sights and sounds. She started toward a cafe on her left when a black limousine pulled up and stopped in front of her. A man got out of the car.

"Faye Unger?"

Faye looked at him.

He pulled open the back door. "Get in."

Faye inched closer to the car and looked inside. The dark interior revealed a passenger wearing a dark suit.

"Miss," the man persisted, "Get in the car." He motioned to the interior with a nod.

Fourteen

"Miss," the sounded impatient. Then, he looked inside the car.

Faye followed his gaze. A woman, seated in the back, leaned forward. She pulled down her sunglasses and looked over them at Faye from inside the car.

Faye got in the car.

"Ms. Unger, I've been looking forward to meeting you." The woman pulled off her sunglasses and looked at Faye.

"I'm sorry," Faye apologized, "I don't think I know you."

The woman pursed her lips together and let out a slow, calculated breath. "Allow me to introduce myself,"she put the sunglasses back on, "I'm Elaine Andrews."

Faye sat up as though her mother had scolded her for slouching. "Nice to meet you, Ms. Andrews."

The car lurched forward.

"I saw your work at the exhibit last week." Elaine spoke from behind her sunglasses.

Faye nodded. "Are you an artist or a collector?"

"Both." Elaine pulled out a long cigarette holder and proceeded to light a cigarette.

"I'm new to the art scene, forgive me for asking, but why am I here?"

"I'd like to have a conversation with you, Faye." Elaine chose a direct approach. "I prefer in-person conversations."

"What would you like to talk about?"

Elaine smiled. "Do you like French food?"

"Excuse me?"

"There's a lovely French restaurant downtown. We can talk there."

They arrived to an empty parking lot. The restaurant appeared to be closed. *At least it's not a loading dock, or an empty storage unit,* Faye thought to herself. Inside the restaurant, the maître d' escorted them to a corner booth in the back. The table, decorated with pressed linens and fine china, resembled Elaine's elegant style. As soon as they sat, someone brought them a bottle of wine along with bread.

"I took the liberty of ordering in advance," Elaine shook her napkin before placing it in her lap, "I hope you don't mind."

Faye shook her head and took a sip from the water goblet.

"They have the best wine in the Midwest. You must try it," Elaine offered her a glass of wine.

"Thank you, but I don't drink. " Faye spoke before thinking and regretted it.

Elaine sat quietly. "There are other delicacies to enjoy."

The food arrived soon after the wine. Appetizers and entrees passed before them while the waiters stood by the tables to replace used china. Faye enjoyed the food and almost forgot that her kidnapper sat beside her.

"You said you wanted to have a conversation?" Faye asked.

Elaine looked up, "Are you enjoying the meal?"

"Very much," Faye dabbed her mouth with her napkin, "It's been a long time since I've had French food. We used to go as a family all the time when I was little."

Elaine grinned. "You have a unique talent, Faye. Do you mind if I call you Faye?"

Faye shook her head.

"I would like to offer you a unique opportunity," Elaine continued, "it would enable you to quit your day job."

Faye looked into Elaine's eyes, but heard Jeffrey's question echo through her mind, *Have you thought about doing this full-time?* She took a sip of water to give her time to think before answering. The calling to teach had been unmistakeable. Faye spent years running from it, attempting one career after another.

"I enjoy my day job," Faye's response did not weaken Elaine's resolve.

"Did you enjoy the exhibit?"

"Yes."

"Did Jeffrey tell you that there were several bids for your paintings?"

"Bids?"

"Yes, Faye, exhibits highlight artists and increase their sales. You had several offers that night."

Faye looked down and tried to hide her excitement. She never considered art as a career choice.

"Faye, this is my profession. I study art and the many methods of painting and sculpting. I have examined artists from all over the world along with their works. I understand and valuate art. Would you like to know how much your paintings are valued?"

Faye stared at Elaine in disbelief. "Elaine, may I call you Elaine?"

Elaine waved her hand in permission.

"Elaine, I am not an artist. I paint as a hobby. A few months ago, I attended a seminar about art and math. It was recreational interest, not a career move. I am a teacher, not an artist."

"Numerous benefactors would disagree with you, I am among them," Elaine persisted. "Why did you enter the exhibit?"

"Jeffrey. We met in Chicago. He's charming and handsome. He convinced me to enter a few things."

"He told you the truth about your work. Why else would he encourage you to enter?"

Faye looked around and tried to avoid the truth, but she blurted it out. "He works for the Auction House. I think he just wants to make a few bucks off of me."

Elaine raised her eyebrows in surprise.

"Well, I heard he got a promotion to look for new talent." She should have stopped there, but Faye couldn't help herself. "I wanted to help him out with his new job."

"Art has both intrinsic and monetary value. I think you understand the intrinsic value of your work." Elaine sipped her wine. "You remarked that prayer was your inspiration. That spiritual element is evident in your painting. You view the canvas and remember the emotions involved in creating it. Others receive similar benefits when they view your paintings. The spiritual element transfers to them providing them with value."

A waiter brought dessert and coffee.

"The monetary value can be determined based on what people are willing to pay for your work. This happens in different ways. Sometimes, people determine what they are willing to pay based on their personal budget for art. The paintings can be valued based on comparisons of similar artists. Other times, an expert will set a baseline price to start for others to bid. These are details of auctions that don't concern you," Elaine took a bite of dessert and sipped her coffee.

The pause allowed her words to settle over Faye. She never considered selling her paintings. The memories hanging on the walls reminded her of how far she had come and the many obstacles she overcame.

"Are there memories you wish to discard?" Elaine's question interjected Faye's thoughts.

"What?"

"You value the memories and the prayers, so you don't think to sell them. What if you could eliminate the unwelcome thoughts?"

"I'm not sure I know what you mean by that." Faye felt a need to defend her thoughts.

"We all have things we regret." Elaine paused and looked off in the distance. "It can be helpful to paint those and sell them to others. Eliminate the memory of the regret and rid yourself of it."

"I don't live with regrets," Faye lied.

"But you are thinking about people purchasing your paintings for the first time. Wouldn't you like to know how others value your work?"

Faye did want to know. She wanted to know the instant Jeffrey told her about it at the exhibit. She looked up at Elaine and nodded.

Elaine pulled out a business card and wrote a series of numbers on the back. She slid it across the table to Faye.

Faye's eye widened as she read the numbers scrolled on the back.

> *$5,000 for the city scape*
>
> *$6500 for the moody dark one*
>
> *Contract with me for 4 paintings worth $50,000*

"The contract is my offer," Elaine started, "four paintings within the next couple of months. You have the freedom to paint anything you like without explanations necessary. If you wish to paint more, we can also put them in the auction."

"Wow. This is a lot to think about about."

"I understand. Take your time."

Faye looked at the back of the card for a number or address. "How will I get in touch with you?"

"No need." Elaine set her coffee cup on the saucer. "I will be in touch with you."

Elaine motioned for the maître d' who spoke to a man before arriving at their table.

"Ma'am, the car is ready for you," he spoke without hesitation.

"Very well. Faye, there is a car ready to take you wherever you like. I will be in touch soon."

Fifteen

Faye heard muffled voices. She tried to walk quietly but the leaves crunched under every step. The voices sounded angry. Faye moved faster. Now, she ran and they chased her. Hurry! Faster!

Faye jolted upright in the bed. She looked around the room and exhaled.

"Just a dream," she repeated aloud to convince herself to calm down.

She looked at the alarm clock, 4:00 am. Slowly, Faye pulled off the blankets and slid her legs to the side of the bed. She took a deep breath and made her way to the kitchen for a glass of water. The cold water extinguished the fire in her belly. She stepped out onto her balcony for some fresh air.

The city slept beneath her while the moon watched. A breeze came her way, and Faye closed her eyes. She could almost hear the river crashing against the pillars of the bridge. The river had a way of flooding her thoughts and carrying off the regrets. Regrets. She'd lied to Elaine. Faye had deep, buried regrets. They hid from her in the day and resurfaced in her dreams.

The nightmares stopped a long time ago. *Why now? Was it the meeting with Elaine? Was it the encounter with the woman at school? Don's attack?* Faye's mind scrolled through the events of the last week searching for the cause. She needed a reset.

"Be transformed by the renewing of your mind," The verse in Romans floated into Faye's mind along with the feeling of regret. Faye hadn't been to church since she returned from Chicago. She usually attended with her parents. She never called her mom. They would want to come to lunch after. Faye spent time cleaning her apartment and prepping for the day.

Attending church also meant coming into contact with students and parents. Teachers in Arlington were akin to movie stars. Faye took extra preparations when it came to her appearance. She also prepared herself for small talk and school discussions. She hoped to run into J.J. and Donna.

Faye did not expect to run into Brandon talking with J.J. She walked toward them when someone intercepted her.

"Ms. Unger," Ms. Brown caught her attention. "I'm glad to see you. I heard that you had an incident at school the other day. How are you doing?"

"I'm ok. Thank you for asking." Faye smiled.

"What happened? If you don't mind my asking."

"I'm not really sure. Sometimes, I just get light headed." Faye grinned in hopes that it would end the conversation.

"Have you been to see a doctor? Mr. Gardner is an excellent physician. He took care of Don when the kids found him in the ravine."

"It's ok, I'm fine, really," Faye tried desperately to leave the conversation.

"Steve! Steve!" Stephanie Brown called him over.

"Hi Stephanie. Oh, hello Ms.Unger," Steve Gardner said as he approached them.

"Steve, I was talking with Ms. Unger here about her fainting spell the other day. She doesn't know what causes it. Do you think you could help?"

"I could certainly try."

"It's really not a big deal." Faye continued to deflect attention. "I'm sure it was an isolated incident,"

"Was it like the one last year?" Susan spoke from behind Faye. "You should let him check it out. He's a fantastic doctor."

"Come into my office one day after school. It won't take long," Steve pulled out his phone and typed a note. "I can arrange my appointments around it."

"Thank you." Faye agreed and made her way to a seat with her parents.

As the music started, Don and Brandon slipped into a seat next to her.

"How are you doing?" Don whispered.

Faye couldn't make sense of the last couple of days. She felt confused and rattled, but she didn't want to tell him that. "I'm ok."

"We can talk later. Coffee tonight?"

Faye smiled and nodded. They missed their last coffee date, because of the attack. It would be good to catch up with him. She would let him go on about his injury and recovery. Maybe he could fill her in on the events of the school day that she missed.

Faye enjoyed the peaceful community in her church. For the first time in a long while, she felt safe. She closed her eyes and inhaled the moment as she would a breath of fresh air. Faye absorbed the music, message, and prayers during the service. Though she'd lost hours of sleep, she felt energized in the moment.

After the service, Faye's parents followed her home for brunch. Her mother prepared the food while Faye set the table. Her father walked around the apartment looking for things that might need repair.

"Didn't you start school this week?" Her mom asked.

"Yes, we did."

"How did that go?"

"Fine."

"That's not what I heard," her dad called from the other room.

Faye looked at her mom. They knew everything. She wasn't sure how the word got out, but she couldn't hide anything from her parents.

"I heard you passed out," her dad said from the living room. "That young man, Brandon, said that he helped you to a couch."

"What happened, Faye?" Her mom asked, "What brought it on?"

Faye shrugged. "I don't know. Some lady said she knew my family. She came at me like Diane did last year. I'm going to see a doctor this week. We'll get it figured out."

Faye's dad turned to look at her mom. Their eyes locked in a knowing glance, but neither said a word. Her mom brought the food to the table and changed the subject.

"These paintings are beautiful. When did you get them?"

"They're mine," Faye happily changed the subject.

"Your paintings are lovely, dear." Her mom smiled. "You've always been so creative."

"Someone at the exhibit helped me with the frames. Aren't they beautiful?"

"Is that antique pine? Those frames are worth a fortune." Faye's dad stood up to get a closer look at the frames.

"This one is different than the others," Faye's mom said as she walked toward Elaine's painting.

"That one was a gift from someone at the auction house."

"The auction house?" Faye's dad sounded alarmed. "Faye, you need to stay clear of those people. Do you hear me?"

"Why? They could probably sell my paintings for me." Faye had no intention of talking to them about Elaine, but she saw nothing wrong with Jeffrey and Jodi working at the Auction House.

Faye's mom looked more closely at Elaine's painting. She gasped as she read the letters EA in the bottom right.

"Jack, it's her."

"NO." Faye's dad walked over to look closely at the painting.

"Who?" Faye asked.

"It's nothing for you to worry about, Faye." Her mom put an arm around Faye and looked up at her dad.

"That's right, Faye, this just looks like something we saw a few years back. Do you know who gave it to you?" Her dad walked back to the table.

"It just showed up without a card." Faye didn't want to worry them with the story about her meeting Elaine, so she kept that part quiet.

"Would you mind if we took it off your hands?" Her dad offered.

"I think it would look lovely in the den," Her mom added.

Sixteen

Don invited Brandon over to his house after church. He wanted to look through the evidence files for any clues that might connect his attack to Julie's murder.

"Don! Hey, you got a minute?" Jason Brown flagged him down and disrupted his thoughts.

"Hey, Jason. How's it going?"

"Great! It's good to see you out and about, Don. Stephanie asked me to bring over this casserole for you."

"Thank you. I appreciate it." Don smiled and looked at Brandon getting out of the car. "We'll definitely be able to use it as we plan for next week."

"Hey, Brandon. It's good to see you again." Jason reached to shake Brandon's hand.

"I've heard some good things about your classes. Well, I'll let you get to work. See you around."

"What's this?" Brandon asked.

"Lunch," Don said with a smile, "The neighbors have brought me something every day since I got home from the hospital."

The men walked inside, and Brandon began to unpack the evidence files. He pulled out a mess of photos and notes mixed with homework assignments and test papers.

"Looks like we might be here a while." Don walked into the kitchen to grab plates for lunch.

"Yeah, sorry about that. I just threw it all into the bag. I brought the homework to beef up our cover." Brandon sorted out the school items from the rest.

Don served a spoonful of chicken casserole onto a plate. "Is everything labeled?"

"Yeah. Let me sort them by dates and crimes. I think we have more than one set of photos here."

Don reached over and grabbed a file folder and thumbed through the paperwork. "This is the case that started it all."

"Back in 2003?" Brandon looked up from the stack of photos. Don nodded.

"Sounds like a good place to start," Brandon handed him a stack of photos and notes. "That's the case that brought you here to Arlington, right? You can fill me in over lunch." Brandon grabbed a plate and filled it with casserole.

"Well, it was cold when we got here." Don filled a glass with sweet tea. "The incident occurred in 2003, but we didn't get the case until 2020."

"Don, it looks like a murder. Cut and dry. Why did they call you guys down here for it?"

"Rogers had intel that the Andrews family had operations in Arlington. The murder was a cover up for the smuggling operations." Don picked up the photos and thumbed through them. He pulled out three photos and set one in front of Brandon. "This is Marcus Andrews. He's the head of the Andrews family."

"Looks like he's posing with a cop."

"He is. That's Frank Schmidt chief of police back in '03."

"So, what's the operation?" Brandon helped himself to more casserole.

"That's the problem. We had intel that they were running drugs through imports. Then, we heard they came clean." Don tossed the file on the table and took a seat.

"How is Faye connected to all of this?" Brandon poured himself some iced tea.

"Did you look at the crime scene photos?" Don slid the file over to Brandon.

Brandon opened the file and flipped a few pages. He pulled out a photo and covered his mouth. A man lay on a pile of leaves in a ravine with multiple wounds. There was a lot of blood.

"I've viewed a lot of crime scene photos, but that one takes your breath." Don paused before he added, "The man was Albert Schmidt."

"No wonder the Schmidts are all fired up. Do you have a list of the suspects? Witnesses?" Brandon flipped through the papers, "Here it is. There are at least 10 names on this list. Most of them Andrews. Some of them very young." Brandon stopped and squinted at the list. "Look at this."

Don grabbed the list. He looked it over and gasped. One name caught his attention: Faye Andrews. "I don't know how I didn't see that before. There's not too many girls that age named Faye. Says here she was only 8 years old." Don leaned back in his chair and shook his head.

Brandon read through the report. "They found her at the scene."

"That's gotta be our Faye. I haven't found anyone else in town who's been here as long with that name."

"I guess that's why the Schmidts hate her. Says here their primary suspect was Elaine Andrews." Brandon kept reading. "How does a 17 year old girl murder a man in cold blood? Don, something doesn't make sense here."

Don looked through the file again. "What about the witness testimony?"

"The report says that they found one witness at the scene, Faye. They were unable to get testimony from her."

"What do you mean, unable?"

Brandon shrugged. "She didn't respond to questioning. The report says that even after the psychological screening, she was unable to speak. They decided not to pursue further questioning."

Faye had been there. It scarred her. *Wait a minute…Faye is an Andrews? No. Why wouldn't she tell me?*

"Did they interview any members of the Andrews family?"

"Hang on, Don, let me see." Brandon scanned the documents. "Ok. They interviewed Marcus Andrews at the time. He was not aware of any disagreement between his family and Albert Schmidt. It says here that he denied any connection to the murder."

"That doesn't mean anything. I'm not sure I'm buying that our Faye is the same Faye on that list. She would've said something by now. Did Marcus have an alibi?"

"Yeh. Says he was in Chicago, along with most of the Andrews family. If this girl did it, she acted alone."

"Do they list any accomplices?"

"Don, the list is two pages here. Of course they list accomplices. And they all have alibis."

Don shook his head. All of these crime families worked the same. He knew that they pinned it on the girl, because she was a minor. He had never come across the name Elaine Andrews in any of his investigations.

Don tried to move onto something else. He didn't want to go through the photos of Julie. He couldn't do that right now. He thumbed through the papers and found a small card similar to a business card, but it appeared to be hand painted.

"What's this?"

"Officers found that on the body in the ravine."

Don looked closely. There was no message on the back. The painting contained dark swirling colors with creepy shadows. It had a texture on it unlike printed business cards. He looked closely for an artist signature and located what appeared to be the letter 'A' in the bottom right.

"They assumed that the A was for Andrews," Brandon read aloud.

"There's something familiar about this painting, though."

Don reached for his phone and opened the photos. He found the photo of the painting in Faye's apartment. The colors swirled in the same way as the tiny card. Both looked creepy. He enlarged the image to look into the bottom right corner. There it was.

"E A"

"What?" Brandon turned to look at Don's phone. "What's that?"

"A painting in Faye's apartment. She said it was delivered by accident."

Seventeen

Faye made her way to the lobby where she'd asked Don to meet her. She didn't want to take any chances after the week she'd had. Don didn't pressure her and it helped a little knowing that he carried a gun. The elevator opened for a new passenger. The smell of cheap cologne made her eyes water. Faye felt the man's giant biceps near her before she looked up. Mazzi's cousin had an unforgettable quality about him.

Faye reached out to push the button for the lobby. The man inched closer to her and smiled.

"Hello, again," he grumbled.

Faye managed a weak smile. "I'm sorry, I don't remember your name."

"Name's Joe." He reached out his hand for her to shake.

Faye politely shook hands. "When did you move in, Joe?"

"Oh, I don't live here. I'm visiting a friend."

Faye took a nervous breath and prayed for the elevator to open. It did. She squeezed through the door and nearly sprinted across the lobby.

"A friend of yours?" Don asked her.

"No, but I see you found a friend." Faye looked back at Mazzi.

"He was waiting in the lobby when I got here," Don stopped.

"What are you doing? Let's get out of here." Faye's attempts to remain calm failed her.

"Give me a minute." Don pulled out his phone to snap photos of Mazzi talking with creepy Joe from the elevator. Then, he turned to escort Faye out of the building. "Does he live here?"

"No. Visiting a friend," Faye said using air quotes. She moved quickly passing the creep, "that guy is so …"

"Shhhh. They are walking behind us," Don said with his teeth clenched and his hand on his gun. "Do you know the men smoking cigars?"

Faye stopped walking and pretended to look for something in her purse. She glanced across the street. Two men stood near a car similar to the one that drove her to the restaurant yesterday. Faye whispered, "I've seen them before, but I don't know them. Maybe they live in the building."

Don and Faye watched Mazzi get into the town car.

Don turned to Faye. "Did that guy say anything to you? Did he hurt you?"

"No. Just small talk. Almost like he was trying to hit on me."

"Do you know his name?"

"Joe. I think he's related to John Mazzi somehow. Cousins? I don't remember. I'm just glad they're gone."

Don and Faye made their way to the coffee shop without further incident.

"It looks like you're healing well."

Don looked down at his arm minus the sling. "It's doing ok. I should probably have worn the sling. Oops," he said with a grin.

Faye smiled and ordered coffee and pastries for the both of them.

"I'm glad to see you are feeling better after that incident at school." He sipped his coffee. "The Schmidts seem to have it out for you. First Diane, then, this lady."

"I know, right?" Faye shook her head.

"The Schmidts have been in Arlington for a long time. Do you remember them growing up?"

"Not really. I mean, I remember the name, but I always tried to stay away from the police."

Don looked up with a puzzled look on his face.

"The Schmidts are synonymous with police in Arlington."

"So, your family hasn't had run-ins with them?"

"Probably." Faye pulled a raisin out of her scone. "You live in a town long enough, you find yourself running into problems with everyone. This city is like a small town, though, people get over it. Neighbors can't live together holding a grudge."

Faye sipped her coffee and took a minute to think about what Don said. A familiar feeling of trouble came to mind. She couldn't tell if it had been from her interview after Don's attack or something else.

"I heard that Stephanie Brown convinced you to go see Dr. Gardner."

"Yeah. I told him that I would stop by this week, but I don't think its a big deal." Faye had never been squeamish or faint, so she dismissed it. "You know how the beginning of the year can be. It's probably just stress."

"No kidding. There has been a lot going on." Don sipped his coffee. "How did the exhibit go?"

Faye smiled, "It went well."

"So, how did it feel to see your paintings displayed? It had to be amazing."

Faye looked up, "You're right. It's hard to describe. I didn't recognize them at first in the frames with the lights on them. It was like I was viewing someone else's paintings. Other people liked them too. They crowded around asking questions."

"That's exciting, Faye."

Faye took a bite of her pastry and scanned the cafe, "Did you know that Brandon came to the exhibit?"

"No." Don sat back in surprise. The raised eyebrows then began to scowl.

"What's that face?" Faye laughed. "Aren't you guys old friends?"

"Yeah, yeah," Don exhaled, "we served together in Afghanistan, but I didn't know he was into art."

"I think he's more into Jodi than art," Faye looked down, "but she doesn't mind."

"If she is anything like the others, it probably won't last, either. Hey, did you ever figure out who sent the other painting?"

Faye shook her head. "I meant to ask Jeffrey, but I totally forgot. My parents seemed to like it, though."

"Really?"

"Yeah, they asked if they could take it with them to hang in the den." Faye paused to sip her coffee and measure her words. "Don, have you ever considered doing something besides teaching?"

"That's an interesting question. Why do you ask?"

"I've had two different people ask me if I ever thought of painting full time."

"You paint beautifully, Faye, but you're called to teach." Don took a sip of his coffee, then looked up at Faye. "Do you mind if I ask, who asked?"

"Jeffrey mentioned it before the exhibit, and someone approached me at the exhibit." Faye took a bite of the scone and sipped her coffee. "It's just that I dreamed of being an artist my whole life. I never thought I could do it before now."

"That must have been some exhibit." Don sat back in the bench. "You think you could do it for a living?"

Faye leaned in close and looked from side to side before she spoke, "someone offered to buy two of my paintings."

Don raised his eyebrows.

"Not only that," Faye continued, "they offered me a contract to paint four others. The contract is more than double my teaching salary." Faye sat back on the bench. "Double."

"Wow," Don took a deep breath, "this was the person who approached you at the exhibit?"

Faye nodded. "We met after the exhibit and discussed the offer over lunch." Faye took another bite of her pastry, "At first, I totally dismissed it, you know? Don, I know God called me to teach. Then, this comes around."

"Are you sure this person is legitimate?"

Faye decided not to mention the part about the car and the kidnapping. "Jeffrey and Jodi seemed to know her. They called her the premier art dealer in the midwest."

"Sounds like you have a decision to make."

"Maybe, I could do both." Faye sat up. "I paint in my free time now. I could probably produce the paintings for the contract and still teach."

"Be careful of compromise." Don looked around the room. "If this person is the premier dealer, they hold a lot of power. Powerful people usually demand more than we are willing to give. Don't be surprised if this person insists that you quit teaching."

"You think she will?"

"It depends on the person. Things that sound too good to be true usually are. Be careful." Don smiled and set down his coffee cup, "Hey, we have an open house coming up in a couple weeks. Are you ready for it?"

"I'm never ready for open house." Faye chuckled glad for the change in subject.

"Last year, they had some pretty good food. You seem to have made friends with the Browns and the Gardners. They're good people to know."

"How so?"

"We're neighbors. They arrived first when… uh… Julie…" Don trailed off. "You know. They've been good neighbors."

Faye didn't take the time to get to know the families. "They seem to really care."

"Do you have good neighbors, Faye?"

Faye shrugged, "I don't really know my neighbors. I keep running into that guy in the elevator, so I should probably start making friends."

Don smiled, "Sounds like you could use some."

Eighteen

Arlington Community School started as a high school. Years ago, a group of graduates from the original Arlington High School formed the Arlington Foundation. They collect money through various events in order to present a scholarship to a new graduate every year. Open House serves as a fund raising event for the Arlington Foundation. The entire community converges on the school campus for an evening of food, drinks, and class reunions.

Each year, the event grows in popularity. This year, Arlington Community School decided to send students home at lunch so that parents and teachers could prepare for the event. The Media Center became party central. Susan and Richard hung streamers and balloons throughout the school. Each hall featured student-designed decor. A large banner hung over the middle of the building to welcome alumni.

Some schools use open house to highlight student achievements and welcome parents into the school. The Arlington Community

School Open House resembled a family reunion complete with pot luck dishes. Parents competed with one another to outdo the others in their extravagant appetizers. The PTA bake sale of cupcakes and brownies held no comparison to the shrimp cocktails and baked Alaska of the Open House.

Susan and Richard organized the volunteers for the event. Parents arrived early in the morning to begin decorating. Many stayed after they dropped off their students. They set up tables with crisp linens and expansive centerpieces. A long buffet table stood in the center of the room for parents to place the food, while they positioned drink stations in the corners of the room. One station, specifically for students, contained sodas and waters. The other stations catered to the adults with spiked punch, bottles of wine, and cocktails.

Faye passed through the media center and overheard the parents gossiping as they decorated.

"How long has she been out of the house?" The first woman asked.

"I don't know. I just heard she's been staying elsewhere. Tariq said that he saw her husband waiting in the lobby in the hopes she would come down," a woman hanging balloons responded.

"You both should mind your own business." Susan attempted to steer the conversation away from teachers in the school. "The Mazzis are new here. Give them the benefit of the doubt."

"Haven't they lived here for a long time?" The first woman persisted.

"I thought they just moved here."

"No. They lived here about twenty years ago," a third parent joined the conversation. "I don't know where they went, but it's like they never left."

"They moved here from Chicago, and they're still getting settled," Susan interrupted. "I know she has a friend that lives close to the river, whom she visits often. They both ride to school together in the morning. I'm sure he just waits for her in the lobby to give her a ride home. It's not a big story."

"Twenty years ago? Wasn't that when they found the man in the ravine?" The first woman started up again.

"Yes! I remember that. Who was it?" The second woman set out a tower of cups.

"Um…his name was…"

Faye walked away from the conversation toward a more interesting conversation happening with her friends.

"Is your husband going to be here tonight?" J.J. asked Donna.

"I'm not sure. He loved those spicy wings last year. So, he'll probably be here."

"Good, I've been meaning to get together with him. What about you, Faye? Is your boyfriend coming?"

Faye sat for a moment and just stared at J.J. She had not even considered inviting Jeffrey to this event. In fact, she couldn't imagine him in the same room with all of these people. The memories of high school clicks and clubs were not especially fond for Faye. She didn't want to relive those days in front of her new boyfriend.

"No. He's not coming."

Donna gave her a look over her glasses. "You didn't even invite him, did you."

"Nope." Faye stood to leave. "I'm going to head out. I have some things to do before tonight. Are you guys carpooling?"

"Yeah. I'll come pick you up," J.J. spoke up, "It's going to be a long night."

Last year's Open House lasted until 2am. Faye didn't want to face any unwelcome visitors in her building at that hour. "Great. See you later."

***

Faye arrived that evening ready to mingle. She began by walking the room to get a feel for the conversations already happening. On her way to the drink table, Faye overheard Don fielding questions about his attack. It had been several weeks since the attack, she was a little surprised that people needed more information. She could have stopped to help, but he seemed able to handle it.

Faye moved quickly past Brandon who stood near the Mazzis. She had little interest in anything that either of them had to say. It was their first open house, so they received the welcome treatment.

"How are you adjusting to the school?"

"Do you live in the area?"

"Didn't you both live here twenty years ago?"

That last question stopped Faye. *Twenty years ago? Everyone seems a little fixated on something from so long ago.* Faye heard John Mazzi clearing his throat. She took a sip of her drink and waited to hear his response.

"Oh yeah, we grew up here. I've been back and forth to this area over the years. My wife has family and friends here."

"Anyone we know?"

"I'm not at liberty to say."

Mazzi dodged the question. He made some excuse to exit the conversation and walked across the room. Faye started to follow him, when someone grabbed her elbow.

"Any run-ins with the Schmidt family?" Brandon asked in a low voice.

"Not yet. You?" Faye attempted to be polite as she spoke to Brandon.

"Just Mazzi."

"I saw. He lived here before? You'd think he would have been back for a reunion before now. Surely, his class would remember him." Faye hoped that remark would end the conversation.

"I think they did." Brandon's response caused Faye to pause. "Mr. Brown knows him from somewhere. He told me to watch my back. I guess they had some kind of rivalry in high school. Did you go to school here?"

Faye thought about his question. "All my life, but I don't remember him."

"He remembers you."

"Faye! Sweetie, how are you doing?" Anna Gardner joined their conversation.

"I'm doing well, thank you."

"I heard about your spill the other day. I'm glad to see you are looking refreshed."

"Thank you. I appreciate your concern. How are the boys?" Faye knew that her son and nephew had been the ones to find Don in the ravine.

"They are doing much better now that school has started. It was a trial while Don was in the hospital. Those boys would do anything for him."

"I heard that they helped with some chores around the house." Brandon just wouldn't leave.

"Yes," she smiled. "They're good boys. It broke my heart what happened with Julie. Don's part of the family now."

Faye excused herself to grab some food. Conversations surrounding Julie and what happened made her uncomfortable. *Murder.* The word sent chills up her spine. She approached a plate of tiny sandwiches and a conversation between Stephanie Brown and an old classmate.

"I've never used them before, but you could try. They're friends of Gina Mazzi. So, you know…"

"I'm not sure I do know." Stephanie turned when she saw Faye. "Ms. Unger, do you know Sarah Baker? I believe you met her sister, Trish Schmidt on the first day of school."

"Oh? Hi there." Faye offered her hand, but Sarah Baker didn't take it.

In fact, Sarah Baker ignored Faye and spoke to Stephanie Brown. "It's your renovation. You can use whoever you like. My guy was dependable. He did the job well. Let me know if you want his number." She walked away without acknowledging Faye.

"I didn't mean to interrupt, Ms. Brown."

"Trust me, you came at the perfect time."

"So, you're renovating?"

"Maybe. We haven't decided if we will do it now or wait until the kids are off to college. Honestly, I never know what to talk about at these things." Stephanie added dip and crackers to her plate.

"Didn't you graduate from Arlington High School?" Faye asked.

"Yeah, but I never cared much for reunions. We live next door to these people. Yet, every year, they pretend they haven't seen me in decades."

The Browns had lived here for years.   Faye remembered them in school. They were older than her. They probably remembered what happened twenty years ago too.

"Do you remember the Mazzis living here twenty years ago?"

Stephanie looked up at Faye. "Gina was my best friend in elementary school. Didn't she tell you?"

"No. I haven't seen her. I keep running into her husband, though."

"Really?" Stephanie paused and then nodded, "He is teaching math this year."

"Yeah, they moved here from out of town, though, right?"

"Chicago."

A lot of people came from Chicago recently: Brandon, Jeffrey, Jodi, the Mazzis, and maybe the creepy cousin. Why do they keep hanging around my building?

"Did they move into the neighborhood or somewhere out of town?"

Stephanie looked at her like she already knew. "They're across the park near the ravine. Why do you ask?"

"He said something about his wife having a friend that lives in my building. I keep running into him in the lobby with his cousin."

"That man is scary, isn't he?" Stephanie looked around. "I think I saw him here tonight, too."

***

Faye moved across the room to join Donna and J.J. As she walked across the room, she looked around to see if she could spot Mazzi's creepy cousin. She passed several classmates reliving the old days with inside jokes and laughter. Faye waved. They pinky-waved back at her giving her permission to bypass conversations.

"Speak of the devil!" Donna said as Faye approached.

"We were just talking about you."

"What did I do?"

"Your artwork is legendary. We want to come see it."

Faye smiled. She knew it was only a matter of time before they brought it up.

"Yes. I hear that you have them framed and on display," JJ grabbed a napkin for wing sauce all over his face.

"As a matter of fact, I do."

"What are we talking about?" Susan approached along with several others.

"Faye is going to have us over for a party."

"I am?" Faye glared at Donna. This could easily get out of hand.

"I'm in." Susan stepped closer to Donna, "When are we doing this?"

"When are we doing what?" Brandon joined the conversation.

"Faye is having us over in two weeks," Donna announced.

"Two weeks?" Faye's glares were meaningless to Donna. No one came to her rescue. "I didn't actually say…"

"I'll bring buffalo chicken dip," J.J. offered.

Random people began to collaborate on what they would bring. Faye snuck away from the group to replenish her drink. Their party planning would continue without her. She walked across the room to be as far away from that conversation as possible.

"Ms. Unger, do you like sushi?"

Faye looked up at Ms. Gardner, puzzled. She looked at the food table and didn't find any sushi.

"Do you mind if I bring sushi to the party?"

"Party?"

Your party. They said you are hosting in a couple weeks?"

Faye nodded, officially overwhelmed. She took a deep breath and a sip of her drink. It stung the back of her throat, and she realized she had made her way to the adult table by mistake.

"It isn't that bad." Don said as he handed her a soda.

Faye shrugged. "It's a collision of my worlds. Until now, I've been able to separate work and art. Separate friends. My apartment was my own," she paused for effect, "happy place. That's all about to change." She took a sip of the soda.

Don nodded and lifted his drink to toast her. In the midst of this friendly reprieve, Faye remembered the ravine. The image of the man lying in the ravine sprung to mind. In her vision, she turned away from the body and looked across the street. The house across the street.

"Don, did you know that the Mazzis live in the house across the street from the ravine?"

"That was a bit random."

"I overheard some folks talking to him about his first year teaching. Someone said he lived here twenty years ago. I asked around. He doesn't live in my building. He lives across from the ravine."

"What do you mean, Faye? I'm not sure I follow."

"So, the Mazzis grew up here twenty years ago. John moved to Chicago. A few weeks ago, he and Gina move back here into the family home." Faye looked at Don as though he should completely understand what she meant.

"Ok. Give me a little more, Faye. Why does it matter that he moved away 20 years ago?"

"Because…" Faye leaned closer to whisper, "the murder at the ravine happened 20 years ago." Her eyes grew wide as she waited for him to connect the information.

"Why is this important to me?"

"Your attack at the ravine," Faye whispered with gritted teeth, "the creepy cousin, or John himself, might have done it. The two might be connected."

"Why would John Mazzi want to hurt me?"

That question stumped her. Faye hadn't thought about motives. "Had you met Mazzi or his cousin before the attack?"

"I don't think so."

"Well, maybe he saw something that could help us catch the guys."

"Good point. I'm sure the police already asked though."

Faye rolled her eyes, "the police?"

"You don't trust the police?"

"Ugh, please."

Nineteen

The cool, night air sent chill bumps on Faye's arms. The leaves crunched under her feet as she walked through the park. She had to find Elaine. She'd already been to the school and the alley behind the donut shop. That other girl didn't know where she was. What was her name? Gina. She told Faye that Elaine had left the party in a hurry.

It was late or was it early? Either way, Faye should be in bed. She stopped before walking toward the ravine and looked down. The red Converse All-Stars had always been her favorite. The flower patches on her jeans reminded her of the ones she wore when she was in the second grade. She heard arguing and looked up.

A man yelled over his shoulder, "It's not gonna fit that a way..."

Faye sat straight up in bed, drenched in sweat. Nightmares again. This time all of the people from the last couple of weeks mingled with images from her childhood. It took her a minute to get a grip on her surroundings.

"It's not gonna fit that a way," a voice called out again.

Faye got up and put on a bathrobe. She stepped into the living room and heard another voice from the hallway.

"You gotta put it on its side."

That voice sounds familiar. Faye stepped toward the peep hole to look out. *Don?* She couldn't see much from the peep hole, but she heard a heavy object hit the floor. Brandon stepped around to where Don was standing.

Faye stepped away from the door and looked at the clock in the kitchen. 8:00am. She crossed to the kitchen and started a pot of coffee. There was no going back to bed. She thought about stepping outside to see what was going on, but she needed to get dressed first. Those guys couldn't see her like this.

Her phone chimed from the other room.

Jodi: Are you excited?

Jeffrey: Today's the big day.

Jeffrey had offered to take Faye's art to the auction today. She was pumped. Last night, the three of them celebrated with too much junk food and old Hitchcock movies. It's no wonder she had nightmares. Today, the public would have the opportunity to purchase her art. There would be value placed on her creative delineations beyond Elaine's quote.

She replied: 😍.

It took her no time to get ready for the day. Faye had prepped an outfit for the occasion days ago when Jeffrey first mentioned it. She had time for a cup of coffee before they arrived. Then, she heard a knock at the door. She tried to ignore it, but the person persisted. So, Faye opened the door to a group of familiar faces.

"Ms. Unger! I thought you lived here," Stephanie Brown said from the other side of the door. "Would you mind if we used your kitchen?"

While Stephanie waited patiently for an answer, Susan and Donna stepped passed her into Faye's apartment.

"Faye! This is beautiful!" Donna said.

"Your party next week is going to be amazing!" Susan added.

"What's going on?"

"I'm sorry, Faye," Stephanie continued. "I hope you don't mind if I call you Faye. Brandon, well Mr. Foster, is moving in next door. We all came by to help with the move."

"Yeah, we need to borrow your sink and counter tops for a minute," Donna spoke apologetically.

The women began to unload armloads of breakfast items and snack foods onto the counters. It took a minute or two for their words to sink in. *They were helping Brandon Foster move in next door!* She knew the people had moved out. The doorman mentioned someone leasing the apartment next door. *I should have asked more questions.*

"Oh." Faye needed to sit down for this. She was shaking her head.

"The counters over there are completely filthy," Donna said. "We need a place to set up food. Those guys have been working all morning to clear out his old place."

"It's 8am? When did you get started?"

"They've been working since about six or seven? Don't worry, it shouldn't take too long."

Faye wanted to protest. Every part of her wanted Brandon far away from her. She tried to ignore his presence at work. It would be impossible for her to ignore him as her neighbor. At least, he didn't come over with Jodi last night, even though she'd invited him. Now, Faye understood why.

"It's just that…"

Faye started to tell them about her plans to leave, but the door opened again. Brandon and Don walked in followed by J.J. and Jason Brown. They wiped sweat from their brow as they made their way to the snacks.

"Thank you ladies, for doing this," Jason said first. The others followed with thank you's and heads nodding.

"Thank you, Faye, for opening your home to us." Don gave her a pat on the back.

"So, where did you move from?" Faye asked Brandon.

Brandon nodded. "Mostly out of storage."

"He was living in a hotel. Can you believe it?" Stephanie poured glasses of lemonade. "We couldn't let that continue."

"I'm thankful for your concern. It wasn't as bad they make it out to be, but it'll be nice to be in my own place."

"How fortunate that there was an opening in my building!" Faye forced a grin.

"And right next door," J.J. looked at them both. "You guys will be neighbors at home and at work."

Everyone smiled and laughed except for Faye. Her forced grin didn't hide her true feelings. Faye moved to a corner of the room and watched them. Their laughter and comfort with one another brought a sense of ease and safety to the room.

Faye's pocket chirped a reminder of her previous plans.

Jodi: Are you ready?

Jeffrey: On my way to pick you up. Then, we can head over to Faye's.

Faye looked at her phone and then at the people in her apartment. She watched and listened to hear when they might be leaving. If they left soon, she could still catch up with Jeffrey and Jodi. Susan held up the carafe from the coffee maker. Several raised mugs indicated a need for more. So, Susan started making another pot.

Faye reached into her pocket and pulled out the phone to respond.

Faye: I don't think I'm going to make it, guys.

Jodi: What?

Jeffrey: You have been looking forward to this all summer?

Faye: Something came up. I can't leave right now.

Jeffrey: Elaine will be there.

Faye looked up at the crowd. This time, the color drained from her face and her stomach fluttered. *What do I tell Elaine? Do I leave teaching?*

"Is everything Ok, Faye?" Don had walked away from the crowd to join her.

"Sure," Faye shrugged.

"I'm sorry we surprised you like this. Really." Don spoke in a quiet voice so he wouldn't draw attention to Faye's condition.

"It's fine."

"We'll get out of your hair soon. I'm sure you had other things to do today."

Faye's mind wandered into the French restaurant with the fancy bread. Elaine sat across from her handing her an offer. *I can't think about that right now.* "I didn't know Brandon was moving next door. What kind of neighbor would I be if I didn't offer to help?"

Faye's phone rang. Jeffrey. She looked at Don, "Let me take care of something first."

Faye stepped aside to talk. Jodi spoke first, "Faye, you're on speaker. We're on our way to get you. Jeffrey says you gotta come."

"I can't."

"What's going on?"

"Some friends and family stopped by." These people certainly acted like family to Faye. "They need my help. You guys can do this without me."

"Elaine will be disappointed. She told me to make sure you come."

"Jeffrey, I'm sure Elaine can run an auction without me. Hasn't she been doing this for a long time."

"It's better for new artists to be there with their work," Jodi said.

"Well, I can't be there."

The call ended. No good-bye or farewell. Faye knew that they would be disappointed, but she didn't expect that. Jeffrey had never hung up on her before. Actually, they'd never argued. It seemed Faye wasn't the only one afraid of Elaine.

Faye overheard conversations in the kitchen, but took a minute to clear her head before she joined the rest of the crew.

"So, how did you manage to secure this apartment?" Jason asked.

"Don't look at me," Brandon pointed to Don.

"It took skilled negotiations, for sure." Don lowered his voice, "I started talking with the super after Julie's accident." He took a sip of coffee, "I thought I might be the one moving in, but…" He patted Brandon on the back. "…this guy needed the place more."

Faye made her way to join the others in the kitchen. She didn't comment on Don's interaction with the apartment. It made sense that he would move after Julie's death. She'd have done the same.

"It'd be different if we had a fourth guy to pull the weight," Brandon looked at Don, his arm still in a sling.

"What? I'm pulling my weight. How else would you all know how to angle it into the doorway?"

Faye slid her phone into her back pocket. "How can I help?"

The moving party lasted into the evening. The Gardners brought over pizza for heavy lifters while the others busied themselves unpacking boxes and setting up the kitchen. The families made plans to bring over meals until he settled. Faye enjoyed the company despite the fact she was helping Brandon. She found herself unpacking boxes along with the rest of them.

The kitchen took the longest to unpack. One particular box gave Faye a hard time. The structural integrity of the box yielded under the weight of it. She decided to leave it on the ground as she unpacked it.

"You cook?" Faye screamed the question as her face lit up in delight.

"I didn't peg you for a cook," J.J. said.

Brandon shrugged, "Sometimes."

"There have to be dozens of cookbooks here. This one was printed in 1965."

"Everybody has a hobby." Brandon's face turned a rosy shade of red.

"I thought the motorcycle was your hobby. You didn't say anything about cooking. After all the take-out…" Don shook his head.

Faye spied a box across the room labeled "Books." She walked over to the box like a child on a secret mission to the cookie jar. Before he could stop her, Faye had opened it. She passed a few crime fiction novels before she found gold.

"High School Yearbook!" She held it up like a champion holds up the trophy.

"No!"

Brandon moved quickly to stop her, but Faye rounded the sofa. The others shielded her from him until she found his photo.

"Awww," the collective response from the women prompted the men to muscle their way in for a view. Several of them nudged him a few times for laughs.

"Your hair is so long here. Why don't you let it grow out?"

"I love that curl it does on top."

"You played basketball?"

"And ran track."

The whole crew had a laugh. "I guess the truth is all out there now," Brandon said. "I've got nothing to hide.

Twenty

After Open House, things settled down at the school. With classes running smoothly, teachers began to relax a bit during their planning time. Once again, the Media Center buzzed with conversations over coffee. Susan and Richard used the opportunity to thin the book shelves for reorders. Several stacks of books appeared on the tables for students and teachers to peruse.

The archives included yearbooks from the High School, which ran from 1980-2015. Evidently, the conversations over Brandon's yearbook prompted Susan and Richard to pull the yearbooks of several colleagues. Faye walked into Brandon and Susan's conversation about her own yearbook.

"There's really only the one photo?" Brandon was asking Susan.

"That's all I could find. It looks like she wasn't really involved in the class."

"Nice photo, Faye."

Faye looked at Brandon with a small grin and skeptical eyes.

"There aren't any secrets in that book," she said. "Most of my classmates attended the Open House. You could have asked them for juicy stories."

"Are there juicy stories?"

"You might find some in this book." Susan pulled out the class of 2001.

Susan started flipping through the pages as though she knew where to look. She landed on a page full of student photos. Faye read through the names until she found one that she recognized, Jason Brown.

"Was his wife in that class too?"

"Sure, but that isn't the curious part. " Susan continued to scroll through the names. Her finger landed on a photo near the bottom, John Mazzi.

"That makes sense," Brandon said. "Mr. Brown told me to watch out for him."

Susan leaned closer to whisper. "But did he tell you why?"

She picked up the book and started to thumb through the pages. She stopped when she reached a section of candid photos from school events. Students stood in the hall near their lockers. Some smiled over food in the cafeteria. Another photo showed a bon fire near the ravine.

"They did bon fires?" Faye said in surprise.

"Oh, yeah. Every year until 2003."

"What happened in 2003?" Brandon asked.

Susan stopped and looked up at Brandon with her mouth slightly open. Everyone knew what happened in 2003. She looked at Brandon as though waiting for him to remember it. When he didn't, she looked at Faye. Faye didn't know what Susan was talking about, so she waited to hear what happened.

"A boy was…" Susan looked from side to side, but didn't dare say the word out loud. She did a lip sync with over-exaggerated gestures, "murdered."

"That's right!" Faye nearly shouted.

Brandon leaned in closer, "What happened? Was it at the bon fire?"

"No. We don't really talk about it." Susan looked up at Faye as she said the last part. Then, she continued, "Some people speculate about who might've been there. Everyone in town has a theory."

"Like what?"

"Brandon, I never pictured you as one for gossip." Faye stood to leave.

"Well." Susan leaned in for effect. "Let's just say that I have on good authority that there's witnesses."

Brandon sat up in the chair, and Faye rolled her eyes.

"And…" Susan paused when Richard entered the room.

"Don't stop on my account." Richard grabbed a handful of books and left.

"They say the killer might have come back to town."

A cold chill ran up Faye's spine. It seemed to move through the room, because Brandon jumped up.

"Oh man! I have a class waiting on me."

Faye stayed behind to look at the photos while Brandon ran out of the room. Jason Brown was standing next to Mazzi near the fire. Jason's wife was next to him. Faye recognized her from the other photo.

"Is this Gina?" Faye asked pointing to the young girl standing next to John Mazzi in the photo.

"I don't think so." Susan leaned closer to get a better look at the photo. Then she turned back a few pages to the junior class photos. "This is Gina."

"Then, who is this?" Faye had kept her finger on the page with the bon fire.

"I'm not sure," Susan said. "You're welcome to look through it. I need to go check on some students."

Faye marked the page with a piece of paper and pulled up a chair. She flipped back through the classes to find another photo of the girl. It didn't take long before she found it in the sophomore class. Elaine Andrews.

Twenty-One

The Browns and Gardners invited Don to his first game night after Julie's death. Over the past year, the families met on the first Saturday each month. This month, Don volunteered to grab dinner for the group. On his way to the store, He stopped by the apartment building to invite Brandon. As he parked on the street, he looked for the black town car that had followed Faye but didn't see it.

"Hello there, Mr. Ambrose," the doorman greeted him.

"Hi, Jay." Don tried to get to know folks in town on a personal level. "I'm here to see Brandon Foster."

"Shall I call him down?"

"Can I go up? He may need some help carrying the drinks."

"Go right ahead."

Don turned to catch the elevator before it closed.

"Gina?"

"Excuse me?"

The doors opened allowing Don to slide into the elevator.

"Aren't you a teacher at Arlington Community?"

"Yes. Should I know you?"

Don Ambrose. I teach Math, with your husband." He offered to shake her hand.

Gina bypassed the greeting and reached to press the button for her floor. "I don't remember seeing you at the school training."

Don raised his elbow still in a sling. "I suffered an injury the night before and couldn't attend. Do you guys live here?"

Gina answered with her face rather than her voice. Her eyebrows raised as she looked at the floor she had already selected. Then, her phone chirped. "Do you mind?"

Don raised his hands in surrender and didn't pressure her for conversation. The doors opened and she exited to the right. Don waited for her to exit before he followed. He pretended to have dropped something and squatted to retrieve it.

Gina knocked on 5C. Don made his was to the other end of the hall and noticed a rather large man answer the door. He waved as he passed, hoping to get a glimpse inside the apartment. The lay-out seemed similar to that of Brandon's. Don stepped into the stairwell and walked up to Brandon's apartment.

"Do you have a mail room here?"

"Hey Don. I'm doing alright. Thanks for asking."

"I need to know who's in 5C. I thought there might be a name on the mail box."

"There is a mail room, but the boxes don't have names on them. What are you tryin' to do?"

"I followed Gina Mazzi to 5C."

"I don't think she lives there." Brandon tossed his keys to Don before picking up the drinks.

"Me either." Don caught the keys with his free hand. "But I want to know who does."

"Just ask the doorman. He knows everybody."

They both headed out the door. As they exited the elevator, they noticed Gina Mazzi approaching the doorman.

"Did you enjoy your visit with Ms. Louise?"

"Very much, thank you," Gina nodded as she left.

***

Don racked his brain to come up with a last name for Louise.

"Come on, Don. It's charades. You have to guess," Jason said. "What's eating at you, anyway?"

"Mazzi."

"That son of a …"

"Jason!"

"Sorry. That guy gets me. How he landed a job at my kid's school, I'll never know."

Brandon looked at Don. "They got a history."

"What do you know about his wife?"

"That's my wife's area. She and Gina go all the way back. Stephanie, tell him what happened with Gina."

"She's dead to me."

"What'd she do?"

"First of all, she stole my boyfriend."

"John?" Brandon looked really confused.

"No. Some other guy, but that's not my point. That actually worked out better for me." Stephanie looked over at her husband and pointed at him as she gave him a wink. "That family, though. Something's not right."

"Come on, Stephanie. You have to give me more than that," Don said.

"I don't have any proof." Stephanie closed her eyes and shook her head.

"There's a way you treat a girl." Jason tried to help them understand.

"I'm not talkin' about John, that's a different issue. Her family ain't right," Stephanie took breath and finished. "The boys never treated girls right. Controlling. Forceful, but like I said before, I don't have any proof."

Don nodded at her response and looked away.

Stephanie left toward the kitchen. She returned with a tray full of snacks and started again, "It's high school, right? The senior boys dated the younger girls. The girls thought it was something to date an older guy until it got to that point. They knew it was wrong. Gina knew it was wrong. She just went along with it. That's on her."

"You said it's the family," Don bit his lip, "what's Gina's maiden name?"

"Schmidt."

"Is this the same Schmidt family in the police force?" Brandon grabbed a plate and loaded it with potato chips and dip.

Stephanie poured a glass of soda. "The same."

"That's why no one reported any assault." Don exhaled with a groan.

"You know how it is." Brandon looked at Don with his mouth full of crunchy chips. Don wanted to change the subject, "So, who is Louise?"

"Louise? Is she a Mazzi?" Jason asked.

"Never heard of her." Stephanie set down her drink and started passing out the playing cards.

Twenty-Two

The pale, blue walls complimented the light gray flooring in Dr. Gardner's office. The housekeeping team also cleaned the artwork from the walls and the magazines from the tables. What might reduce anxiety for some only magnified Faye's apprehension as she approached the tiny window.

"Good afternoon. How can I help you?"

Faye bent down to view the woman sitting behind the desk. "I'm here to see Dr. Gardner."

"You must be Ms. Unger," the woman said with a smile. "He's expecting you. Step over there to the door, and I'll show you back."

Faye stepped back and a door to her right opened. The same woman led her down a short hallway with a room on the right. "You can have a seat. I"ll let him know you're here."

Faye walked into the room and took a seat. The room contained drawings of the human body with bones and muscles. A small model of an ear sat on a counter next to a box of tissues. The longer she sat, the greater her urge to leave. She didn't feel sick, but Faye knew that her visit with the doctor would satisfy her parents.

The door opened, and Faye jumped.

"Hi there, Ms. Unger. I'm glad you came in today." Steve Gardner shook her hand before he took a seat. "How's the new neighbor working out?"

Faye smiled, "I guess it's nice to know at least one of your neighbors."

"Before I look at any paperwork, why don't you tell me how you have been feeling?"

"I feel fine, actually. I probably shouldn't even be here." she started to stand as if to leave.

"Hold on, ok? You're here, so let's check you out." He motioned for her to jump onto the exam table.

Dr. Gardner listened to her heart. He checked her eyes and ears. He even checked her reflexes. Then, he walked over to the computer and started typing. Faye watched as he entered data. She strained to read whatever was on the screen.

"Do you have copies of my medical records?" She asked.

"Sure. All of the hospitals in the region use the same system. It's helpful when I get a new patient. I can see your previous symptoms, allergies, surgeries, and anything else that could cause medical issues."

"Does everything look ok?" Faye couldn't remember having medical problems, but the look on Dr. Gardner's face concerned her.

"Let's see." He turned the screen toward her. "This is all written in medical code, so I may have to translate."

He scrolled down on the computer and typed notes.

"Does it have my family information too?"

"I can probably access it, but it's not on this page. It says here that you are pretty healthy."

"That's good, then, right?" Faye let out a deep breath. "I knew there was nothing to worry about."

"Oh," Steve stopped and stared at the screen. He took a deep breath, squinted, and wrote some things on the chart.

"What is it?"

"Says here that you suffered a grade 3 concussion. Usually, that's when someone is unconscious for a long period of time." He adjusted his glasses and continued. "You weren't unconscious that long, but your symptoms afterwards were similar. Something about amnesia and losing the ability to speak. Do you remember if you ever saw a counselor or psychiatrist?"

"I'm not sure." Faye's apprehension towards doctors started in her teens. "I remember seeing a couple of doctors when I was in middle school, but I couldn't tell you what kind of doctors they were."

"Today, you look pretty healthy. Your heart sounds good, and I don't see any effects of concussion. Could you tell me what happened at the school?"

Faye told him about how Ms. Schmidt confronted her at the school. "She said something about my family. It didn't make any sense to me. I've never met that lady."

"Interesting. Maybe it has something to do with the amnesia. Has anything else out of the ordinary happened lately?"

"I've been having nightmares."

"What happens in the dream?"

"Something about the ravine. Sometimes, I'm just there, scared. Other times I hear voices and someone chasing me."

"The mind is a tricky thing. We found your friend Don Ambrose unconscious in the ravine. That could give you nightmares. My guess, it probably has something to do with the incident when you were younger."

"Could it just be stress?" Faye would rather do anything other than explore her childhood. "I mean, things are different at school, and I have a new neighbor." She smiled hoping to make her case.

Steve shook his head, "There are a few psychologists in town, that you could go see."

Faye took a deep breath.

"I know. Nobody wants to go see a shrink. I'll give you the names of some people. You could also ask your parents about memories that you're missing."

Faye frowned.

"Until then, you could try journalling your dreams. Maybe you'll uncover something."

Faye nodded again. "Sure."

"What about painting? I hear you're an artist. We often release clues of our past in our drawings. You might find the memories in scenes you've already painted."

"That's an idea," Faye nodded as she remembered her painting experience. "Thank you, Doctor."

On her way out, Faye received a text.

Jeffrey: Are you busy?

Faye: Maybe

After talking to the doctor, Faye really wanted to go home and paint. The thought of uncovering the past made her shudder, but she longed for control of her thoughts again. Her mind had gone to so much trouble to hide things from her. However, clues from the past seemed to spill out without her permission.

Jeffrey: Can we meet for dinner?

Dinner with Jeffrey could be a good distraction from the nightmares and thoughts she might uncover. He would probably take her to some posh location, and that would take her out of her head for sure.

Faye: I would be delighted.

Jeffrey: Fantastic. I'll pick you up at 7.

Twenty-Three

Don started putting the pieces together with the Schmidts and the Mazzis, but he couldn't figured out what any of it had to do with The Auction House. Don didn't believe in coincidences. A lot of interesting people converged on Arlington over the past few months. He headed over to Brandon's to get to know this new girlfriend. Chloe, Jodi, whatever you want to call her, she might know something that will string it all together.

Brandon opened the door. "Don! Come on in. We've been looking forward to seeing you."

Don looked at Jodi, whose cheeks were already a shade of pink, "I brought a little bubbly, but it looks like you guys started without me."

"Jodi came over to help me cook. You know."

"Hi." she wiped her hands on a towel and walked over to introduce herself. "I'm Jodi."

"Aren't you a friend of Faye's?"

"Yeah, we're in the art collective together when she's not blowing us off."

"What happened?"

"We were supposed to auction her paintings, but she never showed."

"That's not like her." Don made himself at home in Brandon's kitchen.

Brandon turned toward Don. "When was that, exactly?"

Jodi thrust her hand on her hips. "Saturday morning!"

"Didn't she call?" Don glanced at Brandon willing him to explain to Jodi.

"Yeah, she called," Jodi said and rolled her eyes. "Said something came up. Wouldn't even say what it was."

"Huh," Don's eyes grew wider as he glared at Brandon.

"Um, that's probably my fault."

Jodi relaxed. "How is that your fault?"

"Moving day." Don interjected. "We commandeered her apartment while we set up in here. Were you able to sell her paintings?"

"They didn't even go up for auction. Something about how she needed to be there for it."

"That's a shame. I hear she's pretty good."

"She's alright," Jodi said. Then, she noticed the look of surprise on both Brandon and Don. "That's how it always is in the beginning.

You hype them up so they get involved. Then, they end up helping you promote the business."

Jodi didn't even realize that she'd said too much. They sat down to eat, but Don wanted more information.

"What exactly is the business?"

"We auction things." Jodi leaned into Brandon as she spoke.

Don ignored their exaggerated affections. "Just art?"

"Art. Furniture. Tchotchkes. Whatever we find."

"We?"

"Jeffrey and I make a trip through Kentucky every year to see what they have. They usually have a good selection of hand-made items."

"They also have a lot of drugs and moonshine," Don thought to himself.

"Just you and Jeffrey? I thought he was dating Faye? Are you two involved?" Brandon sounded jealous.

"Jeffrey and I have history, but don't worry honey," Jodi winked at Brandon, "I'm a free spirit."

"Surely you guys aren't the only ones working at the auction house? Who runs the place?"

Jodi stopped and looked at him. Then, she looked at Don. "Are you guys collectors?"

They looked at each other. Their eyes locked and eyebrows raised and they nodded.

"There is another auction this weekend. You should come."

***

"You want me to come to an auction this weekend?" Faye asked Jeffrey. "What happened to my paintings in the last auction?"

Jeffrey sipped his water. "Elaine said you had to be there."

"What? How exactly do auctions work anyway?"

"Usually, the piece goes up on the website with a description. The artist's name can be found with the description. Some artists sell paintings in name only. The auctions begin at a specific time. We often set the first bid."

Jeffrey paused when the drinks arrived. He waited until after the waiter left to continue. "Sometimes, we use an auctioneer. Usually, new artists require an auctioneer to announce their work and gain interest."

"I guess that makes sense. I didn't see why I needed to be present for all of that."

"Elaine wants you to be involved in the process." He shrugged his shoulders and sipped his drink.

The waiter arrived with their food. Faye took the opportunity to think about going to the auction. Elaine wanted to connect with her. However honored, Faye still wasn't so sure about Elaine. Her unconventional methods were intimidating and frightening.

"I'm not sure I trust Elaine."

There. She said it out loud. Faye didn't know if she could even trust Jeffrey, but she threw that out there to see what he would do with it.

"I get that." Jeffrey agreed with her, "but you can't let that get in the way of your art. You're special, Faye." Jeffrey looked deeply into Faye's eyes.

Faye could stare into Jeffrey's dreamy, blue eyes all night. When he looked at her that way, looking into her soul and softening the hard edges, she became a puddle of her former self.

"I'll go with you," Faye said. "Just don't leave me alone with Elaine."

Jeffrey reached across the table and grabbed her hand. "I won't let you out of my sight."

Twenty-Four

Located downtown, The Auction House combined two department stores. The front portion resembled an antique shop. The window display contained items in the upcoming auction. The rest of the room looked like an antique store except pieces sat in auction categories. The back portion of The Auction House resembled a warehouse with floor to ceiling shelving units. Most of the items in the warehouse hadn't been catalogued. Others had been set aside for distribution.

Faye passed by The Auction House dozens of times on her way to the coffee shop. Today, she entered through the back with Jeffrey. They carefully navigated the tall shelves by following yellow, painted paths on the floor. The warehouse operations seemed to be on hold with forklifts parked to her right. Most of the crates on the shelves remained unopened. The path wandered through the maze of packaging until it stopped at the door of an office.

Faye followed Jeffrey through the door. She expected a small office with maybe one desk. She encountered a large room with several tables. To one side, a kitchenette held a cook top, sink, and coffee maker. There was a dining table near it with four chairs. Jeffrey directed Faye to a lounging area complete with plush, leather sofas, arm chairs and a coffee table.

Faye took a seat directly across from a sound proof room. The tiny room, was large enough to include a small photo studio and sound equipment.

"Can I get you a cup of coffee?" Jeffrey asked. "We should be getting started soon."

"This doesn't look anything like the front of the building." Faye's voice matched her surprise.

"People often pick up in the front. During the week, a clerk will meet them there."

"Do people come in off the street to buy from the shop?"

"Not usually," Jeffrey replied, "most people buy online these days."

"Is Jodi coming?"

"She usually works out front." Jeffrey grabbed her hand reassuringly, "I'll let her know you're here. She might come back to see you."

Other people joined them in the large room. Men in suits filed in carrying expertly carved desks and side tables. Two men carried a large painting. Faye watched the men arrange the items for the auction.

She didn't see Jodi. More importantly, she didn't see Elaine.

Jeffrey excused himself to gather small tags to place on each item. Another man entered the room. Wearing a colorful suit and a handlebar mustache, he resembled the ringmaster of the circus. The mustache, along with bushy eyebrows, focused on Faye. She couldn't help but smile at him as he walked toward her.

"I hear you are the artist in residence this morning."

Faye stood and shook his hand with a puzzled look on her face.

"Yes, she is." Elaine said from behind her. "This is Ms. Faye Unger. She has two paintings on display this morning."

"Ah yes. Will she be collaborating with me during the auction?"

Elaine looked at Faye. "I'm afraid not. You may ask her anything you like before the auction. She will also determine the starting bid, however, she will remain with me during the auction."

Faye looked at Elaine unsure how to respond to this. Although happy to be off camera during the live auction, she did not want to spend her time within close proximity to Elaine. She looked around the room for Jeffrey, but couldn't find him. Faye did spy Jodi enter the room from the front.

Jodi appeared to be leading guests into the room. *Brandon.* Even the thought of his name appeared shrouded in disgust. *Is that*

Don with him? What are they doing here? Faye tried to make eye contact with Don. He might help her escape.

Jodi looked at Faye, and Faye gave a wave. Jodi's usual, cheerful expression changed to panic.

Elaine excused herself. Faye watched her glide across the room to speak to a couple of large men in suits.

"What is this?" Jeffrey returned. Then, Jodi approached. "You can't bring your boyfriend to the auction?"

"They're collectors." Jodi corrected him.

"Collectors bid online. You know that." Jeffrey nervously scanned the room. "They shouldn't be here."

"Relax. It's fine. They want to see everything up close." Jodi glanced over toward Elaine. "Trust me, it'll be fine."

Elaine sent the two men their direction.

"Excuse me, sirs," one of the men interrupted, "yous need to come with me."

The men stood close to Brandon and Don and grabbed their elbows, forcing them to move.

"Is this how you treat all your customers?" Brandon spoke with intensity.

Although, she enjoyed watching Brandon squirm, Faye began to feel the tension created by the men.

"We're friends of Johnny," Don cut in.

The men stopped and gave a puzzled look. Don motioned with his head toward the auction booth. Faye followed his glare to Mazzi in the midst of a conversation with the auctioneer.

"Johnny? How do you know Johnny?"

"We work together." Don looked over at Mazzi and nodded hello.

Mazzi looked up from the conversation. This seemed to be all the men needed.

"Oh, sorry bout that sirs." They let go of Brandon and Don. "Right his way."

As they approached Mazzi, Elaine intercepted them. She lowered her sunglasses, and the men stepped back.

"Can I help you gentlemen with something?"

"Of course, do you have any information on the beautifully carved side tables?" Don pointed to a set of tables near Mazzi.

Faye strained to hear their conversation.

"Faye," Jeffrey whispered for her attention.

Faye stepped closer to the conversation. She felt the sudden urge to rescue them from Elaine. Well, maybe just Don.

"The auction is live in an hour. You will receive all the information at that time. All of our auctions take place on the website," Elaine spoke through clenched teeth.

"That presents a problem for me," Don responded calmly.

Elaine looked at him and raised an eyebrow.

"I have no digital signature," He stepped closer and spoke something quietly. Faye strained to hear it, but missed it altogether.

"Ms…," a man placed his hand on Faye's shoulder, "If I may bother you for just a few questions."

She turned sharply toward the auctioneer.

Twenty-Five

Parents often flooded the hallways on Fridays during football season. In fact, parents walked through the hallways in the school every day. Some of the parents worked in the school, while others volunteered in various locations around the building. Today, Faye encountered a small crowd around the Math hall. The flurry of activity appeared to be concentrated near Faye's desk.

From the hallway, Faye noticed bags of groceries and containers of baked goods piled dangerously high on her desk. Someone had lined up sodas and bottles of wine along the floor. Faye stood frozen in the doorway. The shelf that usually held her bag was now the home of a bundt cake and two loaves of French bread.

"I would say that you could use my desk today, but I'm not sure where it is." Brandon spoke from behind a floral arrangement.

"Don't worry, Susan told me that we can store these things in the media center for now." J.J. picked up several containers. He exited toward the media center and motioned with his head for them to follow.

Faye inched toward her desk in an attempt to set her things down. She found a spot in the floor under her desk next to a grocery bag full of tortilla chips. She picked up the bag along with a tray of appetizers and headed toward the media center.

"There might be a space for that in the fridge," Susan told Faye. "I cleared the counter here for the others."

"What is all of this?" Faye observed the flurry of activity in the media center. Teachers and parents came from all directions with supplies. Susan directed and organized all of the materials like she did for the Open House.

"It's for your party tonight," Stephanie Brown arranged the plates in the refrigerator.

"My party?"

"Don't you remember?" Stephanie looked at Faye from the top of the refrigerator door, "at the Open House?" She closed the door and turned toward Faye. "You invited everyone to come view your artwork."

Faye had completely forgotten the conversations about her artwork at the Open House. People drank too much and joked around. She had no real thought that anyone would show up at her place for a party. Let alone the entire school.

"Who did I invite?" Faye looked at Donna who had walked in with a fruit tray.

"It's not about who you invited. It's about who's coming."

"Who's coming?"

"Everyone."

Faye tried to wrap her head around how many people would actually be showing up at her house. She enjoyed parties, really. In fact, she hosted members of the Art Collective on more than one occasion. Everyone, though? Faye worked hard to separate home and work.

"Don't worry," Mrs. Brown said, "We'll come over after school and help you get ready."

Faye thought about the condition of her apartment. Usually, her apartment, like everything else in her life, appeared clean and ordered. However, Faye had decided to go through some of the personal items after she left Dr. Gardner's office. She had emptied old photo albums and photo boxes on the dining table. She even opened a safe hidden in her closet. Faye planned to go over these items thoroughly after school.

Faye left the media center and headed toward the math office.

"I need to leave early today," Faye announced.

"What's wrong?" Don walked up beside her.

"Can you cover my class?"

"Sure. What's going on?"

"There's a party at my house tonight! I need to prepare."

The apartment seemed worse than she remembered it. Photo boxes stacked on the floor spilled onto the carpet. Other stacks of photos covered the dining table. Nearly all of her storage bins jumped from the shelf for examination. Faye looked over the photos on the table trying to remember them. She tried to stuff them in boxes, but her brain ordered them according to dates written on the back. Faye moved quickly to sort photos and tuck them back into their album.

All of these photos held superficial memories. Homecoming photos with friends. Football games. Nothing sparked panic or stress. Faye tucked them into their boxes and placed them back on the shelf. A few of the boxes would go into the bedroom with the safe. The safe held more clues. Faye couldn't remember the last time she had opened it. Probably, tax season. She unloaded the sensitive tax documents and bank statements, and set them aside. Next to the stack, she placed a program from the circus and concert tickets from her 18th birthday. Similar to the other photos, the things in this safe seemed more trivial than stressful.

A tiny book of pressed flowers sat near the bottom of the safe. Apprehension along with a cold sweat swept across Faye. She remembered making this book with her mom when she was 10. Her hands started to shake as she reached for it. Perhaps this earlier memory had something to do with the amnesia.

Faye stroked the lace on the front of the book. She closed her eyes and took a deep breath. Instantly, she was in her mother's bedroom gluing the fabric to the front. She could picture her mom's face and even hear the sounds of laughter in the room. The book held all of the pressed corsages from high school. Homecoming freshman year. Prom. Aunt Jackie's wedding. The last one had a simple white carnation with the label, "Funeral."

Faye tried to remember this funeral without any luck. She smelled it in case the scent sparked the memory. Nothing. So, she continued to look through the safe. She found her senior homecoming crown resting on top of a jewelry box. She placed the crown on her head with a smile and reached down to pick up the box.

Faye opened the box along with a sense of dread. A heart-shaped locket rested on the bottom. The locket looked familiar, and Faye found herself searching the room to be sure she was alone. She picked up the locket and saw a class ring attached to the chain. Faye looked closer at the ring. A man's ring, Class of 2001.

Faye's hands trembled as she attempted to open the locket. She pictured herself fastening the clasp of the chain around someone else's neck. Her fingers slid over the silver loops in a familiar way. She opened the locket and saw a tiny photo of two teenagers on the right side. She didn't recognize them. The left side held an inscription, *"Yours Forever."*

Faye closed her eyes for a moment to try to remember what this meant or why she had it. The image of the ravine flashed across her mind. Then, she heard someone knocking at the door.

Twenty-Six

"I'll be right there!" Faye called over her shoulder as she scrambled to gather her things and lock them into the safe. She carefully hid the safe in the back of her closet before going toward the door.

Faye opened the door to Stephanie and Donna carrying trays of food.

"Susan is right behind us with flowers." Stephanie walked straight to the kitchen. "The men have the other food with them."

Faye left the door unlocked so that the others could find their way inside.

"Your apartment is beautiful!" Donna said on her way to the kitchen. "I'm not sure what else we need to do here."

"Thanks," Faye said as she cleared the television stand. "We can move the T.V. to the bedroom and use this for food. You can also place trays on the coffee table and side tables."

"You've done this before." Susan set the flowers on the table.

Faye nodded and headed to the balcony with a broom. It didn't take long for them to transform the space for the party. Last week, Jeffrey installed lights for the paintings. Faye walked around and plugged them in for the first time. She had several lamps around the room with ambient lighting for the party.

"Perfect," Donna said, "we've got it from here. You go back in there and get dressed."

Faye hadn't thought about what she would wear. The sounds of guests in the hallway prompted her to move quickly. She grabbed a sequined cocktail dress and heels. Emerald earrings and red lipstick completed any party look. Faye made sure to clean up her bedroom in the off chance they needed space for coats. Then, she entered a room already full of people.

Faye's colleagues mingled seamlessly. They spoke on a regular basis, so there were few awkward pauses in conversations. Everyone made efforts to compliment Faye on her paintings. She returned the favor with compliments on the food and floral arrangements. Someone turned on the stereo with light music that added to the casual atmosphere.

The guests held no distinctions between faculty or parents. The Browns and Gardners had helped decorate and provide food. All of a sudden the conversations paused. The music echoed minored chords complimenting Ms. Schmidt's entry. The sinister guest brought the dark mood as her plus one. As far as Faye knew, no one had even invited Ms. Schmidt. Of course, most of these people arrived without invitations.

"The nerve…"

"Anna…," Steve Gardner attempted to calm his wife.

"Seriously, after what that woman did to Ms. Unger. She has the nerve to show up here?"

"It's ok, Mrs. Gardner. I'm fine," Faye looked over at Steve. "Your husband checked me out. See?" Faye smiled in an effort to convince Anna and herself. She started toward the door to greet her new guest. Then, she saw John and Gina Mazzi walk in behind her.

"No," Stephanie Brown said.

Faye held up her hand to calm the Browns as she passed. *The host remains gracious no matter who decides to show.* She continued toward the door to welcome the guests. Mazzi's cousin was the last to enter. Faye took a deep breath.

"Hello. I'm glad you all could make it tonight. Please come in," Faye said with a counterfeit smile.

"Thanks for having us." Gina Mazzi handed her an overcoat.

"Please, make yourselves at home." Faye took their jackets to the bedroom.

Stephanie met her at the door. "Let me take those. Go get a drink. You need it."

Faye smiled and handed off the jackets. On her way to the kitchen, she overheard Don talking to the new guests.

"John. Gina. How are you this evening?" Don greeted them as old friends.

"Mr. Ambrose, it's nice to see you again," Gina replied.

"I see you remember me." He smiled and held out his hand, "Who's your friend here?"

"This is Trish Schmidt. We were in school together. Now, she has a 6th grader."

"Nice to meet you, Ms. Schmidt. Are you a fan of Ms. Unger?"

"Not particularly." Trish scowled.

Don avoided the snarky comment. "Let me show you her latest paintings." He led them across the room.

"I don't know why she even bothered to show up," Stephanie said as she joined Faye to replenish her beverage.

Faye looked up at her quizzically.

"That Schmidt woman," Stephanie continued, "clearly has a problem with you, but this is not the time or the place."

"There is definitely an agenda." Brandon joined them.

"I don't remember ever meeting her or anyone in her family," Faye added. "Maybe I should just talk to her. I'm sure it's just a misunderstanding."

"You could try." Brandon didn't sound convincing.

"Are you guys crazy?" Stephanie interjected. "Don't you remember what happened during your encounter at school? No way. She means to take you down."

Faye looked their direction at her friend escorting them through the apartment. Mazzi and his cousin opted for a different tour of the room. Mazzi whispered something to his cousin. The two located Faye and waved in her direction.

"Faye!" He shouted as they walked toward her.

Faye lifted her chin to acknowledge them, but didn't move. She watched Elaine do something similar at the Auction House. She hoped it would intimidate the creepy man.

"Ms. Unger," John's cousin started, "I thought you lived on 8?"

"Have we met before?" Faye asked.

"We met in the elevator."

Faye interrupted, "and you took notes on what floor I visited?"

"Listen. It's not like that."

"Oh? Then, explain it to me."

"I think we may have gotten off on the wrong foot." Mazzi sounded apologetic.

"Excuse me." Faye slid past them toward the door.

"Darling!"

Faye stood in shock as Jeffrey kissed both cheeks.

"I couldn't resist a good a party." He walked past her.

"Check it out!" Jodi came through with the kiss on each cheek, "Are these your colleagues?"

"Some of them." Faye managed.

In one evening, no, in one moment, Faye's worlds collided. The efforts she maintained to separate work from social life proved meaningless in this moment. The carefully sculpted teacher persona disrupted in an instant. Her elegant, artful world shattered by the glue sticks and construction paper of simpler people. Don and Brandon interrupted this world when Brandon started dating her friend. However, the two arenas remained separate until now.

Faye looked up to find Jeffrey introducing himself to Gina Mazzi and Trish Schmidt. Her heart dropped along with her knees, and she nearly fell. She made her way to a stool along the wall and distracted herself by listening to conversations.

"So, how long have you two been married?" Don asked Gina.

"20 years this September."

"Oooo, great question!" Jeffrey interjected, "Did you guys date in high school?"

"No. We started dating a few years after graduation," She sipped her drink.

"Nothing beats an exciting love story." Jeffrey toasted his new friends.

"We're a close community around here." Don looked at Trish. "Have you always lived here?'

"What do you mean?" Trish spoke harshly as her eyes darted around the room. "Why all the questions?"

"Well, I know John and Gina moved back recently. I wan't sure if you stuck around after high school and recently moved back also."

"Yeah, been here most of life." Trish looked at Gina. "I got family here."

"I see." Don excused himself to another conversation.

Faye wasn't about to leave Jeffrey alone with the two of them. She grabbed a beverage and joined the conversation.

"I'm so glad you both could make it." Faye smiled warmly at Gina. "Have you been able to settle into your new apartment?"

"Apartment?" Gina looked puzzled.

"Don't you live in the building also? I've run into John and his cousin a few times."

"Oh." Gina looked into her glass before she spoke. "I have a friend in the building that I visit from time to time." She glanced at Trish and they gave one another a suspicious look.

"So, you live in a house nearby?"

"Yes, near the park." Gina looked annoyed. "My family kept their home as a rental. We were able to move in right away."

That's right, Faye remembered the ravine. She pushed the memory aside in favor of information about Trish's grudge.

"Do you also collect artwork?" Jeffrey asked them both.

Trish pressed her lips together tightly.

"Jeffrey has done a wonderful job displaying mine." Faye slid her arm around him and squeezed. The gesture distracted her from

Trish's anxiety. Faye wanted one moment alone with her. Just one. "Why don't you show them the lights that you installed?"

Jeffrey raised his eyebrows and pulled away from Faye, "Yes, of course. Lighting makes all the difference."

"Trish." Faye hoped to grab her attention before she followed after Jeffrey.

She stopped to look at Faye.

"Is everything alright? You seem upset or irritated." Faye didn't waste time. "Have I offended you in some way?"

"Well, it's just that, um." Trish stumbled on her words and looked for Gina's help. She took a drink, then, stared at Faye. "He was my brother. My brother." She shook her head.

Faye looked at her blankly. "What do you mean?"

"You tellin' me you don't remember?"

Faye looked at Trish and slowly shook her head.

Trish leaned close for Faye to hear the deep rasp in her voice, "You murdered him."

Faye stepped backwards and tried to catch her breath. *Murder?* Two tall gentlemen dressed in expensive suits stepped in between Faye and Trish. One of the men placed his hand at the small of her back providing support. The other spoke something to Trish while he escorted her to Gina. The man whispered something to Jeffrey, before they both excused themselves.

Faye, thankful for the man's assistance, sipped her drink and regained her composure. Out of the corner of her eye, a woman approached.

"I see the gang's all here." Elaine spoke in soft, jazz tones.

Faye looked at Elaine and nodded.

"You met, Frank." Elaine smiled at the gentleman supporting Faye.

Faye looked at the man and smiled. "Thank you. Frank."

Frank continued to stand near Faye providing support without assuming any other connection. Faye couldn't recall a time when she had a body guard, but she could get used to it.

"Have you thought about my offer?"

"Some."

"And?"

"I enjoyed seeing others appreciate my work." Faye looked into the distance and delighted in that image.

"Shall we get a drink and talk about it?" Elaine looked over at the second man in a suit and gave him directions with her eyes. "Shall we?" Elaine motioned for Faye to join her on the balcony.

A small crowd of people stood on the balcony pointing at landmarks. Frank walked head of them and whispered something to them. Faye watched them exit the balcony while the other man brought them drinks.

"You seem tense." Elaine looked beyond Faye to the city skyline.

"Maybe a little. Some folks came uninvited." Faye looked into the apartment at Trish. "And they brought drama with them."

"There is no shortage of drama in Arlington." Elaine pulled a cigarette out of an elegantly carved case and began to light it. She offered one to Faye.

Faye shook her head.

"I'm sure you've heard the rumors surrounding the Auction House."

"I'm not sure what you're talking about."

Elaine sighed. "I do my best to keep them at bay."

"Would this contract be with the Auction House?"

"No." Elaine proceeded to light her cigarette. "Rest assured, when you are under contract with me, you will garner my full protection."

Faye looked at Frank then at Elaine who gently pressed the cigarette to her lips.

"Is there something I should know about?" Of all the things running through Faye's mind, she hadn't bothered to look into the Auction House.

"I don't work for the Auction House."

"I thought you ran it"

Elaine gave a nod to validate her rule over the Auction House. "I'm more like an agent." Elaine took a moment to continue smoking. "This is good news for you. You sign with me and I assure your success. I can sell your paintings at the Auction House here in Arlington like you've already seen. I can also transport them to new markets as needed."

"Would I be able to continue teaching?"

Elaine smiled, "When you're ready, come by the restaurant."

Twenty-Seven

The soft jazz music filled the spaces in Faye's mind as she walked through the crowd in her apartment. The ambient lighting created shadows around the guests. She smiled anyway.

"This is a beautiful party, isn't it?"

"It certainly is," Elaine responded.

"You know, these people planned the whole thing. I didn't even cook." Faye smiled again as Elaine handed her another drink.

"I've been thinking, Elaine, and uh. " Faye paused for moment and just stared, "Where would I put an Auction House? My apartment...," Faye's voice trailed as she gestured with her hand across the room.

"Faye, focus."

Faye looked at Elaine whose face was blurry, "Why are we whispering?"

Elaine turned to the tall, handsome gentleman and whispered in his ear. Faye put her hand on Elaine's arm to get her attention.

Then, she looked at Elaine as if remembering something from a long time ago.

"Chicken Butt," Faye whispered and laughed. She said it again, "Chicken butt," and laughed. Then, she leaned in closer for a hug.

Faye rolled over trying to wake from this dream, but her eyes proved too heavy this time. She lay there to sleep it off, however, her mind didn't get the message. Eyes closed, she could hear voices, but wasn't sure whether she slept or not.

"Don."

"In here, Brandon. Keep your voice down."

"Don't worry, she's out." Brandon walked in on Don in the middle of Faye's closet while she slept. "I don't know what they gave her, but it must have been strong."

"Good job, by the way. Nobody knew she'd passed out."

"Thanks, I was trying to stop her from talking to Elaine Andrews."

"Elaine was here last night?" Don looked up from the safe he was attempting to crack open.

"Yeah, the Mazzi crew had you preoccupied. Did you ever find out why they showed up?"

Don grunted, "Na, John claims he wanted to support a fellow teacher. I guess the Schmidt lady knew his wife."

"Who keeps a safe anyway?" Brandon handed Don a lock-pick set.

"I guess we're about to find out."

Faye heard the safe open. *Come on arms. Move. Wave at them.* Papers rustled. *Hey! Stop that! That's personal! It's locked for a reason.*

"Check this out."

Papers rustled. File folders opened. *Why are they looking through my things? Am I dreaming again?*

"What's this? Bonfire? That's not Faye." Brandon's voice echoed in Faye's ears.

Get out of my safe!

"Its says, 'Elaine and Stephanie 2001.' I s that Stephanie Brown?"

"Oh yeah." Don spoke with confidence.

"She knew Elaine?"

"She knows a lot. I don't think I could've gotten this far without them. I want to know why this is in Faye's safe?"

Faye wanted to know that too, but she hadn't had time before the party to figure that part out yet. *If they could just close it up and ask me like normal people...*

"Yeah, me too. Elaine gave her a hug last night before she left." *Wait. Did Brandon just say that Elaine gave me a hug? Was that real?*

"I couldn't hear what she said to her, though. There's a similar photo in the yearbook. Susan recognized the Browns along with Mazzi, but she didn't recognize the girl."

Faye heard more rustling. Then, the silver chain zipped along the metal sides of the safe.

"Class of 2001. When did you say Faye graduated?"

"2012," Brandon responded. "Does the locket open?"

Don fumbled with the locket. *Don't break it, please. That's important.* Then, it popped open.

"That's the photo from the yearbook!" Brandon nearly shouted. "That's Elaine with Mazzi."

At some point, Faye dozed off again. She woke to the smell of French toast and coffee. She looked around and sat up slowly. Her head ached with the light making it worse. She stumbled into the kitchen and stopped when she saw Brandon.

"Good morning," Brandon said from the kitchen.

"How did you get here?"

"I think you had a little too much to drink last night. Some guy helped you to your room."

Faye gave him a puzzled look.

"Don't worry, he stood near the door until most of the people left." Brandon placed a plate full of French toast on the dining table. "I didn't know you had a body guard, Faye."

Faye walked toward the table with the blanket still wrapped around her, *"Body guard?"* She vaguely remembered Frank helping her to the balcony. That must be what Brandon meant.

Brandon handed her a cup of coffee. She breathed in the aroma of the liquid and tried to remember his conversation with Don. She only remembered being angry with him. He and Don had been in her bedroom. How did they get past the body guard?

"Thank you," she said finally.

Brandon placed hot maple syrup on the table.

"Were there any other problematic guests after I left last night?" Faye had difficulty remembering anything to do with Jeffrey and Jodi. She didn't even remember them leaving.

"Mazzi stayed for a while, but I think it was more about his wife than anything else."

"What happened to Jeffrey and Jodi?"

"Something about an early auction this morning. They ducked out early."

"Early?"

"Well, midnight or so."

"What time did I fall asleep?"

"I'm not sure. It's 6:30 now. I think you went to your bedroom around 2:30?"

"Oh. That explains why I'm so tired. It's a good thing we have a long weekend."

Faye jumped at a noise coming from behind her.

"Good morning." Don called. "I'm almost done cleaning up here."

"Thanks." Faye surveyed the room. "It looks great. Did you clean up all by yourself?"

"I had some help" he said.

"Did you find anything unusual?" Faye's memory of Don and Brandon started to return.

He looked surprised. "Unusual?"

"I don't know. Remember, the extra painting?"

"Oh, right. Nothing like that. You might want to check around, though."

Faye finished her breakfast before she stood to check the apartment. She turned pillows and felt between sofa cushions. She checked behind paintings and photographs. Faye stopped looking and stood frozen.

"Did you find something?"

"This little card was in the corner of my painting."

"Oh? Do you mind if I take a look?"

She held up the front of the business card. Don could see why he missed it. The artwork on the front matched the painting exactly.

"How did they do that? It blends into the corner perfectly. Is there a name or a message?"

Faye read the back and didn't respond. She held it out for Don to take a look.

Chicken Butt,

Call on me when you're ready. You know where to find me.

"Chicken Butt?"

"This doesn't make any sense." Faye stopped at the words. She said something like that in her dream. The words felt familiar, but she couldn't place it. Faye turned and shrugged her shoulders.

"It sounds like a code for something. Are you sure you don't know what it means?"

Faye shrugged. "The truth is that I don't remember much. The doctor said it's something about amnesia from a concussion. Maybe it'll come back, or maybe it's gone for a reason."

"I'll go with you."

"Where?"

"To meet up with Chicken Butt."

Faye giggled. She tried to speak, but couldn't finish a statement, because she was laughing so hard.

"I mean…," Don tried to remain serious, but the lack of sleep combined with the silly nickname on the card. He bust out laughing. Tears streaming down their faces, they laughed until they couldn't laugh any more.

"Thank you, " Faye said. "I needed that."

"I meant it though." Don stopped before they both started up again. "You don't have to do any of this alone. You have people who will back you up."

Twenty-Eight

Don waited for Brandon at the coffee shop early Sunday morning. He'd gotten a notification that intruders had entered the school. He sat in disguise sipping a pumpkin spice latte to avoid making a scene. Don nodded at Brandon when he walked through the door. He stood and held out a coffee for Brandon. Neither man spoke until they hit the sidewalk.

"Did you walk here?"

Don nodded "They know my vehicle. This needs to be under the radar."

"Copy." Brandon sipped his coffee. "So, how long have you been tapped into the school security feed?"

"Rogers arranged it on Julie's request."

The men turned down an alley next to the CBD store. The path between the buildings continued through the woods behind it. They carefully walked through the trees along the path toward the school.

Don held up a hand for Brandon to stop. He, then, reached into his jacket and pulled out a tablet. "I can access the outside cameras from here, but we need to get to the servers for the inside."

He tapped the screen several times, then motioned with his hand to move forward. The men scanned the area around the school, and chose to walk near the tree line. They approached on the back side of the building near the cafeteria.

Brandon pulled a lock pick out of his pocket and went to work on the door. He turned the nob and a light began to flash over head. Don removed the alarm panel and disconnected the wires. With the alarm silenced, they moved forward toward the front office.

"Aren't the servers in the media center?" Brandon whispered.

Don nodded. "But we can access the security feeds through the office. I want to see the view from the cameras and erase our entry."

"Copy."

They continued through the dark building unnoticed. Don rounded a corner and stopped. He backed against the wall frozen. The faint sound of voices echoed through the building.

"I'm tellin' you that was the alarm. We gotta hurry up or the cops'll be onto us."

"Really? 'Zat some kinda joke er somethin'?"

"Yeah, sorry, you know what I mean."

Don held up a hand with a finger over his mouth. He strained to hear the rest of their conversation.

"This place gives me the creeps. I wanna get outta here."

"Hold yer horses alright? I'm almost done here."

"Hey, you sure nobody gonna be mad 'bout dis?"

"Of course, they are, but that don't matter. They'll get theirs. That's what counts."

"Alright, alright, let's go."

Don looked at Brandon and motioned around the corner with his head. They waited for the rustling in the hallway to subside.

"Did you see where they were?" Brandon continued to scan the hallways.

"Negative. Your guess is as good as mine. Everything echoes in this building." Don motioned forward with his hand.

"Should we try to follow them?"

Don shook his head. "Local law enforcement are on the way. I want to know who sent them and why?"

They approached the office without incident. Brandon tried the door handle. Unlocked. They looked at one another moved in slowly.

Once inside, Don opened the computer and went to work on the security system.

"Can you link it to our phones?"

"It shouldn't be a problem."

"Did you recognize the men with Faye at the party?"

"Negative."

"I don't think they were ours."

"Private security firm." Don typed a few things on the keyboard. "That's my guess anyway. Do you think we'll be able to get eyes on her apartment?"

"I'm working on it. She's not one for routine. I'll have to move in when she leaves."

"I'm done here. Let's go." Don put the tablet back into his jacket and made his way out of the office.

"We might even make it to church today." Brandon smirked.

"Or we make it over to Faye's while she's at church."

"Won't people be expecting us at church?"

Don nodded. He had a point. Jason and Stephanie would ask about him. Not to mention the other faculty members.

"Let's head out," Don pushed the chair around and straightened the desk. "Should we lock the door?"

Brandon shook his head. "Like we found it."

"Copy."

The men retraced their steps through the school. Don repaired the alarm by the door before they exited the building. "Did you, by any chance, see the footage from the other intruders?"

Brandon paused before making his way to the tree line. "Nothing clear. I'll have to clean it up when I get home."

"Let me know what you find."

Brandon darted across the grass to the trees. Don followed close behind. He had seen the other men in the school. They looked familiar, but not the men from the party. He wanted to be sure who they were before he said anything to Brandon. The men at the party were pros. They'll either provide good protection for Faye or put her more at risk. Either way, they wouldn't show at the school.

Twenty-Nine

Time flies through the first half of the school year. The hectic schedule in Arlington with football and fall soccer seem to make it go faster. No matter how quickly the time goes, some moments pause as though frozen in time. Faye looked up from her tablet at the students before her. Pencils in hand, they readied themselves to tackle the next equation. She never tired of seeing their eager expressions. *My calling.*

After all the time she wasted aimlessly wandering through jobs and courses, she finally felt at home. Sure, she enjoyed Math. She tolerated the teaching courses. However, it wasn't until she sat in front of a student for the first time that she truly felt alive. Something awakened in her like she belonged here.

"Don't forget: take at least 10 seconds to read the problem before you start." They didn't take their eyes off the board. "Ready?"

Frozen. The entire room awaited the command to begin. Faye held onto it for a second longer.

"Go!" She flashed the equation on the board. Students scribbled quickly on the pad. Then, one stood.

"Ah! Man!" Grumblings sounded through the room.

"Don't give up, now." Faye encouraged them. "You don't know if he's right. Keep working. You get points for every correct response. The points will add up."

They continued to work, but Megan Brown raised her hand, "Will we all be on the same team or divided into different teams this year?"

"It depends on how many students want to participate." Faye replied. "We have a lot of eligible students this year."

The bell surprised them all.

"That's right. We have conferences today." Faye announced, "Have a good day, everyone."

"See you later, Ms. Unger!" Several students shouted as they left.

Donna peeked her head into the door. "Have you got a crowd coming this afternoon?"

"I'm not sure. I was hoping to get things together for the Math Tournament." Faye gathered her papers from the table.

"You're starting early. That's not until January."

"There are a lot of pieces at play, Donna. I don't want to wreck it my first time out."

"What do you mean first time out? You practically ran it last year."

"I fell into the middle of it when I stepped in for Don. This year, I'll be prepared."

Donna shook her head. "We have a room set up for conferences in the Science hall." She looked down at her clipboard. "I have you down from 12:30-1:45. Is that good for you?"

"I'll see you there." Faye made a mental note to ask J.J. about 8th grade conferences before heading to the office.

She passed several colleagues on her way.

"Where is everyone going?"

"Someone brought barbecue for the faculty members." Don shoved his car keys into his desk. "Are you coming?"

"Sure. I'll just put these things down." Faye opened her desk drawer to store her grader and noticed something strange. She pulled out a piece of paper with a photo attached.

"Is everything ok?" He stopped at the door.

Faye shook her head as she read it aloud. "Obituary." She didn't recognize the name, so she glanced at the photo. It was the same as the photo in the locket. Her head throbbed in frustration. Seeing the photo again did not bring back the memory.

"What is it?" Don walked closer.

Faye turned the photo to show him. Then, she read the names on the back: Elaine and Albert 2003.

She looked up at Don. "Why would someone put this in my desk?"

"Is there a note?"

"An obituary."

"For who?"

"Albert Schmidt," Faye spoke the name, and her heart sank. Don reached for the paper. "Do you mind if I read it?"

Faye handed him the obituary.

Albert Rufus Schmidt

Albert Rufus Schmidt, 19, was found dead in

Arlington Community Park Saturday, November 2,

2003. The police ask that anyone with information

useful to this investigation tocontact the station.

He is preceded in death by his grandparents, Rufus

and Alfia Schmidt. Albert is survived by his parents

Rufus Schmidt, Jr and Louise Schmidt, his brothers

George and Scott Schmidt, and his sister Trish

Schmidt.

Albert played quarterback for his high school football

team the last three years. He served on homecoming

court in September. Funeral services for Albert

Schmidt will be held Monday at Arlington

Community Church.

Don looked up. "Did you open your desk before class
this morning?"

Faye nodded. "I pulled out my grader. Someone planted this in
my desk during class."

"I didn't see anyone come in."

Faye exhaled, then, she tossed the papers into the garbage.
"What?"

"Are you ok?"

She shrugged. "What can I do? I don't know what any of it
means. If someone has issue with me, they should tell me."

"Did they solve that murder?"

"I don't know. I was like 10 years old." Faye continued to put
her things away. She cringed at the thought of someone rummaging
through her desk.

"Do you think they would try to blame you for it?"

"Trish already blamed me for it."

Don cleared his throat and waited for Faye to continue.

"The other night at the party, Trish said that I murdered her brother." Faye closed the desk and started to walk out. "Don. she's crazy."

They walked out of the office without another thought.

The barbecue smell wafted down the hallway drawing them toward the Media Center. Faye piled a plate too high with meat and potato salad and headed toward a table with her friends.

"Excellent party the other night, Faye." Susan brought them a pitcher of lemonade.

"Thank you, but you all made it great. I can't believe how everyone pulled together like that."

"I told you not to worry." Stephanie pulled up a chair and joined them for lunch.

"So tell me, what did you really think of my art." Faye asked the question for the sake of conversation, but she secretly wanted to know what everyone thought of her Art Collective friends.

"Everything was beautiful, Faye," Donna said between bites. "Your apartment is the perfect backdrop for a cocktail party."

"A fancy cocktail party at that," Stephanie added. "I didn't know you liked to dress up, Ms. Unger."

They all laughed.

"It's like you live in a different world outside of these walls," Donna said with a wink.

"It'll catch up to you one day." Don's advice silenced the laughter. "I'm just saying, it's a good idea to be honest with your friends about your life. Keeping secrets usually comes back to haunt you."

"Ain't that the truth." Susan took a seat. "Can't nobody keep a secret around here."

"Yeah, I heard that a certain Mazzi has eyes for Faye." Brandon poured a glass of lemonade as all eyes landed on him. "The word in the building has it that he waits in the lobby for her."

Faye's cheeks turned rosy pink as she glared at Brandon.

"Who was that lady that came with body guards last night? She looked important." Donna munched on some chips like she was at the movies.

"She's with the Art Collective." Faye tried to answer with a straight face.

"And what about your date? He's dreamy!" Susan held up her glass to toast to anyone who agreed with her.

"I saw you cozy up with him." Donna grinned at Faye.

"Look at the time." Don held up his watch. "8th grade conference in the Math hall."

Don's sense of urgency failed to transfer to the rest of the crew. The teachers stood to leave but took their time making their way to the conference. Faye headed toward the Science wing for the 9th grade meetings.

"You're late." Gina Mazzi glared at Faye.

"Excuse me." Faye directed her apology at the parents.

"No problem." Stephanie and Jason Brown smiled at her from their place at the table.

"These are my favorite conferences," J.J. began. "Megan works hard and has a bright future. I enjoy helping families plan for futures in education."

"I agree," Faye added. "Megan has done well in Math this year. In fact, I think she will be a good leader for the tournament in January."

"I'm not seeing the same progress in Science." Gina started a descent into negative comments.

This completely sounds like a Mazzi issue. I'm not sure why she called us all here. Faye's mind continued to wander. *Was the corsage marked 'funeral' from Albert Schmidt's funeral? I'm glad Frank came last night.* Faye sat in that thought for a moment. She enjoyed the feeling of security he provided her in the midst of the Schmidt accusations. For the first time in a long time, she didn't have to guard herself.

"Ms. Unger?"

"I'm sorry, what did you ask?" Faye had a difficult time connecting to Gina's questions.

"Would you be willing to tutor Megan in the Math portion of our Science class?"

"Of course, I enjoy working with Megan."

They stood to leave, but Gina grabbed Faye's elbow. "What was that?"

"What?"

"You completely zoned out, and made it look like I was the one with the problem."

"You were the only one with a problem." She wrenched her elbow loose from Gina's grasp. "Seriously? Megan Brown? She can not be on your list of troubled students."

"You're on my list." Gina looked at Faye and squinted her eyes, "I heard about you and Trish. Stay away from her."

"Ok." Faye's eyebrows raised along with her sarcastic tone.

"I'm serious. You tell your goons to back off, or this'll get ugly." Faye put her arms up in retreat.

"My goons." She mumbled under her breath. *Goons?* Faye remembered the man in the suit who went to speak to Trish as Frank stood by. Then, she smiled. *I have goons.*

Thirty

Faye marked the last quiz and straightened the stack of papers on her desk. The mumbled conversations stopped, and students waited for the results.

"These are some of the best yet." Faye walked through the room and handed them back. "Take a moment to locate your mistakes."

Students compared papers and scribbled changes.

"I keep forgetting to check my work." Gus announced in frustration.

Megan looked at his paper. "I think you rushed through them. You should choose the tests without timers."

"Huh?"

"That's a good idea." Faye returned to the front of the room. "As a team, you get to decided which tests you'll do. Some of them aren't timed."

"Ok, I'll take that one." A smile grew across his face.

Faye could feel that one. Elaine's proposal sauntered into her heavily weighted mind. *I can't stop teaching.* She and Jeffrey had plans for dinner. *He's going to bring it up again. How can I make this decision?* She felt the buzz of her phone in her pocket.

"Ok, everyone that's our meeting for today. Don't forget to practice. We'll meet again next week." Faye moved to the front table to gather her things.

"Thanks, Ms. Unger." Megan waved as she followed the others out of the room.

Faye pulled out her phone.

Jeffrey: Are we still on for dinner tonight?

Faye looked up from her at the array of pencil shavings and bits of notebook paper. An equation remained unsolved on the board. *Maybe I can do both?*

Faye: I think I need to pass on tonight. I have some paintings to prepare for Auction.

Jeffrey: Sounds exciting! I'll check in with you tomorrow, then.

When she arrived home, Faye prepped her space for painting. She kept her painting supplies in the basement storage area. Elaine mentioned that she often sold the painted scenes that she wished to forget. So, tonight, Faye would paint a forgettable scene.

If only she could find her key to the storage locker.

She usually kept it on the key holder next to her car keys. *They probably knocked it when they cleaned up for the party.*

Faye searched the change dish on the coffee table. She even looked on the bedside table. Eventually, Faye threw convention to the wind and searched every cabinet, drawer, and shelf. She even looked in the photo bins.

The safe?

It seemed unlikely that anyone could have opened the safe to hide her key in it, but she looked there too. Examining the contents of the safe reminded her that Don and Brandon had searched it. *That could have been a dream. Or they aren't who they say they are.*

Faye dismissed the idea for the greater purpose, painting. the doorman kept spare keys for this reason.

"Good afternoon, Faye." He welcomed her as she approached. "Uh-oh. What happened? You don't look so good."

Faye looked at him and then around the lobby.

"Something with that party? I heard it was a late one."

"No, Jay. I need a key to my storage area."

"In case of emergency, like I always say." He began to unlock a drawer in the reception desk.

"It's not an emergency."

"You need in and you lost your key. It's an emergency."

"I just want to get a few things out, and I didn't lose my key," Faye took a deep breath. "I don't lose things."

Jay held up his hand. "No explanations needed. Just bring it back when you're finished."

Faye thanked him and headed to the basement for her things. She had two totes for supplies: one for paints and brushes, and the other for blank canvas. Faye relied on the service elevator to avoid making multiple trips. She loaded the elevator without trouble and headed upstairs.

Inside her apartment, Faye placed a drop cloth on the hardwoods and set up the easel. The concept of forgettable images brings a sense of freedom. Unwanted memories, even forgotten ones, can reek havoc on ones' mental state. The time had come to be rid of it. *How do I do this? Do I even want to bring these images to mind? Lord, show me what I need to know and only that.*

Faye closed her eyes. Usually, this helped an image come to her. Nothing. She thought about Chicken Butt and smiled. She stayed in that thought. *Had it been a dream? Is that real?* Memories of her childhood came to mind. She could see the fabric of her favorite dress flowing out as she twirled around in it. Beautiful colors appeared in her mind. She painted soft pinks and purples highlighted with yellows and whites. It reminded her of playing outside until the sun went down.

She painted her favorite blue dress. The one with the little red flowers. The brushes in her hands followed along with soft, meaningful strokes. Faye continued to paint in this way with images coming one at a time. Her painting resembled her memory with bits and pieces in different locations on the canvas. She would have to wait to see the big picture.

When she finished, Faye could not put it all together. The act of remembering and expressing the memories exhausted her. She picked up her brushes and stepped away. Things usually had a different outlook from a distance. Faye decided to include time with distance on this one. She set down her brushes and headed to the kitchen for a coffee break.

When she returned to the painting, she noted the elegant brush strokes and improved techniques of her painting. The event of the painting still seemed unclear. The color choice included brilliant contrasts of pink with red, blue against purple, and subtle shades of orange and yellow. The girl in the blue dress no longer seemed as prominent as Faye originally thought her to be. She was one of many people standing around at an outside picnic. The spinning girl did so with other children around. Some spinning, while others jumped rope and tossed marbles.

The adults interacted in their own conversations. Some of them stood holding glasses of wine, engaged in serious conversations. Others sat at a table full of food and drink. The table, in the midst of the outdoors, was covered in a beautiful table cloth and expensive china. Many of the adults at the table smiled and laughed.

Faye stood at this painting trying to feel some emotion of memory. *It reminds me of a Renoir. What was it called?* She took a break to search it. *That's it: Luncheon at the Boating Party. Is this a memory of a real event or just my memory of the famous painting?* She leaned it against the patio doors. Perhaps, the memory would come later.

Faye decided to pack up her paints and return Jay's key. She moved things around in the tote to organize it better. Then, her hands ran across something wrapped in brown paper. *Are these chalks? Oil pastels?* She pulled it out of the tote. A solid brick of something wrapped in brown paper tied up in string. No markings.

Faye unwrapped it. She removed the brown paper and dropped the package onto the floor. The white powder protected in plastic fell like a brick.

"What?!"

She stood back and looked at her hands.

"What?!" She whispered-yelled it this time. She didn't need to attract any attention. Someone is clearly playing a joke on her. This can't be real.

Faye walked to the kitchen to put distance between her and the powder. She poured herself a glass of water and stared at it from the kitchen. It didn't move.

"Someone stole my keys and hid this in my storage locker. That's the truth. It's not mine. I'll turn it in to the police. I'll be fine."

"No, I won't be fine. They're not going to believe me," Faye continued the conversation with herself. "I'll lose my job! I'm a teacher. They don't let drug addicts or drug dealers or drug people teach children. I'll probably go to jail. I can't go to jail."

There was a knock at the door. She probably should have had that conversation in her head.

"Faye, is everything alright?"

Brandon. *What do I do? He can't see this. I need time to figure this out.*

"Yeah, Brandon, I'm fine, " Faye yelled through the closed door. "Just spilled some paint. Got my hands full. Big mess." *Now, I lied.*

"Do you want some help with that?"

"No, no." She tried to be calm. "I got it. Thanks."

She heard his footsteps and ran over to the package in her floor. She needed to wrap it up and get it out of here before he decided to come back. She hid it in the safe until she could figure out some other plan.

Thirty-One

"I can't believe I agreed to this," Stephanie Brown stood outside the Mazzi front door holding a casserole dish.

"We couldn't let him go alone." Jason pressed the doorbell.

"Oh." Gina answered the door with her eyebrows raised. "Come in, please."

John stepped up to the door and greeted them warmly, "I'm glad you folks could make it."

"I'm sorry I didn't come sooner," Stephanie told Gina. "I should have been here when you first moved. When was that exactly?"

"It took us a while to figure out where we wanted to live. This house belongs to Gina's parents. She's not too thrilled to be living here."

"It'll do until we get a place of our own." Gina took their coats and hung them on the tree.

"I love what you've done with the place." Stephanie attempted a compliment.

Don stepped up to the doorway in the sitting room and knocked. "Is that oak?"

"Maple," John said with a grin. "It's nice to meet a man interested in fine finishings."

"This home has no shortage of fine finishings."

They made their way into the sitting room, and Jason made an attempt at polite conversation. "Great party the other night, over at Ms. Unger's. Did you guys know she was an artist?"

Gina looked over at John and headed into the kitchen for drinks.

"That one threw me for a loop." Don took a seat near the fireplace.

Stephanie shook her head. "You think you know a person. Honestly, it's like she leads a double life."

"I know the four of you know each other, but did you all know Faye when she was younger?"

"Sure, Don, I knew her family when we was kids. We all," John gestured to everyone in the room, "go way back."

Gina walked in with a tray of drinks. "John was better acquainted with Faye's sister."

"I particularly liked that painting of the city." Jason opted to change the subject.

"The colors in that sunrise." Stephanie paused and closed her eyes. "I could look into it all day long."

Don interrupted the scenic reflection, "Faye has a sister?" This information may have been news to Don, but no one else paid attention to his question.

"Did I hear she was going to sell her paintings at the Auction House?" Jason took a drink from the tray.

"I saw her there once or twice." John took a sip.

"What are you doing at the Auction House?" Jason responded.

Don knew this could get ugly fast. He sat up on the edge of his seat ready for anything.

"I spend some time there helping them get set up."

Gina glared at him giving Don the impression that he spends more time there than she would like.

"Doesn't Elaine work down there?" Stephanie glanced at Gina for effect.

John nodded her direction. "I work mostly in furniture." Then, he looked at his wife. "But like I said, I'm only helping out until they get on their feet."

"John started with the Auction House in Chicago. We decided to change direction when we moved to Arlington." Gina stood a little taller. "A fresh start."

"I'll drink to that." Jason lifted his glass, "To a fresh start."

"A fresh start." Stephanie raised her glass to Gina.

Gina ignored Stephanie's gesture of peace and ushered them toward the table. "Now, let's eat."

"You have outdone yourself, Gina." Don said, "this smells delicious."

"That was a good thing you did for my cousin, Trish. I wanna return the favor."

Don struggled to recall what he did. "I was just being friendly. That's what this community is all about, right?"

"Used to be," Stephanie said in a cough before grabbing a drink of water.

"What's that supposed to mean?" Gina dropped the bread basket.

Stephanie raised an eyebrow in her direction.

"I thought we were all friends here" Don reached over to pick up the bread. "What happened?"

John shook his head. "It's water under the bridge."

Stephanie started to speak, but Jason intervened. "Nothing a good, old-fashioned apology couldn't help." He turned toward Gina, "I know we caused you and your family a lot of grief back in high school. I'm sorry about that."

Gina turned to Stephanie, "I'm sorry for stealing your crush, Stephanie, but Al never would have gone for you."

Stephanie glared at Gina. "I understand. You were going through a lot." Stephanie looked at John.

John excused himself to the kitchen to grab more bread.

Don followed him into the kitchen. "Whew, you can cut the tension in there with a knife."

"Ain't that the truth." John fumbled with the cabinet door. "She's still hung up on a high school fling." He pulled down a bottle of bourbon. "Interested in something a little stronger?"

Don held up his hand. "No thanks. So, who was the girl from high school?"

John shook his head. He peered around Don toward the other room to be sure nobody could hear him. "Elaine. She had this way about her, you know? Elegant. Beautiful."

"So, what happened to her?" Don sipped his drink.

John shrugged. "Eh, family. I was too old or something. I don't know. It's here or there. Am I right?" He held out a glass for Don.

Don waved off the glass. "I get it. You probably haven't seen this girl since high school."

"Well," John shrugged. "She works with the Auction House, but it ain't like that. She's sophisticated. She doesn't waste time with guys like me."

John led the way toward the living room. "So do you prefer antiques or custom-built?"

"Both, actually." Don understood the need to change the subject, "We live in these beautiful, old homes. I like to fill mine with character pieces."

"I prefer the furniture to the artwork as well." John took his seat at the table. "Do you have plans to purchase something?"

Don nodded. "I spoke with a woman there the other day. I'm not much of an online shopper."

"I can arrange a meeting, if you like." John patted his mouth with the napkin.

Gina had started collecting dinner plates while the men gathered in the living room. The stacked plates crashed. Gina marched over them into the kitchen.

"We should probably go." Jason picked up his jacket.

Don nodded and headed to the foyer to collect his coat. He stopped in the kitchen on his way. "Thank you for a lovely meal, Gina."

She turned to face him. Her eyes red, she closed them tightly. "I'm sorry for all of this." She waved her hand.

"Don't mention it." Don looked into her eyes. "Really, we can do this again sometime." He smiled and walked to the door.

"John." Don reached out his hand. "Thanks for having me." He leaned into the handshake and gave him pat on the back.

"I'll be in touch about the Auction House," John patted him on the shoulder.

No one spoke as they walked to the car. The tension appeared to follow them out. Don spoke first.

"Thank you, Jason. I know that was hard for you guys. Whatever it was, though, you have to forgive them." Don shook his head and chuckled.

"We just didn't want Gina to poison you." Stephanie fake-smiled.

"There's something else going on there." Don put on his hat. "I don't think that had to do with high school."

"It never did," Stephanie looked away.

Thirty-Two

Faye rehearsed possible scenarios while she cleaned the apartment. *This has to be a mistake. An accident. Someone accidentally placed their drugs in the bottom of my organized storage bin.* Of course, they would have had to break into her locked unit and remove the contents of the bin before accidentally placing it inside.

Too many accidentals for that scenario.

A lot of people attended the party. Someone likely found her key with an intention of using her storage. *Why?* They might want to pick it up later. If so, she should put it in the bin where she found it. However, they may attempt to set her up. If that's the case, moving it to the safe is a good idea.

Faye paused to examine her apartment. The once tranquil retreat felt unstable. She had moved the package to the safe, but it may not be safe. In her dream, Don had no trouble opening it. Even as a dream, the thought frightened her. If someone were trying to set her up, they wouldn't stop at the storage unit. They would find a way to send the police to her apartment.

Who would do this?

Faye scrolled through the contact list in her mind. Trish Schmidt hated her in obvious ways. Hiding the drugs in her storage took time and secrecy. Faye didn't think Trish capable of secrecy, let alone the ability to find the key and sneak through the building. It had to be someone capable of sneaking through her building.

Her watch chimed with an alert. *Dinner.* Faye went to the kitchen to start on dessert. She couldn't stop her mind from reeling. *Who do I know that is sneaky enough to do this?*

Don and Brandon snuck through the safe in her dream. *Was it a dream?* They didn't say anything to her about going through the closet, but they also cleaned up after the party. They could have found a lot of things in the clean-up. It would have been easy to spot them while people cleared out.

Mazzi and his creepy cousin also had opportunity. They know their way around the building. Jay recognizes them from the times they visit their friend. *Whoever that is.* He wouldn't question them. That creepy guy might have been checking to make sure they had the right unit. He had mentioned that he thought Faye lived on a different floor.

Elaine showed up unexpectedly. She walked in with an air of mystery. It's possible that she lifted the key after Faye went to bed.

Brandon said that Frank guarded the door. Maybe, he guarded the door while the other guy lifted the key. *Why would Elaine offer protection if she were going to set me up?*

The surprise package remained in the safe for now. Faye attempted to put it in the back of her mind as she prepared the dessert for Brandon's dinner party. However, she jolted at the knock on her door.

"Jeffrey." Faye smiled, her hands still shaking. "Come in."

"Smells good. What are we making?"

"Coconut cake."

Jeffrey grabbed an apron to help. "That was a great party the other night."

"Yeah. How did you hear about it?"

"You invited me."

"Did I?" Faye turned to look at him.

"Didn't you?"

"I forgot about it until the day of. They. Planned. Everything."

"Everything?"

Faye turned to face him. "Everything." She whispered as she leaned in for a kiss.

"Well, I had a great time with you. Maybe we can revisit it after the dinner tonight."

Faye pretended like she knew what he meant, but she couldn't remember anything happening with Jeffrey at the party. Brandon said she'd had too much to drink, but Faye didn't drink. Sure, she enjoyed carrying a champagne flute, but she usually filled it with seltzer water. *Had someone spiked my drink?*

She smiled at Jeffrey and touched his nose with cake batter.

He laughed and headed to the bathroom to clean up his face.

"Did you paint yesterday?"

"Hmmm?" Faye said from the kitchen. She didn't want to think about yesterday.

"This painting, is it new?"

"Yes. That one is new. What do you think?"

"I like it. These people appear to be locals." Jeffrey stepped closer to the painting and squinted his eyes.

"What do you mean? Do you know them?"

"Well, it's just that…" Jeffrey paused for a moment. "that gentleman." He pointed to a younger man in a serious conversation. "He resembles John Mazzi. You know, about twenty years ago."

Faye leaned closer and squinted. He looked like that kid standing next to the bon fire in the yearbook. She looked at the other faces, and stopped. Elaine. Gina. Stephanie. They were all there. The young yearbook photo came to life in this painting.

"Do you recognize any of these other people?" She had to know who else she had painted. Maybe she just remembered the yearbook, or maybe she remembered being there.

"This guy looks familiar." He pointed to the man in the conversation with young Mazzi. "And this gentleman… on the other side of the painting seated at the table. The man laughing with people."

"Who are they?"

"I saw the one come into the Auction House. Let me think of his name." Jeffrey took a minute. "Schmidt?"

The name hit Faye's stomach like a sack of concrete. Her face curled into a visible frown.

"What's wrong, Faye? What did I say?"

"It's nothing." Faye shook her head and tried to catch her breath. "That family keeps following me. I don't know what it is."

Jeffrey stepped closer to Faye. "What do you mean by following you? Like Brandon followed you in the summer?"

"Nothing like that." Faye shrugged. "I just keep seeing them around."

"It's a small town, Faye. Nothing like Chicago. You're bound to run into people." Jeffrey opened the oven for Faye to insert the cake.

"Elaine said something to me at the party that I keep thinking about." Faye tossed a hand towel on the counter.

"I noticed the two of you talking at the party." Jeffrey grinned like a little boy. "Does this mean I'll see more of you?"

Faye brushed off the comment and continued her thought. "She said something about protection."

Jeffrey stepped back as the smile left his face.

"Do you know what she could have meant by that?"

Jeffrey shrugged, but the hopeful curiosity left his expression. His tone grew serious. "Elaine has access to people and places beyond my pay grade. Whatever she said to you must be for your ears only. I can't even attempt to guess at the meaning."

Faye marveled at the diplomatic tone he took with her. For the first time in their relationship, she felt like an asset or colleague rather than a girlfriend. She didn't know what to make of it. So she shrugged.

"I guess, I'll have to ask her next time I see her."

"Good idea." Jeffrey smiled again. "Will you be seeing her soon?"

Faye set her apron aside. "I'm still considering my options."

Thirty-Three

Christmas in Arlington resembled a cheesy movie. Arlington Community School took Christmas a step further.

"Wait here." Susan squeezed Faye's arm in the dark hallway. "You gotta see this." She flipped a switch that lit up the halls.

Faye gasped. "It's so beautiful."

Christmas lights had always made Faye smile. Simple white lights adorned the outside of the school. Beautiful as they may be, they didn't touch the grandeur of the interior. Large strings of fresh garland connected the halls with the media center in the middle. Giant, colorful ornaments hung from the garland along with tiny, white lights.

"You have outdone yourself this year, Susan."

"Come on, help me fill the stockings."

"Stockings?"

"This year, I made stockings for the teachers. Well, I have one for each department. There were so many new faces, I couldn't keep track."

They walked into the media office that had transformed into Santa's living room. The fireplace, which consisted of colored butcher paper, took up the entire back wall. Stockings hung from its mantel. Faye maneuvered around the Christmas tree to gain access to the stockings.

"Are those gifts under the tree?"

"Yeah. It's for secret Santa." Susan handed Faye an envelope. "We didn't play last year. I guess, we all got distracted with what happened to Julie."

"What's this?"

"Your person."

Faye wasn't sure what she meant. "My person?"

"You never played Secret Santa?"

Faye shook her head.

"You buy them small gifts but don't write your name on the tag. Then, at the party, we all try to guess our 'Santa.'"

Faye nodded and opened the envelope and read the name, Brandon. "Can I trade?"

"Nope. You are stuck with 'em. It's only for a couple of weeks. Small gifts. It'll be fun."

Faye rolled her eyes as she put the card back into the envelope, "When do we start?"

"Everyone else will get their envelope in their mailbox. You can deliver them if you like," Susan handed Faye a stack of envelopes.

She took the envelopes with a grin.

"Don't even think about it," Susan ordered. "They're sealed for a reason."

"Does anyone else know everyone's Santa?"

"Faye, it wouldn't be fun if everyone knew." Susan stuffed the remaining decorations into the storage bin. "Try to have fun with this."

Faye made efforts to enjoy the Santa game. She had always been pretty good at keeping secrets. Everyone discussed it at length over lunch. Faye listened closely for her name or any clues.

"This time of year, I enjoy reading mysteries," Donna announced to the table in the hopes of gaining the attention of her Santa.

"Chocolate goes well with a good book, too Donna." J.J. added.

"Relax." Faye sipped her water. "I don't know who your Santas are."

"I just hope I get someone that pays attention." J.J. opened his chocolate milk. "We got too much junk at our house already."

"It's about the mystery of it all, J.J." Donna stabbed her jello, "The gifts are just a bonus."

"In that case, you should be able to solve that mystery." J.J. looked at Faye, but she didn't respond. "What's up with you, Faye?"

"Yeah, you're quiet today." Donna tapped her mouth with a napkin. "Is everything ok?"

"Oh, sure. I'm trying to think of something to buy my Santa that won't give myself away." Faye smiled the kind of smile that hopes no one can see what you're really thinking. *Maybe, I just give him the drugs hiding in my safe.*

"That's a good strategy." J.J. didn't press her for more information.

The next day, Faye arrived early to start decorating her classroom. She hoped decorating would be better than nervously waiting for the police to show up. *I can't believe they haven't come search the storage units by now. The best course of action will be inaction for the time being.* It had only been a few days, but so far no police.

"Do you have any wrapping paper?" Faye asked Susan.

"I think I have some gift bags in the cabinet."

Faye grabbed a medium size bag along with a few sheets of tissue paper. "I'll be right back." Faye headed down the hall to the math office. She rummaged through her desk for a gift. It had completely slipped her mind after she left lunch yesterday. She found an extra Easy Grader, and an old candy bar. She tossed them both aside when she remembered the CBD oil she purchased at the beginning of the school year. A smile crept across her face as Faye enjoyed the irony of it all.

Faye placed it in the gift bag with extra tissue paper. Then, she rushed to place the gift under the tree before the other staff members arrived. Some folks had already gathered around the tree.

"Good morning, Faye." Donna stood from the bottom of the tree. "We were all just talking about our plans for Christmas break. So, where are you headed this year?"

Faye hid the gift behind her back. "I'm not sure." Faye eyed Brandon kneeling on the other side of the tree. She would have to wait until he turned his back or left the room.

"Didn't you go up to Chicago last year to be with family?" Susan looked at Faye.

"Not for Christmas." Faye spoke while her eyes scanned the room. "I'll probably just have dinner with my parents." She walked around the other side of Brandon to place the gift without him seeing.

"Have you been to the office yet, Faye?" Brandon looked directly at her.

Faye leaned sideways to hide behind the tree. "Um, yes, I have."

"I put the homework on your desk, but I don't have much confidence." He continued to speak to Faye as she did her best to avoid his gaze. "I tried to grade it, but Geometry is not my thing."

"No problem." She poked her head from the behind the tree to look him in the eye. Perhaps, direct expression would satisfy him enough to leave the room. "So when do we get to open our gifts?"

"Lunch time," Susan called out from the circulation desk. "You can get out of the tree, Faye. Nobody gets anything from under the tree until lunchtime. That way everybody gets a fair shot."

"Oh, I couldn't find mine anyway." Faye called back. She waited for Brandon to turn his back, and she slid the gift behind a much taller box under the tree. She made it halfway down the hallway before she heard a voice behind her.

"Faye, wait up." Brandon rushed to catch up with her.

"Can I help you with something?"

"I just wanted to say how much I appreciated you helping me with my classes this year. I think we started off on the wrong foot." He cleared his throat. "Was that coconut cake I smelled the other night? Maybe I could get your recipe?"

Faye smiled. "In your dreams."

Brandon laughed. "Hey did you ever get the paint cleaned up?"

"Paint?"

"The other day, you said something about a paint spill."

Immediately, Faye remembered the package hidden in her safe. *Breathe.* She took a sip of her coffee to slow her breathing. "Oh, yeah. It came straight up. Water based, you know."

"That's good news," Brandon kept pace beside her.

Brandon's memory surprised Faye. She didn't want him to remember the moment she discovered the package. She needed to get rid of it, or at least get help with it. When she got to her desk, Faye pulled out her phone and set a reminder to contact the French restaurant. Then, she looked at the stack of papers on her desk.

"You're right, Brandon, geometry isn't your thing."

Thirty-Four

Don followed Brandon home from school. They entered the lobby together and waved to the doorman. He looked up from his phone conversation. "Good to see you there, Mr. Foster. Mr. Ambrose."

They smiled and waved as they passed the front desk toward the elevator.

"So," Don started to speak, but Brandon held up a finger.

"The weather certainly has taken a turn for the worse, hasn't it?" Brandon said aloud. He looked up toward a security camera in the elevator.

Don nodded. "It certainly has."

They didn't speak to each other until they were inside the apartment.

"Ok, so tell me about that photo you sent me."

"I think you know what it was, Don."

"Tell me the story. I need the whole story here."

"Alright, alright. A couple of weeks ago, Jodi came over and well…"

Don stared at him.

"I'll get to the point. We heard something from Faye's place. I'm thinking its nothing. Sounded like a conversation."

"Ok with who?"

Brandon started walking to the kitchen to brew some coffee. "I don't know. I didn't see anyone over there."

"Were you able to get eyes on her place?" Don pulled out a chair.

"Yeah, no problem, but I couldn't check it at that moment." Brandon pulled some cookies out of the pantry. "So, I made myself presentable and went over there to check on her. She says everything's alright. Something about spilling paint. So, I let it go."

"That still doesn't explain the photo."

"I'm getting there." Brandon places cookies on a plate. "Next day, I check the footage."

"Next day?" Don's voice rose. He tried not to judge Brandon for his cavalier lifestyle, but, sometimes, his indiscretions get in the way of the job.

"Yeah, next day, I check the footage. She painted alright, but she didn't spill any. The footage shows her pulling this out of her storage container. Unless, I get up close to it, I'm not going to identify completely, but I think you know it."

"Can I see this footage? I mean did she know about it? Do you think she's stashing drugs in her storage unit?" Don grabbed a cookie off the plate.

Brandon went to the bedroom and brought out a laptop. He sat at the table and began to type something into the keyboard.

This doesn't make any sense. Faye plotted and planned her life. She took precautions when it came to legal responsibilities. She told me that she never wanted to do anything that might jeopardize her job or her testimony.

Brandon turned the computer toward Don to show him the footage from inside the apartment. The common areas showed up clearly visible. Don could see the kitchen and the living room.

"Nice quality." *Brandon never cut corners when it came to surveillance.*

They watched Faye set her paints down to view her work.

"I'd like to take a look at that painting."

Brandon paused the video and zoomed in to view the painting, "That looks like…"

"Mazzi." Don looked closer. "But younger. This came from some time ago."

"I think I saw yearbook photos similar to these. This scene is different, though."

Brandon started the video again. Faye stands back to view the painting again before cleaning the paints. She opens the container and pulls out a package.

"This is it." Brandon slows the footage so they won't miss her reaction. "She's surprised."

"And angry. Check it out." Don points to Faye pacing through the apartment. "What does she do with it? Come on Faye. Do you call somebody? Do you put it back?"

Brandon shook his head as the video continued to play.

"Where's the bedroom feed?"

Brandon shook his head. "I didn't put in a bedroom feed, Don. She deserves a little privacy."

"Privacy? Now, you want to give a young lady privacy?"

"Hey, that's too far!" Brandon sat back in the chair. "I may be loose in my relationships, but I can be a gentleman. This is Faye we're talking about."

Don closed his eyes and took a deep breath.

"Besides, you told me to access the exits and have eyes in the common areas. Remember, we want to protect her."

"Maybe we need a new goal."

"You don't believe she's running drugs." Brandon got up to pour some coffee. "We need to talk about this rationally. Somebody is setting her up."

Don shook his head.

"Don, you know somebody's setting her up. Let's talk this through. What do we know? Who would do this?"

"Where is the package now?"

"As far as I know, still in her bedroom. Probably in the safe. That's where I'd put it."

Don took a sip of coffee. "Where were the storage bins? Who had access?"

"She pulled them out of the basement storage. So anybody with a key."

Don nodded. "Anybody could've swiped that key at her party. Let's make a list of who would do this."

"Trish Schmidt is top of my list. She threatened Faye at the school and the party."

Don wrote the name. "Do you think she could gain access to the drugs?"

"Do you know someone else who could?"

Don looked at Brandon. "The Andrews family. That's why we're here isn't it? Elaine showed up at the party that night. She brought security. Any of those guys could have done this."

Brandon went into the other room and returned with a box of files. "I thought I saw something about the Schmidts in these files."

"Good idea. We need to know who is capable of this." Don scribbled a name on the pad. "We should add Mazzi to the list."

"Isn't John connected with the Andrews through the Auction House?"

"I'm thinking Gina. I'm not sure why, but she has it in for Faye."

Brandon looked through the files. "I don't see anything here about Gina."

"She's connected to Trish. Cousins, I think." Don sipped his coffee and began calming down. He tried not to get so involved with this case. He and Julie investigated the Andrews connection. They'd hit a dead end. From all appearances, the family had shut down their organization. Then, Julie uncovered something that stirred the pot. *It couldn't have been the Andrews. Elaine came to Arlington this summer…after Julie.*

"Trish married into the Schmidt family in 2010." Brandon kept reading. "Ew."

Don looked up at him.

"Says here she married her cousin. That's so gross."

"Real cousin? Keep reading."

"Ok. Ok." Brandon turned the page over. "The family adopted her in 2007. So, I guess that's not a blood relative."

"So, what do you know about the Schmidts? Does it say anything?"

"Aha!" Brandon slapped the table. "The Schmidts run the police force in Arlington. They have for years."

"That's not new information, Brandon. We knew that already."

"Yeah, but that means they have access to illegal drugs."

Thirty-Five

Faye pulled up to the her apartment building and noticed two police cruisers parked in front. Immediately her heart dropped along with all the blood in her head. She pulled into the garage slowly and took her time parking.

I have to think. Breathe. They're probably looking through storage units. Breathe. They have to have a warrant to look in apartments anyway.

She took a moment to gather her thoughts and calm her heart rate. The plan was to go straight to her apartment and not spend time in the lobby. *But I want to know why they're there. It could be for a totally different reason.*

Faye grabbed her bag and headed into the building. A sense of determination replaced her fear. She could solve this thing once and for all. She opened the door to the lobby and made her way to the doorman. The lobby seemed empty compared to the cars parked in front.

"What's going on?" She didn't waste time with her questions to Jay.

"Good afternoon, Ms. Unger." He offered his usual pleasantry.

Faye pointed to the police cars. "What's up with the police?"

"Oh, that's nothing for you to worry about, Ms. Unger. They need to check out a tip they received."

Faye nodded slowly.

"Don't worry, Ms. Unger. They are checking the basement. Your floor is clear." He smiled, but Faye doubted his sincerity.

She returned his nervous smile. "Ok. Thank you." Then, she crossed to the elevator to check out her apartment. The police could really be anywhere. The back stairwell and the freight elevator go straight up from the basement.

Faye took a deep breath as she exited the elevator. She didn't want to appear nervous should she encounter the police. Keys in hand, she slowly unlocked her door, but jumped when Brandon's door flung open.

"Faye," he whispered, "did you see the police cars out front?"

She looked around and nodded.

"Do you know why they're here?"

"What did you do?" All of her anxiety focused into the scowl across her face.

"Me? Nothing. I thought you might know."

Faye forced a chuckle. "Relax. Jay said that they are checking on a tip. Nothing for us to worry about. Unless, of course, you planted a bomb in the basement."

Faye checked his reaction closely. *If he planted it, he might give himself away.*

"Scouts honor." Brandon held up two fingers.

"You're such a dork," Faye grumbled and left him in the hallway.

She cautiously stepped into the apartment. The door closed behind her, and she glanced around the room. Everything looked the same as she left it. Faye walked over to the table and set her bag on it. She paused to observe the area. No change. She crossed to the kitchen and took a glass from the cabinet. Everything seemed in order.

Faye poured herself a glass of ice water and considered going into the bedroom to check the safe. *I'll never know unless I check it.* She took one last drink and walked toward the bedroom. As she passed by the front door, she heard voices from the hallway. She stopped to listen.

Is that Brandon? Maybe. A woman. No, a man.

Faye tiptoed to the door to look through the peep hole. She saw the back of someone wearing dark clothes. *Police?* They were talking to Brandon.

"No, sir. Everything's quiet around here. I'm not sure if everyone's home from work yet though."

The officer mumbled something in return. Faye heard keys and steps. Someone walked near her door.

Definitely cops.

He turned toward Brandon. *I wish I could hear better.* The policeman changed direction and moved toward the apartments at the other end.

I can't check the safe now! I need to stay put. Maybe I get comfortable. Faye walked toward her bedroom. *At least I can see if anyone has been here.* She didn't waste time. She practically ran into the bedroom to look around.

"Thank God!" Her sigh of relief echoed through the room. "Just as I left you."

The fact remained, the police had searched the building. Whoever wanted to set her up had tipped the police. Faye needed to take action. She pulled out her phone to contact Elaine, but a message popped up on the screen.

555-999-4268: You need to get out of there. Exit through the lobby and walk toward the coffee shop. There is a car waiting for you.

Faye started to question the text, then she heard the police knocking on doors. She grabbed her purse and left. The police were talking to the neighbor across the hall. Faye walked quietly behind them toward the stairwell.

She felt safer behind the door, but didn't waste time. The text said to exit through the lobby. Faye found the door for the second floor. *Surely they have finished questioning these people. Or maybe they were only questioning people on her floor.* Her heart stopped as the elevator opened. She couldn't turn back, so she stood up straight and pretended to belong there.

An older couple stepped out and waved to her. Faye smiled, but held her breathe until the door closed. *One floor. I can do this.* The door opened to the lobby where the policemen gathered around the doorman.

Faye glanced his direction, but didn't slow her pace. The door to freedom was within reach. To her benefit, Jay didn't break from conversation. He simply nodded and continued. Faye made it safely to the street. Two other officers had noticed her.

You belong. Don't look guilty. She smiled at them both. One officer tilted his hat toward her as she strode past them to the black town car. Frank stepped around the vehicle and held the door open for her.

"Thank you, Frank." Faye had never been happier to see these goons.

Thirty-six

Faye rode in complete silence for a while, but it settled her racing heart.

"Are you hurt?" The driver called out.

Faye continued to stare out the window.

"Miss, are you hurt?" Frank repeated himself.

"No." Faye adjusted the hair around her face.

"There's a bottle and a glass." Frank motioned toward a compartment between the front seats.

"No, thank you." Faye looked up to reassure him that she would be fin. "Where are we going?"

"Somewhere safe, Miss."

"How did you know to come get me?"

"You'll have to ask the boss that one. I just do what I'm told." Frank's tone comforted Faye, but his words caused her to second guess her decision to meet with Elaine.

She looked out the window to see the French Restaurant coming into view. The car pulled around to the back of the building. Frank got out to open the door for Faye. They entered the building through the back, and she followed him down a dark hallway lined with mahogany paneling. Two chandeliers lit the passage from above. Then, Frank opened a door, hidden by the panelling, and motioned for her to walk through.

Faye looked behind her for possible exits, but another man stood guard in front of any doorway. She walked through the hidden doorway into a dimly lit stairwell.

"Follow me." Frank slipped past her and descended the stairs.

Faye followed him. The stairs led to a long corridor. Pendant lights hung from the ceiling revealing three doors. A short, stout man guarded one of the doors. Frank nodded to the man, and he stepped aside.

Then, Frank knocked three times. A window in the door slid open. Eyes from inside the door focused on Faye, and the little window closed. The door opened to a room larger than the restaurant above. Mahogany paneling covered the bottom half of the walls while elegant wallpaper covered the rest. Tiny lights cooperated with the silvery wallpaper to highlight framed paintings on the walls.

Artwork filled this space like an art museum. The placement of artifacts encouraged Faye to walk into the space. She saw statues on pedestals and curio cabinets with delicate porcelain sculptures. The lighting helped frame the pieces and set the atmosphere. Faye felt oddly comfortable in the room. *Maybe I've visited too many art museums.*

Faye wandered the room waiting for her host. Most of the art appeared modern, but she didn't recognize any of the paintings. One particular painting captured her attention. *Where have I seen you before? The colors and style are so familiar, but I can't place it.* Faye gazed into the painting determined to remember where she'd seen it before. Like a name on the tip of the tongue, the painting both haunted and threatened her. The hair on the back of her neck stood up as a cool sweat approached her forehead.

"Do you like this one?"

Elaine's voice pulled her away from the painting but only just.

"There is something compelling about it." Faye hoped to hide her sudden distress.

"What do you see in that painting?"

"The forest? It's nice," Faye wanted to sound aloof and unfettered. "The colors are rich and vibrant."

Faye took a step toward the painting to get a closer look. She would have done the colors just like that. In fact, a lot of the strokes for the trees looked like something she had learned in art school. Something else, though, seemed familiar about the scene. She had been there, but she couldn't remember the location.

"The colors are similar to the ones in your paintings. Do you see it?"

"The place looks familiar, but I don't remember seeing this painting before. Do you know the artist?"

Elaine nodded and pointed to the lower right of the painting. It was signed, FA. "Do you recognize this artist?"

"No. I'm afraid not."

"Definitely one of my favorites." Elaine smiled as she changed the subject. "Come, let's have a drink. You've had a difficult afternoon."

Faye followed her to the table. As they sat, a waiter brought them a glass decanter with two glasses.

Faye had so many questions. She took a breath to launch into them, but Elaine held up her index finger. "I know. I will do my best to answer your questions, Faye. But first," Elaine picked up her drink and motioned for Faye to do the same. "Don't worry. It's non-alcoholic."

The caramel colored beverage smelled like rotten fruit. Faye sipped slowly. The carbonated liquid tickled the back of her throat going down. *Apple soda?* She looked up from the glass and waited for Elaine to explain.

"Now, how are you doing?" Elaine sounded sincere, but everything about her screamed 'run away.'

Faye had already located the exits, so she kept her eyes focused on Elaine. She took another sip of her drink to contemplate her response. She decided to play it cool. After all, Elaine could be the mastermind behind this whole set up.

"So, why have you summoned me? Was I in danger?"

"Weren't you?"

"I mean, the police were in the building checking on a tip, but I didn't do anything."

Elaine casually looked up at Faye. "Some of us don't have to commit a crime to be in trouble. Tell me about your friend, Trish."

"I wouldn't exactly call her my friend."

"Do you know why she keeps coming after you?"

Where is the this woman getting her information? How does she know about my history with Trish?

The surprise must have shown all over Faye's face.

"There are a lot of people concerned about you, Faye." Elaine looked over her shoulder at the waiter. "People talk. Especially in Arlington."

"I don't know anything about Trish or her family, do you?"

Elaine exhaled. "You don't remember. Do you?"

Now, this woman knows about my memory? Either she's been talking to Steve Gardner or she was there. Either way, Faye wanted to get out of there.

"I think I need to go now." Faye put her napkin on the table and pushed her chair out. "Thank you for the drink, and the ride."

Frank came to stand behind Fay, and a waiter brought Elaine a sealed note on a silver platter. Elaine looked at the note and held up her index finger for Faye to wait. She opened the note and proceeded to read it.

"Thank you." Elaine placed the letter on the tray. "I don't think you should go home just yet."

"And why is that?"

"I haven't answered any of your questions. Please, let me explain." Elaine motioned for Faye to sit. "Please."

Faye took a seat.

"You see, I grew up here, in Arlington. So, I have a lot of friends in different places. One of my friends has connections to the police force. That is how I knew about the tip."

Faye nodded and thought for sure everyone in the room could see the lightbulb over her head. "Did you go to Arlington High School?"

"Yes. Now, you answer one of my questions." Elaine took another sip. "Is there any truth to the tip?"

"What was the tip?"

Elaine looked at Faye sarcastically. "Someone found drugs in the basement storage area."

"How do I know that you didn't call in the tip? Maybe you're trying to set me up?"

"I would never set you up, Faye." Elaine closed her eyes and shook her head. "You have the drugs, don't you?"

Faye didn't respond. She took another sip of the apple soda.

"Don't talk to anyone. I'll send you instructions. I just need a few hours."

Faye sat, and the room stilled. Her phone buzzed in her pocket.

Don: Where are you?

Faye looked up at Elaine and didn't respond to either of them.

Don: Are you ok?

Faye looked up toward Elaine who had already gotten up and exited the room. She wan't sure if she should stay at the table or leave. Her phone rang.

"Faye?" Don sounded frantic.

"Yes?" Faye whispered into the phone, "I can't really talk right now."

"Are you ok?"

"Yes. I'm having dinner."

"So, you haven't been home, yet?" Don's voice started to calm, but his questions troubled Faye.

"Home? Why? What happened?" Her quiet whisper rose with the questions.

"The police searched your apartment."

Silence on both ends of the line.

"Meet me for coffee?" Don sounded calm. The words he didn't say concerned Faye. *Did he know? Did the police find it?*

"Ok. Give me thirty minutes."

***

Frank insisted on waiting for Faye outside the coffee shop. One police cruiser still parked in front of her building. Faye didn't mind waiting for them to leave before returning to her apartment. She swallowed hard the thoughts and fears of what they might have found. Then, there was Elaine. She started planning something. Faye could only image what it could be.

Don stood as she approached the table. He stepped around and pulled her in for a hug. In all her anxiety, she hadn't stopped to imagine what he might be experiencing. She didn't have to wait to find out.

"I'm so glad to see you." He sounded relieved. "I didn't know what happened, and Brandon wasn't any help at all." He handed her a coffee. "I went ahead and ordered your usual."

"Thank you." Faye took a sip. "How did you know that the police searched my place?"

"Brandon told me that much. He said they looked for you, but no one knew where you'd gone."

"I got a phone call." She paused unsure of how much to share.

"Well, I'm just glad you're ok." Don's hand shook slightly as he picked up his drink.

Faye started to feel bad for not sharing her location. "The police make me nervous. I can't really explain it, but, for as long as I can remember, I get queasy and sweaty when they're around."

All of this was true. Faye couldn't remember when it started, but she avoided the cops at all costs. Seeing the text gave her a way out.

"I understand. Oh, I almost forgot." He pulled out her school bag and handed it to her.

"My bag?" Faye grabbed it from across the table.

"Yeah, Brandon saw it when the police were there. He grabbed it just in case you weren't allowed to go back inside."

Faye sat up straight. The anxieties she had swallowed came back to the front of her mind. "You think I might not be able to go back inside?"

Don shrugged. "I found a gift under the Santa tree with your name on it. I put it in your bag."

"Thanks. I almost forgot about that." She peered into the bag and pulled it out. "Did you bring yours? We could open them together."

"Good idea." Don reached into his jacket pocket. "We could use a little laughter today."

Faye watched Don peel open the paper. "So, what'd you get?"

"Christmas socks. I'm pretty sure it's Richard."

"I didn't know you liked crazy socks."

"I don't, but I think Richard does. He has worn a different pair every day."

Faye chuckled.

"Open yours." Don's smile lifted the dark mood. "Let's see it."

Faye looked into the gift bag.

"What is it?"

She pulled out a locket, and dropped it on the table.

"Ooo, looks like you have an admirer." Don reached over and and opened it ."This isn't new."

Faye shook her head, and kept shaking her head. "No, it isn't."

"Faye." Don reached over and grabbed her hand. "What's wrong?"

"That was from my safe," Faye looked at Don with tears filling her eyes.

"You have a safe?"

"Someone has been inside my apartment, Don." Faye tried to hold it back, but tears streamed down her cheeks.

"Faye, let's focus."

Faye grabbed a napkin to clear the tears from her cheeks. She closed her eyes to think. *My peace I leave with you.* The prayer had helped so often in the past. She needed to focus on it now. She remembered hiding the gift for Brandon under the tree, but couldn't recall getting one from the tree.

"Who would do this? Why?"

"I don't think it's your Santa." Don looked around the room. "Who's in the locket?"

Faye picked up the locket and looked at the picture inside. She recognized the young man she painted a few days ago.

"This is Mazzi." Faye pointed to the young man. "I'm not sure the name of the girl."

Don nodded. "I think I know it. Gina mentioned an old girlfriend from high school."

Faye looked up at him. She had been tryin to figure this out for a long time.

"I think that's your sister, Elaine."

"My sister? I don't have a sister."

Don looked confused. "Well, I had dinner with the Mazzi's the other night. Gina mentioned that John might be better with your sister than with you. Later, John mentioned a high school fling with someone named Elaine."

"You had dinner with the Mazzi's?"

"That is a whole other story, but let's get back on topic."

"Yeah Don, I don't know anything about a sister." Faye completely dismissed the idea.

Don changed the subject for her, "Looks like the police are gone."

Thirty-Seven

Don held the door for Faye out of the coffee shop. *There has to be more to this than what she's telling me.* They walked bundled and silent as the wind blew fresh snow at them. He didn't ask if he could come up. The elevator opened, and they both stepped inside.

Don pressed the button. "I hope you don't mind me going with you. I just don't feel right sending you up alone. I want to check the apartment to be sure no one is there and the locks work."

"Always the gentleman."

Don would probably go up and check it even if she had said no.

Faye tried the handle before using her key. "At least they locked it back for me."

The apartment looked untouched. Don had searched apartments before. He never bothered to put them back in order afterwards.

"This place is a mess!" Faye shouted. "I can't believe they would do this! Just go through my things and turn everything inside out!"

"So, can you tell what they looked through? Maybe what they were looking for?"

Faye marched around the room reorganizing shelves and bins. She mumbled complaints as she straightened paintings. Then, she headed toward the bedroom. Don hadn't cleared that room, so he followed after her.

"You can't come in here." Faye jumped as she said it.

What are you hiding in here?

Don reached his hand into his jacket to grab the revolver. "I just want to make sure no one else is in there with you."

Faye looked at his hand and stepped aside. Don checked the bathroom and even behind the curtains in the bedroom. He started toward the closet, but Faye stepped in front of him.

"What are you doing? The closet is one of the first places people hide."

"It's just…" Faye mumbled something.

"What?"

"The safe is…is in the closet."

"Then, what are we waiting for? Open it up. Let's see if your locket is in there."

Faye had a puzzled looked on her face. Whatever she's hiding must be in the closet. She stood there frozen, so Don stepped forward and opened the door.

Faye yelped, but Don couldn't figure out why. "Ok, the closet's clear."

Faye stood frozen.

"Everything's ok. Nobody's in the closet."

"Um, sure." Faye didn't sound sure or ok.

"Shall we check the safe? I'm thinking if your locket is still there, then the gift might have come from Mazzi himself." Don tried to sound hopeful, but the look on her face didn't show it.

Faye slowly approached the safe. Her hands trembled as she turned the combination lock. Don couldn't wait to see what she might be hiding in there. *It's gotta be the package from Brandon's photo.*

Faye paused before opening the door. "You can't judge me by what we may or may not find in here."

"Ok," Don spoke aloud, but inside he screamed, *OPEN THE SAFE ALREADY!*

Faye opened the safe to reveal a large, brown package. She reached around the package and pulled out a necklace. Ignoring the package, she lifted the necklace that held a locket and ring.

"It's Mazzi!" She squealed with delight.

"That's great! Do you think he's the one trying to frame you?" *We have to address the package.*

"It could be Gina or Trish. Neither of them like me."

"What's the brown package? Was that there before?"

Faye's face went from jubilation to white as a ghost. She pulled out the package and handed it to Don. He started to open it, but she put her hand out to stop him.

"I found this in my storage unit. In fact, my key is missing. I had to use the extra from Jay."

"When did your key go missing?"

"After the party."

Don knew this package, but he pretended to be surprised. "Did you open this at all?"

"Yes. I took the brown paper off, but I put back on."

"Is it explosive?"

"Explosive? I didn't even consider that."

Don gently removed the brown paper to reveal the white brick wrapped in plastic wrap. He pulled out a pocket knife to cut a slit in the plastic. A white puff escaped into the air. He reached his pinky into the powder and tasted it.

"Definitely drugs, but you knew that didn't you."

"Why did you just taste it?" Faye sounded completely disgusted.

"Well, isn't that what they do on tv?"

"How do you know what drugs taste like?"

Don had to think of something quick or he would risk blowing his cover. "I learned a thing or two in the military." He paused before he offered a solution, "I think we need to turn it in."

Faye put her face in her hands, "I can't go to jail, Don. It would ruin me. Ruin me."

"Don't worry. I have a friend in the FBI. We can call him. I'm sure he'll handle it discretely. No one at school will need to know."

"They'll know when I don't show up, because. I'm. In. Jail!"

"Faye, it's ok. Remember, someone stole your key. Jay can testify for you. You won't be alone. You have friends."

"Not like that, Don. My friends are all superficial. Jodi? Jeffrey? They just care about making money for the Auction House."

"Look," Don pulled up his contact for Agent Rogers and showed it to Faye. "I'll call him from here. You can listen to the call."

"Are you sure?"

"Yes, I will help you. I'll stay right here until I know you're safe."

"Ok, you can call him. It's the right thing to do."

Don put his phone on speaker and dialed Rogers. He could hear Faye mumbling a Psalm under her breath.

"Though I walk in the midst of trouble, you preserve my life. You stretch out your hand against the anger of my foes, with your right hand, you save me."

"Hey there, Don. How's it going?" Agent Rogers said from the other end.

"I'm doing well, Agent Rogers. I have a situation here that is a little sensitive."

"Oh?"

"I'm here with my friend, Faye. It seems that someone tried to hide a brick of cocaine in her apartment storage locker."

"Really? How did she come across it?"

"It was in a storage tote in the basement of her building."

"Does she still have it?" Rogers did not sound surprised. Don appreciated the discretion from him. He knew the details of this case, and this call could easily blow his cover.

"Yes, sir. Is there a way to investigate without drawing attention and pulling her out of work? She is a teacher, and this could ruin her career."

"I'm not sure, Don. I'll see what I can do. I'll send a couple of agents to the apartment to look around and ask a few questions. Will you be there?"

"Yes, sir. I'm not going anywhere."

"Alright, then. Send me the address, and I'll tell them to look for you."

Don watched Faye wander out to the balcony. He sent the details to Rogers, along with an update for Brandon. Then, he walked out to join her.

"You have a great view out here."

Faye nodded, tears filling her eyes.

"I always enjoyed looking at the city lights with Julie. I miss that sometimes." He stepped closer to Faye.

She reached around him for a hug. "I'm scared."

"I know." Don held onto her.. "I'm here."

Thirty-Eight

Dressed as repairmen, the agents arrived conspicuously and hid their investigative instruments in tool chests. Faye changed into comfortable clothing with the assumption that they would cart her off to jail. They had no real reason to believe her story, and she had no proof to back it up.

"Ma'am, where did you say you found this again?"

"It was in the tote with my art supplies."

"Are those supplies in your apartment?"

"No, they're in the basement. The building has a storage area for each apartment."

"I can show around down there." Brandon offered. "I live next door. We can talk to the doorman about a key."

Don brought her a cup of coffee, "You're doing great. I think they're almost done in there."

"Did you have to include Brandon in this? I was kinda hoping we could not include the people from work." Faye took the coffee, but kept her eyes on the agents going through all of her belongings.

"Sorry about that, he sounded worried about you."

Faye rolled her eyes.

"Have you heard anything from Jeffrey? Or Elaine?"

Faye shook her head. This was the time she needed friends and goons. *Where is Frank now?* She looked up from the coffee at the agents carrying files and paperwork from the safe. A dried flower dropped from the pile and fell to the floor. The man stooped to pick it up and caught her eye as he stood.

Suddenly, Faye experienced a sense of déjà vu. She had never met the the man, but something about the context felt familiar. Faye stepped out to the balcony for some fresh air.

"You ok?" Don pulled out a chair for her to sit down.

"Just a sense of déjà vu. I can't explain it."

Don grabbed the cup from her trembling hands. "Do you remember the attack in 2003?"

"How do you know about that?"

"Faye, this is Arlington. People talk."

"Ok, well. I only remember bits and pieces. Mostly feelings of being scared."

Brandon walked in with the other agent. Faye excused Don to go speak with them. She didn't want to talk about the ravine or anything

she might have seen. Right now, she wanted to everyone to leave.
She wanted this whole nightmare to end. She could be an artist full-
time. The art community is full of people with questionable pasts.

Don stuck his head out the door. "Faye, can you come inside for
a moment? The agents have a few questions for you."

Faye took a deep breath and stood up. *I can do this. I've been in
this place before, and I got out then.* She walked inside where an
agent directed her to take a seat at the dining table.

"Ma'am, you said that you found this in your storage unit. Is that
correct?"

"Yes, sir."

"Did anyone else have access to this storage unit?"

"I have a key and the man at the front desk has a spare. So, I
guess he would also have access to it."

"Do you have the key with you?"

"No sir. I lost my key a few weeks ago."

"You lost it?" The agent scribbled vigorously onto a note pad.

"I think it may have been stolen during a party I hosted." Faye
conveyed the information even though it seemed unlikely to her that
they would believe any of it.

"Do you , by any chance, have a guest list for this party?"

Faye shook her head. So many other people planned the party. It
would be impossible for her to remember everyone in attendance.

"I attended that party." Don spoke up from behind her. "I can forward you a list of people who were there."

"Thank you, sir." The agent seated at the table completed his form. "Now, we just have a few forms for you to sign for the things we need to take with us."

Faye glanced at the door to see her painting tote ready for departure. She didn't bother reading the papers before she signed.

"That's all we need here, Miss." The agent collected the paperwork and started to head out the door. "We'll let you know if we need anything further."

Faye waited for the inevitable. She watched them intently. The two agents gathered their things. They spoke to Don and Brandon and gave them fist bumps. No one moved toward her or even bothered to take out hand cuffs. They nodded in her direction and started to leave. Faye stepped toward the door in surprise.

"Wait." She stopped before she spoke further, "shouldn't I go with them?"

Brandon and Don looked at her.

"Isn't this where they put the handcuffs on me and take me to jail?"

"No." Don said as he put his hand on her shoulder.

"We asked them while you were outside. Basically, they don't have an arrest warrant, so you stay here until they do." Brandon added as Don nudged him.

"Faye, they don't have any reason to take you in handcuffs. You cooperated with them. Answered their questions and let them search your apartment. You're safe."

Thirty-Nine

Faye decided to stay with her parents through Christmas. The break from her apartment and the inevitable jail time brought her peace of mind. The snow outside matched the thoughts swirling in her head. Faye peered through the frosted window for a glimpse of snow, but decided to walk in it. She enjoyed the eerie quiet. When she closed her eyes, she could hear the snowflakes landing on the trees and shrubs. *This must be what heaven is like.*

"Would you like some hot chocolate, dear?" Judy offered.

Faye nodded and grabbed the cup.

"The snow is peaceful." Judy put her arm around Faye. "It will be ok. These things have a way of sorting themselves. You'll be fine. Don't worry."

Faye lifted her eyebrows. "I wish I could just decide to not worry."

"You can. It takes practice, though"

Faye set the table while her mom put the finishing touches on the sides. Her dad carved the turkey and displayed it on the table. A knock at the door caused Faye to jump.

"I'll get it." Judy moved from the kitchen to the front door and placed her hand on Faye's back and whispered, "Relax."

A young man stood at the door with a sealed envelope. He walked away as Judy took it from him. She stepped inside and read it to herself.

"Same as last year?" Jack asked.

Judy nodded her head and placed the note on the side table by the front door.

This wasn't the first time a messenger delivered a note to the house. Faye didn't pay attention the other times. Today, everything mattered. Every decoration had a clear design and significance. Event this messenger stood out in her mind. After she placed the silver, Faye made her way to the table to read the note for herself.

> Merry Christmas. I am not able to join you at
> this time. I wish I could be there. Soon. I
> will see you soon.
>
> - EA

Faye took the note with her into the kitchen. Judy wiped her hands on a towel and looked at Faye.

"Who were you expecting for dinner?"

Judy stood shocked at Faye's question.

Faye held up the note. "Who is EA?"

"Your sister, Faye."

"What sister?"

Judy looked beyond Faye into the other room. "We invite her every year, Faye. This is why we have the extra plate setting."

"I know you don't want to think about it." Jack walked into the room and placed his hand on her shoulder. "She's been gone a long time now."

"It's not that I don't want to think about her. I don't remember her at all." Faye looked at her parents willing them to explain. Both of them looked at her as though she were joking.

"Let's go sit down and talk about this." Judy spoke softly and ushered them to the dining room.

"You can start by telling me her name." Faye's disrespectful tone demanded answers.

"Her name is Elaine." Judy answered, but didn't offer any other information.

"Is she married?"

"No, she's not married," Jack answered. "At least, I don't think so."

"Then, why does the card say E.A.? Shouldn't it be E.U.?" Faye closed her eyes in frustration. "Look, guys I need information. I've got people trying to frame me. I need to know what's going on."

"Ok, ok. We haven't been hiding things from you Faye." Jack started. "We thought you already knew." He took a deep breath and a sip of water. "E.A. stands for Elaine Andrews. Years ago, after the incident, we changed our name to Unger."

"We needed to do it, Faye. We didn't see any other way out," Judy added.

"What incident?"

"The murder in 2003." Jack paused. "I know you remember this."

Faye looked at the design of the flowers on the plate in front of her. Images from the ravine kept coming to mind, but she couldn't put the pieces together.

"They tried to frame Elaine for it." Judy wiped a tear. "We couldn't let the same happen to you."

Jack placed his hand on Judy's. "So, we got out."

"Got out of what?"

"The family business." Jack pursed his lips like he did when he had finished talking about a thing.

Faye never asked about the family business. Something deep inside her told her to leave it alone. Things were different now. Today, she needed to know. "What was the family business?"

"No." Judy shook her head.

"I'm already involved. I have people telling me that they know about my family. Shouldn't I know about them too?"

Jack patted Judy's hand. "No secrets." Then, he took a deep breath. "The family business is imports and exports. At one time, we controlled the traffic of goods in and out of Arlington."

"What's with all the secrets, then? That's not dangerous."

"That's the surface of the business. Beneath the surface, the family organized the traffic of illegal goods and services. The family made sure that all business went through us."

"Like the mafia?"

"Not like it, dear." Judy's tone was serious and her eyes darted across the room. "That is the family business."

"So, did we murder Albert Schmidt?"

"No!" Jack pounded the table with his fist. "We did not murder Albert Schmidt. They tried to pin that one on us."

"Jack." Judy attempted to calm him down.

"No, we had an agreement." He pulled his hand away from hers.

"Why do I remember the ravine? Was I there?"

"Yes. You were there, but we can't say what happened to you. You never told us."

Jack stood up and crossed the room. "You probably know who did it."

"Let's calm down. This won't help her remember, Jack." Judy looked at Faye. "Your sister chose to stay with the family business. That's why she moved to Chicago."

"She's back now." Jack yelled from the other room.

"I know." Faye considered telling them about the offer and about Elaine's help with the police, but her phone buzzed in her pocket.

She pulled it out to check the message. Her mom got up and went into the kitchen.

Don: Are you coming to the Christmas party tonight?

Faye had forgotten about the party. Last year, she worked hard to develop her private life. She didn't attend any parties. She looked up from her phone. Her parents were nowhere in sight. So, she responded:

"I'll be there."

Forty

Don carried jugs of apple cider across the street to the Browns. The jugs weren't particularly heavy, but he took his time. Something about the sound of snow crunching under his feet brought with it memories of Christmas past. He smiled, *those were good times.*

"Hey! Don's here, everybody!" Jason took one of the jugs from him. "It's good to see you, brother. I hope you brought your appetite."

The party was in full swing. Christmas carols rang out from the stereo with a chorus of folks singing along. Appetizers adorned the table along with candies, nuts, and garland.

"Hey, Don, good to see you." Brandon patted him on the back, "I've been meaning to get with you the last few days, but I've been a little preoccupied." Jodi walked up beside him and snuggled under his arm.

Don greeted Jodi and started toward the others in the kitchen when Brandon grabbed his arm.

"There have been some developments." Brandon spoke into Don's ear, "we need to talk."

Don eyed the study off to the left, then headed toward the kitchen.

"Hey! Faye's here, everybody!" Jason shouted from the living room.

Don looked behind him near the front door. Frank stood behind Faye removing her fur coat. She smiled at Don from the doorway then proceeded to mingle through the crowd. Don placed the cider on the counter and headed toward the study. Brandon met him there.

"You're free?" Don pretended to look for Jodi.

"Very funny, but we probably don't have long to talk."

"What's so important?"

"I got a call from Rogers." Brandon looked around the room.

"Oh?" Don wasn't sure why Rogers would call Brandon and himself.

"It doesn't look good for Faye." He looked down. "They're getting a federal warrant."

"Federal? She has no priors, and I don't think this is federal either."

"On account of her family, Don."

"Her family?" Jack and Judy couldn't hurt a fly.

"It seems Julie knew things she hadn't shared with any of us, Don."

Don stood taller at the mention of Julie's name,. "This better be good, Brandon."

"She's an Andrews."

"What?"

Brandon nodded, "They're going to try to take down the whole family. Rogers thinks Elaine might be in on it."

"What does that have to do with Julie or the 2003 case?"

Brandon scoffed. "Julie had secret meetings with Elaine. Didn't you know she went up to Chicago to interview the family?"

No. He didn't know that, but he wasn't about to confess that to Brandon. Don clenched his fist ready to pop Brandon's smug little face, but a call from the other room stopped him.

"It's Secret Santa time! Everyone meet around the tree!" Susan called out through the house.

Don took a deep breath to calm himself and walk away from Brandon. He went through the kitchen to grab a drink before meeting the others in the living room.

Faye snuck up beside him and whispered, "It's the big moment."

Don turned to look at her. *Andrews.* But he didn't see it. He just saw Faye: happy, innocent, and beautiful.

"You look great, tonight." Don couldn't help inhaling her perfume as he spoke to her.

"Thanks." Her smile started melting his anger toward Brandon. *It can't be true. There's no way she's part of that. Not Faye.*

"Come on." Faye grabbed his arm. "Let's go catch the look on Mazzi's face when he reveals himself."

Don joined her in the other room where they had already begun uncovering the secret identities. Brandon pulled his gift and opened a new cookbook with Faye's name on it.

"I can be nice, too." Faye laughed.

Don opened a pair of Christmas slippers from Richard.

Then, Faye's turn came. She pulled her gift and glanced toward Mazzi. She opened a set of canvas and water colors.

"Brandon?" Faye's surprise brought laughter through the room.

She made her way toward Don and whispered, "I thought for sure it was Mazzi."

"Me too." Don's brain worked over time to arrange the clues to make sense. "Whoever sent the locket meant to scare you for sure."

"But they had to know that I had the other one." Faye's face paled in the dark room.

"Let's go somewhere less crowded." Don led her to the study grabbing a glass of punch on his way. "Here, drink this. You look pale."

"Thanks." Faye paused and readied herself. "Do you think Brandon could have done this?"

Don had to think about his answer. He and Brandon had worked together for years. Top agents. Don trusted no one else in the agency like he trusted Brandon. However, he had never wanted to punch him like he did moments ago.

"I don't know Brandon had knowledge of the locket."

Faye sipped the punch and looked up at him. "He went to Arlington High School. He might have known."

Forty-One

Winter break never lasted long enough. It had been a week since the FBI confiscated Faye's painting tote. While she had some answers to her questions about Elaine, Faye remained in the dark about events in the ravine. She still had no clue who was trying to frame her. She needed order in her life. Starting a new semester could help. Faye walked into the school hoping to quietly prepare for her day.

"Good morning!" Susan sat behind Faye's desk. "I'm glad I caught you."

Faye stood in the Math office and looked around the room.

"I have a list of ideas here for the Spring Formal, but I need your input." Susan stood and handed Faye a binder bursting with colored papers and ribbons. "Faye, bring it with you to lunch. Tell me you'll look it over before then?"

"Maybe. I have class today, and I think we're meeting about the Math Tournament."

"That's tomorrow." Don mumbled from across the room.

"Don?" Faye looked over at Don who sat face down at his desk.

"I gotta go. See you at lunch?" Susan stopped briefly to wait for Faye's answer before heading out the door.

"Ok, I'll look at it." Faye walked over to Don.

"Don? Are you ok?"

"Hmm?" He sat up and looked at her with one eye closed, "Yeah." He cleared his throat. "I'm ok. Just didn't sleep much last night."

"Oh." Faye felt the weight of his insomnia.

"I'm ok. I've just got a lot on my mind. The break seemed more busy than restful for me."

"I understand. I'm not at all prepared for the tournament tomorrow."

"You'll do great. I remember my first tournament." Don smiled and looked off into the distance.

"That bad, huh?" Faye brought him back to the present.

He shook his head. "Not at all. Just remember, something always goes wrong."

The math tournament meeting involved the entire school. Math and science teachers organized the tournament brackets and judges. English and social studies teachers took care of the hospitality rooms. Susan took on the responsibility of organizing everyone else. Every year, math teachers fought over who would MC the event.

Usually, none of them wanted to host, because the host becomes the go-to person for questions and complaints.

This year, J.J. would lead the meeting about the tournament as head of the math department. Faye, however, had been selected to MC this year's tournament. She had wanted to review her notes about last year's tournament over the winter break, but things didn't go as planned.

"Is everyone here yet?" J.J. started all of their meetings.

"I think we're missing John," Don spoke up.

"He had to leave early, so he won't be here." J.J. looked around to see if everyone else was there. "We're going to go ahead and get started. Last year, everything went smoothly. I went ahead and photo-copied the list of responsibilities. We'll pass that around and you can sign next to where you want to serve. Faye is our MC this year. Do you have questions, Faye?"

"I just have a few things to clarify. So, I give the rules at the beginning of the day. When do I need to say anything else?"

"Every day, there will be some kind of announcement. Usually, Susan writes it down. But we'll give you that at the beginning of each day. You will bring everyone together during lunch while we tally scores. You also need to gather the crowds before the next round."

"Got it. That doesn't sound like too much. I don't know why you guys hate it?"

"It was a lot better last year," Don chimed in, "more organized, so people had fewer questions."

"Do you have a copy of the rules?" J.J. flipped through a manilla file and pulled out an extra copy for her.

"Thanks. I guess I'll need that."

***

The day of the tournament arrived without issue. Usually, the issues came with the visiting schools. Susan had organized the floor plan and all of the faculty members served to welcome visitors. Excitement filled the building. Faye looked forward to her role as MC. It seems the cloud of winter break had finally lifted.

"Ms. Unger, do you have any information for Washington School?" Megan Brown approached Faye in a panic. "They think they're first, but we don't know for sure."

"Don't you have a teacher assigned to you?"

"I think so, but I don't know who it is."

"Don't worry," Faye looked around the media center for Susan, "let's find someone who can help."

Faye located Susan and the list of host teachers and students. She took an extra copy for herself.

"It says here that Ms. Mazzi is supposed to be helping you."

"I haven't seen either of the Mazzis today," Susan whispered to Faye.

"Is there another teacher who can step in to help?"

"Don't worry, dear," Susan said to Megan, "Ms. Donna is on her way to help."

Satisfied, Megan went on her way to pass along the message.

"Neither of the Mazzis are here? Did something happen?"

Susan shrugged. "All I know is that they didn't show up to pick up their packets. Good thing I had alternates."

Faye stepped back to check her paperwork and locate the opening remarks for the day. Schools began making their way to the Media Center. Students reserved seats in the center for the math teams. Other students mingled with the visitors and introduced themselves. Many of the students talked with their friends from years prior.

"This is amazing." Faye mumbled.

"I know, right?" Brandon stepped beside her. "Are you ready?"

Faye nodded. "I think so. It's not that complicated. I'm listing out rules and encouraging teams to do their best."

"Well, go get 'em." He patted Faye on the back and nudged her forward.

Faye walked up to the microphone and began her speech. "Hello, everyone." Faye raised to her hand to get their attention. Then, she tried again. "Welcome to Arlington Community School. We are excited to welcome all of our visiting schools to this year's math tournament." She paused and looked around the room.

The students stopped fidgeting, and conversations ended. Faye had the room. A sense of power swept over her along with dread and nervous energy.

"Before we get started, I want to go over a few procedures." Faye began to identify the restrooms and trash cans when she noticed movement out of the corner of her eye.

"Your host teachers should have your schedule of events." Something moved toward the crowd surrounding the media center.

"The judges will update the tournament bracket regularly."

The crowd began to part.

"Remember to keep negative comments to yourselves. We want to keep a safe, friendly environment at all times." Faye neared the end of her speech when someone tapped her on the arm.

"Faye Unger."

She turned to see a police officer. Two other officers circled around her.

"Get on the ground and put your hands behind your head."

"Please?" Faye gave the man a bewildered look.

He drew out his hand gun. "Face down. On the ground. Hands behind your head."

An officer from behind her put his hands on her shoulders forcing her to the ground.

"You're under arrest for possession of illegal substances with intent to sell."

Forty-One

On the morning of the math tournament, Don arranged to meet Brandon at the school early to clear the building before visitors arrived.

"It's all set. Did you download the app to your watch?" Brandon showed him the icon for the app on the watch.

Don glanced at Brandon's phone and entered some info into his own. "Got it. Now, we have mobile eyes on the building. Anything else from Rogers?"

"He had to pass the case to the local police."

Don stepped back. "What?"

"Relax. It's a formality. You know how they have to alert local law enforcement of any investigation."

Something about that news didn't sit well with Don. *Why didn't Rogers communicate any of this to me?* Movement from a camera in his phone caught his attention.

"What's this?"

"Probably just the other math teams arriving."

Don looked toward the front entrance. "I'll go check it out. You stick close to Faye."

"I doubt she needs it." Brandon pointed to Frank keeping watch near Faye.

Don rolled his eyes and headed toward the office. He welcomed a school from Louisville and another from Cincinnati. Then, he noticed the police cars pulling up. Don's interactions with the Arlington police taught him two things: they run their own investigations and they don't work well with others.

This is a formality? Don pulled out his phone to message Rogers for back up. *This could get ugly.*

Officers took their time before exiting their vehicles. Don watched from a safe distance as three additional police cruisers arrived. He could hear Faye testing the microphone behind him. The last visiting team filed past him into the school. If the police were there for protection, they could go. No incidents inside or outside.

They waited in their vehicles. Don stepped inside the school, but kept watch from the entry doors. Two unmarked cars pulled up in front of the school. He looked down at his phone. Nothing from Rogers. He watched them exit their vehicles.

As they approached, Don opened the door to greet them. Several officers pulled their guns.

"Detective George, I didn't expect to see you here."

"Mr. Ambrose." The detective nodded. "I have no business with you today. I would appreciate it if you stepped aside."

"That all depends." Don stepped directly in front of him. "On your business. This is a school. Is someone in danger?"

"Like I said, Mr. Ambrose, it's not your business."

"Whatever your business, I'm sure you won't require guns." Don motioned to the officers who had pulled their guns.

The detective motioned for the officers to put the guns away. "I quite agree. However, Mr. Ambrose, you are well aware of the dangers in Arlington. We don't want anyone to get hurt."

"Is there a way to conduct your business discretely?" Don looked into the detectives eyes unapologetically.

"Arrests are rarely discrete, Don." Detective George placed his hand on Don and pushed him aside. "Now, step aside."

Three officers stepped around Don to enter the media center. By the time Don caught up to them, they had Faye face down on the ground. His phone buzzed.

Rogers: Hey, sorry I haven't gotten back with you guys. We are still investigating on this end. No need for an arrest.

He looked up at Brandon who was already making his way toward the microphone.

"Now that you're all awake." He paused for laughter, but the crowd remained silent. "Ahem." He tapped on the microphone, "now that you're all awake. Let's give it up for Ms. Unger and our local police officers." He started clapping his hands. "That might be a little over the top, guys. I think they made their point, though. Don't you?" He motioned to Faye and the officers.

The crowd applauded loudly and students cheered for Faye.

"We will definitely remember to follow the rules that Ms. Unger outlined for us, won't we?"

Again, the crowd applauded her. Brandon looked over at Don and thrust the microphone into his hands.

"It's time for our first round of competitions." Don tried to sound confident. "Your hosts have the schedule. Good luck!" Don returned the microphone to Susan and exited the building in hopes of finding Faye outside.

Brandon stopped him at the front door, "They already loaded her into the car."

"What? Did they even have a warrant?"

Brandon shrugged.

Don pulled out his phone. "Hi Jack, how are you?"

He listened on the other end. "Yeah, do you remember what we talked about last night?" He looked away and nodded. "Um hum, well, yes it's happening now. So, you…Oh? He's already at the house?"

Don smiled at Brandon as he listened to Jack Unger on the line. "Excellent. Ok, I'll be here at the school. Call me when you want me to come down."

Another pause to listen, "Ok, great. Thank you."

Forty-Two

Faye sat with her hands cuffed behind her in the back of the police cruiser. There might have been enough room for her feet had the officer in the passenger seat not reclined it all the way back. An officer climbed into the seat next to her her and gave a creepy grin. Every muscle in her body tensed as she tried to keep a straight face.

"So, what exactly happens at a math tournament?" The nonchalant tone would have been more appropriate at a cafe.

Faye refused to answer.

"Probably math. Hahaha." The driver laughed way too hard.

"So, do you like being a teacher?"

Faye tried not to roll her eyes as she ignored their conversation. *Breathe. You can do this. You are sitting in a car. Breathe.*

When the car stopped, the officers helped her out of the back. They escorted her through the back door of the station and into a small room.

"Have a seat." The officer adjusted her hand cuffs from behind her back to the arms of her chair. "Can I get you something to drink?"

Faye shook her head without saying words. Then, he left.

Alone in the room, Faye's mind began to race. She shuddered at the prospect of jail and the loss of everything important to her. *Breathe. Don't jump to conclusions yet.* Faye observed the room and tried to locate the cameras. She knew they would be watching her. She didn't want to give them any reason to think her guilty.

She jumped at the sound of the door knob. Detective George walked into the room accompanied by an officer with a laptop.

"Ms. Unger, we need to ask you a few questions for processing. Please tell the officer your full name."

Faye looked up at Detective George, but said nothing.

The officer looked at Faye waiting for her response.

"Ms. Unger, please state your name."

No response.

Detective George slammed his hand on the table. Faye would have jumped out of the chair had she not been shackled to it. "Your. Name."

Breathe. Faye took a deep breath and closed her eyes. All of this felt familiar. She'd been here before. Done this before. *Help.* The small prayer came through her mind from a place deep within her, the place that remembered. She sat still awaiting the next instruction. *Ask for a lawyer.*

"State. Your. Name." Detective George leaned over the table with all of the veins in his neck bulging.

"Lawyer." The words slipped out as a whisper.

"Can you say that again, miss? I don't think I got it." The officer leaned closer to hear her quiet voice and record her response.

"Lawyer. L-A-W…"

Detective George stomped out of the room and the officer followed.

Faye sat in the dimly lit room for an eternity. *Thank you.* The second prayer, easier than the first, reminded Faye of her dependance on God. She recalled the stories from the Bible about the apostles sitting in jail. *I am still loved. God will not leave me here alone.* She began to hear mumbled voices outside the room.

"You can't keep her here."

"Sir, calm down."

"I'm her lawyer. Let me see my client."

"We don't know your client. Sir, I'm going to have to ask you to leave."

"Let me talk to my client."

Faye recognized as Detective George's voice through the door.

"The suspect we have in custody refused to give us a name. We will need to run the finger prints to determine identity. If you will wait outside, an officer…"

The voices grew too quiet for Faye to understand. They must be walking away. A few minutes later, a female officer entered the room to fingerprint her. Then, she left. After an hour or so, a different officer entered the room. He unshackled her wrists so she could stand.

"Come with me." He cuffed her hands behind her back and opened the door. With a firm grip on her arm, the officer escorted Faye down a dark corridor to a holding cell. He removed the cuffs from her wrists before locking her inside.

She stood in the center of the cell and looked around. She expected to find a flimsy mattress, but a concrete bench would have to do. Next to it, Faye found a toilet along the concrete wall opposite the bars. No toilet paper. No sink. She stepped toward the bench and noticed stains in the concrete which explained the horrible smell. Faye found a cleanish spot on the concrete and sat.

"I'm thankful to be here alone," Faye whispered to no one in particular. "There would be no one to watch me use that toilet."

A door opened at the end of the corridor. Faye heard more than one set of footsteps. She turned to see who might be coming.

"Sounds like you two have had quite an ordeal." The officer made small talk as they walked.

One of the people, maybe a man, started to speak, but a woman stopped him. "Shhh, that's enough outta you." She muttered his direction.

The closer they came to passing in front of Faye, the more she longed to see who it was. She composed herself and resigned to sit forward, even though her body itched to jump up and run to the bars.

John and Gina Mazzi passed before her along with two officers. Gina marched in front with her face to the ground supporting her scowl. John followed behind and turned his head toward Faye as he passed. He slowed and looked her in the eye, but said nothing.

"Mazzis? What are they doing here?" Faye whispered.

In what felt like hours, an officer arrived with handcuffs.

"Miss Unger? Come with me."

Faye stood in surprise and offered her hands. He led her down the long hallway into another tiny room.

The door opened to a room full of people. Unlike the interrogation room, the conference room had a long table down the middle. Faye noticed a pitcher of water in the middle of the table with glasses. The people around her scrambled to give her a chair. A young lady poured her a glass of water.

"Officer, the handcuffs are unnecessary. You can remove them. Be sure to turn off your surveillance cameras as well. I don't need to remind you that what we say is confidential."

The officer nodded as he removed Faye's handcuffs. Then, he exited the room.

"Alfred Xavier Eldridge, Chicago's finest legal counsel. You can call me Al." Al offered to shake her hand. "You must be Faye Unger."

Faye nodded.

"Please, have a seat." One of the other people pulled out a chair for her as the young lady handed her a glass of water.

"This is my legal team: Tina, Jessica, Robb, and Alex." They each waved as he called their names. "Your father, Jack, has done some business with our firm in Chicago. We represent the entire Andrews family. As you can imagine, we have attorneys in every area. I handle matters of criminal law."

Faye took a drink of water. She hadn't realized how dry her mouth had become.

Al opened his briefcase and pulled out a legal pad along with a file. "I understand that you are good with keeping your thoughts to yourself."

Faye gave a wry grin.

"I'm going to ask you a few questions. I encourage you, as long as we are here, to answer only the questions I ask."

Faye nodded.

"Did the police show you a warrant for your arrest?"

Faye shook her head. "No, sir."

Al looked at his team. "Alex, would you do us the honor of retrieving the warrant?" Alex left the room and Al continued, "Did they charge you or tell you why you were arrested?"

"They said I was under arrest for possession of illegal substances."

Al nodded and wrote some things on his legal pad, "Did they ask you any questions?"

Faye nodded, "They asked me my name."

"Did you answer their questions?"

"No." Faye took another drink of water.

A knock at the door interrupted their discussion. Alex entered empty handed. He shook his head.

"Typical." He pulled out a few typed documents and handed them to Jessica, who pulled out a stamp and signed it.

"What do you mean, typical?" Faye asked.

"Sometimes, the police make an arrest before they have been able to get a judge to sign the arrest warrant." Al ordered the papers and clipped them. "Robb run this to the DA's office. The second copy is for the judge."

Faye sat back in the chair and took a deep breath. The legal team typed and chatted on their phones and laptops.

"Faye, I want you to be honest with me about a few things. First, understand that I work for you. I will do my best to give you the best legal advice, but the decisions are yours to make. I advise you to tell the truth, no matter what that may be. Secondly, I advise you not to talk about this case with anyone. Do you understand?"

"Yes, sir. I understand."

"Great. Do you know anything about illegal substances in your possession?" Al stopped writing notes and waited for Faye's response.

"Yes."

The entire room stopped. Everyone waited for her to finish her story, but she didn't.

"Please tell me what you know."

"I found a package in my storage bin. I think it was probably cocaine."

Al scribbled some notes. "And how did you come into possession of this package?"

"Like I said, I found it in my storage bin."

"Did anyone else have access to your storage bin?"

Faye looked around the room. She didn't want to retell the story again. She had already been through this with the FBI.

"The storage bin is in the basement. I had lost my keys after a party at my apartment." *Which now seemed to be a mistake.* "When I accessed the bin, the package was in the bottom."

"I see." Al scribbled a note and tore it off to hand to one of legal aids. "Does anyone else know about this."

"Yes, my friend Don."

"Don?"

"Don Ambrose. He called a friend with the FBI. They came to ask me questions and collected the tote."

"Did you get that name, Jessica?" Al spoke to a woman on a laptop computer from across the room. She looked up an nodded.

"Do you remember the names of agents that came to your house?"

Faye shook her head. "The only name I remember is Rogers, but I don't think I met him."

"That's ok. We have enough information to get started." Al flipped through some papers and checked his phone for messages. "Do you have someone who can give you ride a home?"

Faye stared at him from across the table. She hadn't thought about going home. Until this point, she had been sure that she would stay in jail for a long time.

"I can go home? No court or judge or anything?"

"That's the plan. We will know for sure when Robb returns with the judge's signature."

Faye ran through a contact list in her mind of people she could call. She recoiled at the thought of telling Jeffrey that she had even been here. Jodi might think it's hilarious, but would not be reliable enough to pick her up. She really didn't want to ask her parents. She would never hear the end of it.

Robb entered the room with a signed paper. Al read the paper before speaking to the room.

"Looks like we are good to go." He stood and knocked on the door for the deputy.

The deputy opened the door. Al spoke to him quietly. He nodded and closed the door again.

Jessica looked up from her laptop. "Al, I got a hold of a Mr. Don Ambrose."

Al lifted his chin giving Jessica the cue to continue.

"He's legit." She paused. "Says he's on his way down here."

Forty-Three

Faye walked out of the building, and the crisp, winter air smacked her in the face. She shuddered. No coat or hat. She removed her cell phone from the clear plastic bag the deputy had given her. The battery was only at 20%. They must have gone through her phone while she sat in the cell. She turned and began walking She needed distance from this place.

Don pulled up and stopped at the end of the corner. He got out of the car with her coat and rushed to wrap it around her. Faye slid her arms in the sleeves, and immediately felt comforted.

Don't cry. Not here. She wanted to cry, though. Her worst fears realized: arrested and no real friends to call for help. The homecoming crowns and lavish parties had little yield on what really mattered. She looked over at Don as he opened the door for her.

"Thank you."

Don smiled and went around to the other side of the car. "Are you ok?"

Faye looked out the window unsure how to answer.

"They could've waited until after school." He shook his head as pulled into the traffic.

Don continued to drive past Faye's building. She sat up and looked over at him, but he didn't say anything. He just kept driving.

Faye didn't protest. She had done enough talking with the lawyers. The view outside captured her attention. Don had taken them along Riverside Drive. Mansions faced the river on one side of the street while a park sat on the other. Snow blanketed the lawns, and the river glistened in the fading sunlight. Down stream, a tiny tug pushed giant barges full of freight. The scene waxed poetic against the sunset.

In the midst of her struggle, life carried on. They passed the shops on main street, and Faye watched children throw snow at one another. The stress of her day began to pass in the silence of the drive. *He knows just what I need.*

"It's time to let others in."

Faye paused her thoughts. "What?"

"I went to see a therapist after Julie died. I needed to talk with someone before I went back to work. You know." Don paused.

Faye turned toward him.

"The therapist told me, 'it's time to let others in.' All this time, I didn't know what he meant by that. The Browns had invited me over a few times, so I took them up on the offer. It wasn't until I saw you lying on the floor of that school that I understood."

He parked the car. "We can't do this on our own, Faye."

Faye listened to Don, but heard God speaking to her through his voice. *It's time to let others in, Faye. You can't do this alone. I am with you, but I also sent Don.*

Faye looked at Don, eyes wide open filling with tears. "You're right. I'm sorry."

She didn't know whether she spoke to Don or God. Either way, she couldn't do this alone. She needed real people in her life. Real friends. A contact list full of people to call for help. She needed game nights and Christmas parties. Neighbors who came over to check on her. No one came to her aid at the school. Even Frank stood by as the police detained her.

Don patted her on the shoulder. "Let's go inside."

Don turned on a light in the living room and ushered Faye into his home. Faye surveyed the room taking it all in. She admired the prairie style architecture with its geometric designs and symmetry. The wooden accents gave the space a cozy feel. The modest home suited Don, but Faye noticed the feminine touches in throw pillows and silk flower arrangements. She'd met Julie at the beginning of that school year, but didn't know her very well. Seeing Julie's touch on the room brought a stab of grief to her already sensitive demeanor.

Don hung the coats on a hook by the door. "I have dinner heating up for us."

"Smells good." Faye made her way to the dining room. She noticed stacks of photos and file folders on the buffet.

"Don't mind all this." Don moved more things from the dining table to the buffet. "Let's eat dinner first. I'll bet your starving."

Faye looked at the time on her phone, 5:45. She hadn't eaten all day. "Can I help?"

Don handed her plates with silverware on top. "Thank you." Then he retreated to the kitchen for the main course.

"I didn't know you cooked."

"I don't. Stephanie brought it over after the tournament today. She started to get concerned when she hadn't seen you after the morning announcements."

"How can I…," her voice trailed off.

"Don't think about that right now." Don placed the casserole dish on the table. "I'm not sure what kind of casserole we have here, but Stephanie's a pretty good cook."

They talked about nothing important during dinner. Faye appreciated this about Don. He was good at small talk. In fact, the small talk brought with it a sense of normalcy. Faye imagined he knew the kind of stress she had been under. He understood that she needed to ease into difficult conversations.

"So, what's with the stack? It can't be homework. Everyone participates in the tournament."

Don looked up and swallowed hard. "I've been doing an investigation of my own."

"An investigation?" Faye enjoyed solving problems. "Is this about the attack over the summer?"

"Among other things."

"Other things? Can I help?"

Don smiled. "I'm counting on it."

Faye stood to clear the table. Don went over to the buffet to sort the papers and photos.

"Where did you get all of this?"

"I have my sources. I arranged the photos and files according to suspects. This is Trish right here." Don placed his hand on a small stack in front of him. "I tried to group the information by family as well."

Faye started looking through the photos. She stopped suddenly. The boy in the photo looked familiar. Faye had painted him in the dinner party of her last painting.

"Who's this?"

"That's Albert Schmidt." Don paused. "Have you seen him before?"

Faye nodded. She opened her mouth to speak, but took a deep breath instead. Images of the ravine came to her mind. She closed her eyes to block them without success.

Don grabbed her hand, and it brought her back. "Do you want to talk about it?"

"Not yet, I don't think I have words for it. I can't seem to make connections between the images in my mind.

Faye set it aside and opened Trish's file. She flipped through school records and marriage certificates. Then, she moved onto the next stack. Gina Mazzi. She flipped through photos until she landed on the birth certificate.

"Gina is a Schmidt? How did she end up John Mazzi?

Don shrugged, "I haven't figured that out, yet."

"Mazzi dated my sister in high school, and our families don't get along."

"I know. I was kind of hoping your sister might have told you a thing or two that would shed some light on the subject. Do you remember when they broke up?"

Faye shook her head. "I only found the photo of them in the locket. That's how I knew they dated. Maybe Susan told me. I don't remember."

She continued to thumb through the file and came across old family photos. "Did you know Gina had siblings?"

"Is it labeled on the back?" Don asked.

Faye turned the photo to view the scribbles on the back.

"Gina, Gio, Albert, and Louise"

Don pointed to the older woman in the photo. "I know this is Louise. I'm not sure about Gio and Albert."

"This is Albert Schmidt." Faye picked up the photo she had set aside to compare. "I don't get what this has to do with your attack over the summer, though."

"I think my attack has to do with Julie's murder."

"Julie was murdered?" Faye couldn't contain her shock. "I thought it was a break-in gone wrong."

Don paused for a while, and Faye thought it must be hard for him to talk about Julie.

"Faye, I need to share something with you, but you can't share it with anyone."

Faye stopped thumbing through the photos. "What is it?"

"Do I have your word?"

"Of course." Faye couldn't imagine what he might want to share with her. Don led a simple life. He never talked about going places or doing anything. She thought it had something to do with horrible things that happened to him in the service.

"I'm an agent for the FBI."

Faye waited for the punchline, but Don continued, "Agent Rogers is my supervisor."

"But Julie..."

Don nodded his head. "Julie and I met through work. We were sent to replace a rogue agent. We had information about illegal imports coming in and out of Arlington in connection with the murder in 2003."

"Do you think they killed Julie?"

"I do."

"Who was this rogue agent? Is he still around?"

Don looked around. "I'm not sure. That information is above my classification."

"Why are you telling me this?" Panic from the police station filled Faye as she remembered her lawyer's advice. He told her not to trust anyone. Now, her one friend turns out to be a spy from the FBI.

Forty-Four

Don saw the look of panic return to Faye's tired eyes. Her face grew pale before him. He needed to say something before he lost her trust.

"Faye, I'm on your side, here. I know you didn't have anything to do with the murder in 2003. I also know that someone is trying to frame you for the drugs." Don stepped toward her to provide comfort, but she backed away from him. "Faye, the FBI didn't arrest you today. The police did that on their own. I need your help to sort this out, though."

Faye closed her eyes and shook her head. "He said not to trust anyone."

Don didn't know what to do with that. How does he convince her to trust him, when he's been lying to her about his identity all this time?

"I'm sharing confidential files with you." He pointed to the stack of folders and photos on the table. "Ask me anything."

"Were you really in the military?"

"Yes. The FBI recruited me from there."

"And Brandon? Did you meet him there or is he a spy too?"

Don recoiled at the term 'spy,' but he determined to gain her trust. "Yes. We worked together on a special project. He was responsible for recruiting me to the agency."

"Why me? Did you pick me out to investigate me all this time?"

"No. No, Faye. It wasn't like that at all. They told me that I was going to teach math way before you started teaching at Arlington." Don could see some color returning to her cheeks. "I didn't learn anything about your involvement until after I started going through Julie's notes."

"Julie took notes about me?" Faye shouted.

"It's not like that, Faye. For some reason she thought you might be in trouble. I've been trying to protect you this whole time."

Faye took a seat at the table. Don could almost see the wheels turning in her head. He didn't blame her for being upset with him. In fact, he wished he had told her sooner. Under cover ops made it difficult to live a life of honesty and integrity. It felt good to come clean with one person. Hopefully, this honesty would pay off.

"Will you tell me everything you know?"

Don smiled.

"Everything?" Faye gave a stern look. Don knew she meant business, and she still had the full support of her family behind her.

Whether she knew it or not, she had the power to ruin people's lives in Arlington.

"I'll tell you everything you want to know, but you cannot share any of it with anyone in your family."

"Alright. What do you know about the murder in 2003?"

Don pulled out his laptop and logged into the FBI database. "Police found Albert Schmidt dead in the ravine October 24, 2003. He had three gunshot wounds. Police reported two witnesses at the scene: a young girl, Faye Andrews and her sister, Elaine. Lawyers prevented police from questioning the witnesses."

Faye looked at the floor. "I still see it, sometimes."

"See what?"

"A dead man lying in a ravine." Faye closed her eyes. "My visions have fall leaves covered in blood. I thought it was you at first, but your attack happened in the summer."

Don scrolled through a screen on his computer and turned it for Faye to see. "Like this?"

Faye gasped!

"I'm sorry." Don moved the screen away quickly. "I'm so sorry, Faye. That must have been terrible. You were so young."

Faye straightened herself. "It's ok. I need to deal with it, so it will stop haunting me."

"Did you see anyone else at the scene?"

"Maybe. Dr. Gardner said that I received a concussion. I think whoever did it, might have hit me. Knocked me out."

"I have some other photos here from Julie's file. Maybe something there will jog your memory." Don closed the gruesome crime scene photos and opened another file. "I enhanced the photo so we could see the people in the background."

"Was this Open House?" Faye noticed the people dressed warmly and trees without leaves. "There are a lot of people here."

"These were taken a couple years ago. Just before Julie's attack. Look closely at the right side." He zoomed the photo to the right.

"Is that who I think it is?"

"Looks to me like Jeffrey and Jodi."

"It can't be. They didn't move here until last summer, and they wouldn't have a reason to show up at Open House." Faye scanned the rest of the photo hoping to find anyone else who could be involved. "Look over here." Faye pointed to the opposite side.

"Mazzi? Yeah, well it was Open House."

"But didn't they move here this year? And who is this?" Faye pointed to a tall, slender man. Dressed in dark, autumn colors, his face shielded from the camera.

Don pulled up four similar photos and set them all on the screen for comparison. "Are all the same people in these photos?"

"I can see the Mazzis in all of them, and his creepy cousin. Looks like the tall stranger is in all of them too." Faye pointed to the left side of the screen.

"We need to find out about that guy," Don suggested.

"Maybe, a rogue agent?" Faye gave him the side eye.

Forty-Five

Faye saw Frank's car sitting on the street outside Don's house. She knew he would give her a ride home, but she didn't trust it. She felt safe with Don. She still didn't know if she could trust him, but at least he gave her answers. Don offered to give her a ride home, so she took him up on it.

"I can go up with you and make sure its safe." Don parked and turned off the engine.

Faye placed her hand on his to stop him. "No need." She looked over her shoulder at the tall man standing feet away from the car. "Frank will take care of anyone that tries to come after me. I'll see you tomorrow at school."

Don pulled back. "Ok, then. Do you want a ride in the morning?"

"I'll hitch a ride with Frank here." Faye smiled, enjoying the idea of someone keeping an eye out for her.

Frank accompanied her to the apartment. They didn't speak. The doors opened on the eighth floor, and Mazzi's cousin stepped inside. Frank inched toward her and glared at the creepy cousin. Faye kept a cool grin and exited for her floor. No need to pretend she lived elsewhere this time. She kept a confident gait as she stepped inside the apartment.

"Faye!"

Her name sounded like a gunshot through the apartment. She turned quickly to see Frank holding Jeffrey by the collar and whispering something to him.

"Frank! It's ok." Faye attempted to intervene. "Jeffrey, what are you doing here?"

"I heard what happened and came straight over."

"You heard? What did you hear?" Faye didn't want Jeffrey knowing anything about her day, especially the part about her arrest.

"Jodi said the police picked you up." Free of Frank, Jeffrey rushed to embrace her.

His arms did little to comfort her. "How did you get into my apartment?"

"Jodi let me in."

Faye still puzzled pressed him for information. "She doesn't have a key."

"Anyway, you must tell me how things went. Are you ok?"

"Jeffrey, I can't do this right now. Maybe we can do dinner tomorrow. I just want to forget about today."

"Come, I know what you need," Jeffrey took Faye by the arm and brought her to the couch. Her poured her a glass of wine and handed it to her.

"Jeffrey."

He ignored her protest and lifted her leg to remove her shoes.

Faye set the glass on the end table. She needed to relax, but she had a feeling that Jeffrey had other plans. He started to massage her feet. She should have enjoyed the attention, but this was weird.

"Jeffrey." Faye pulled her feet away from him. "You need to go. This is not the time."

"Of course, it is, dear." He moved closer and kissed her.

Faye pushed him away. "Not tonight."

Jeffrey persisted, but two hands reached from behind the couch yanking him up.

"The lady said to go." Frank's words matched his actions as he pulled Jeffrey toward the door.

"I'll call you tomorrow, Jeffrey." Faye managed before Frank closed the door.

Faye didn't feel bad about making him leave. She turned to Frank, "Do you think we're safe?"

"I'm not sure how he got inside, Miss."

"Me either."

***

Faye stood in the ravine amongst the blood-spattered leaves. A chill crawled up her spine and her stomach dropped. She looked up at a dark figure standing over her.

"Nobody likes a tattletale, little girl. So, keep your mouth shut." The deep, growling voice echoed.

Then, Faye felt a pain on the left side of her head. She fell to the ground and waited. Her head still ached from the blow, but she didn't dare cry. No, she pretended to sleep until she no longer heard the man's footsteps.

Faye woke up with the left side of her face on the remote control. She reached over to the night table and pulled out a notebook to sketch the man. He resembled the figure from Don's photos. She closed the book and put it out of her mind. Today, she would face the crowd of students and colleagues. She needed to face them in order to put that fear behind her.

She stepped out of her bedroom toward the kitchen. "Good morning, Frank." He'd slept on her couch in case someone attempted another break-in. "I'll call to get the lock changed this morning."

He nodded in approval. "I have a car ready downstairs for us."

"Thank you, but Don offered to drive me this morning."

"Are you ready for this?" Don slipped the car in gear and pulled onto the road.

Faye shrugged and looked out the window.

"It's not easy to walk into a building filled with rumors." Don raised his eyebrows and looked away. "I've done it a couple of times, and it's never as bad as you think it will be."

"Do you have an update on the tournament for me? How will I know what to say?"

"Brandon is on his way with the standings. Susan will have the other announcements ready for you. You might want to open with something about following the rules."

Faye gave Don a quizzical expression.

"Trust me, it'll break the ice."

Faye found her car still in the parking lot. Her mind replayed the scene of her arrest, as she approached the front of the building. Closing her eyes didn't stop her from remembering it. A silent gasp had filled the room when the officers called out the charges. In her memory, she got onto the floor in slow motion. *How do I recover from this?* Faye prepared herself to be dismissed. Perhaps the decision to work with Elaine would be made for her.

She took a minute to gather herself again before stepping into the building.

"You got this." Don whispered in her ear.

Faye nodded and walked through the front door. She stepped slowly toward the space where the police forced her into handcuffs. She took a deep breath and remembered the smell of the carpet when she was facedown on the floor. She coughed and a shiver went down her spine.

"Faye!" Susan came up and grabbed her into a hug. "I'm so glad you're here early. We have quite a few announcements this morning before we get started."

Faye looked at her a little shocked. *Does Susan know what happened?*

Don looked at her and shook his head.

"What's going on?" Faye pretended nothing had happened.

"With John and Gina out yesterday, things were completely messed up. We got it straightened out though. I called Gina yesterday."

"You called Gina?" Faye suddenly remembered them walking past her in the jail.

"Yeah, they'd been gone for two days and nobody knew where they were. I had to find out." Susan spoke matter of fact.

"Well? Where had they been?"

"Something about visiting family or a family emergency." Susan shook her head along with the rest of her body. "She wouldn't tell me. She said that they would be back today, though."

"Here are the standings from yesterday." Brandon came up behind Faye and held out a file folder.

Faye took the folder and nodded. "Are we ready for announcements?"

Students and teachers filed into the media center and took seats around the room. Faye looked at their faces with mixed emotions. She never thought twice about talking in front of students before today. Her knees quaked as she picked up the microphone.

"Good morning, everyone."

The crowd fell silent as all eyes connected with her own.

A knot developed in Faye's stomach and a lump grew in her throat. She remembered Don's advice. "Have you all been following the rules?"

The room erupted with laughter. Faye eyed her own students cheering for her around the room.

Once the students were on their way, Faye settled into the office of the media center for coffee and donuts. The friendly smiles greeting her made the break all the sweeter.

"We didn't even get to catch up from the holidays." Susan pulled up a seat next to her. "Any art exhibits or auctions?"

"Not this time around," Faye answered, "just dinner with my folks." Susan reminded her about Jeffrey. She made a mental note to text him later. "What about you?"

"Nothing at my house, but I can't say the same for our friends, the Mazzis."

"Why didn't you say something earlier?"

"In front of Brandon?" Susan shook her head and sipped on her coffe. , "I done a little diggin' on my own 'bout that one." She shook her head. "Nah."

"What do you think happened at the Mazzis?"

"They had the full police force over at their house."

Faye picked up a donut. "I think Gina might be related to some of the guys."

"True, she is a Schmidt, but family doesn't usually show up with red and blue lights." Susan stopped for effect.

"Do you know why?"

"Can't say." Susan sipped her coffee while Faye's mind filled with questions.

"So, what's the deal with Brandon? I have my own reason for doubts, but what did you find out?"

Susan leaned closer to whisper, "Turns out, he is much older than I thought he was."

"Oh?"

"Graduated in the class of 95."

Faye sat back in the chair. "So, the yearbook is legit, but why doesn't he know what happened in 2003? Everybody around here knows that."

"I think he's faking it, but I'm not sure what he's tryin' to hide."

"How did you find out about this?" Faye sat impressed at Susan's ability to take gossip to the next level.

"Your parents told me!" Susan laughed. "You should talk to them every once in a while. They know things."

The principal knocked on the door frame and stepped into the room. "Ms. Unger? Can I see you for a minute in my office?"

Forty-Six

Don's thoughts ran wild while he monitored the math test. Faye brought up a good point about a rogue agent. This person had to still be in Arlington. Somehow, this agent avoided him yet knew his next move. He pulled our a notebook to record his thoughts. Agents could easily hack into his phone or laptop.

Don scribbled a few questions:

Did the same person attack both me and Julie?

Could it havre been an agent?

Do our attacks have to do with the 2003 murder?

Don looked over the questions. The only thing he knew for certain was that Julie had more information than he did about the 2003 murder. The agent had gone rogue before he and Julie arrived, and neither of them knew his cover name.

What information did Julie have in her files?

Don couldn't trust anything in those files to be accurate. He got them second hand.

1. Verify the information in Julie's files

At this point, everyone in town presented as suspect to the crime. He needed to start ruling them out and determine who to trust.

2. Eliminate suspects

All of the reports indicated the attacker to be a grown man, so women could be eliminated. Well, petite women should be eliminated. He could also eliminate anyone who graduated after 2003. They would have either been at the bon fire or too young to commit the crime.

This can only be true if the same person committed all of these. *I graduated in 2008, and I fit the description for both Julie's attack and my own.*

3. Create a profile for the person of interest

Don began a list of facts that might be present in the person he searched:

Andrews Family - someone in Elaine's crew could have done this. Even if she were too young, another member of the family could be involved.

Schmidt family - the police force usually posed a threat to illegal activity, but may or may not be corrupt.

"Mr. Ambrose." Mazzi knocked on the door.

Don closed the notebook and looked up.

Mazzi pointed to his watch and closed the door.

Forty-Seven

Faye looked up at the principal. Then, she looked at Susan. "Excuse me."

"No worries." Susan winked her.

Faye knew there was no pulling one over on Susan. She gathered her confidence and followed the principal to his office. Going to his office for a chat did not phase her. She had done this many times over. The thing that bothered Faye was the thought of losing her students.

The walk did not take long, but it was long enough for Faye to examine her life's choices. Of all the careers, she landed on teaching. She'd never sought to be a teacher, and never saw herself as a good one. On the contrary, Faye attempted numerous other careers with no success at all. She learned her strengths and weaknesses while going through the process.

She had no doubt that God had called her to teach. While she made every attempt to avoid trouble, she knew that she could not avoid this. This moment of reckoning caught her by surprise and left her with no recourse. Faye prepared herself to be fired on the spot.

The principal opened the door for her. Faye walked inside to find two of her lawyers seated near the principal's desk.

"I'll just leave you to it, then." The principal closed the door behind Faye.

"Please, have a seat Miss Unger." Al pointed to a chair while he stepped behind the principal's desk. "We have some good news for you."

Robb opened a briefcase and pulled out a few folders while Faye sat in amazement.

"This morning, we filed a motion to dismiss the case against you." Robb handed Al a folder. "The district attorney did not present sufficient evidence to convene a grand jury."

"What does this mean?" Faye couldn't see the good in the legal jargon. Her mind still reeled from the thoughts of getting fired.

"They dropped the case." Al beamed with triumph.

Faye continued to look at him puzzled.

"You're free to go." Al opened the folder and pulled out a few forms.

Faye sat back in the chair and let out the breath she had been holding. "No trial?"

"No trial." Al pulled out a pen. "I will need to get your signature on a few forms, though."

"Sure," Faye sat forward to sign the forms.

She attempted to read the pages, but the legal headings made little sense to her. She had so many questions. She stared at the page while her mind raced.

"Do you have any questions?" Al had been thorough, Faye knew he had a lot on the line with her case.

"Do you know who accused me of this?"

"Good question." Al flipped through some pages in the file. "Let's see, the first note lists complaints from a neighbor. Something about noisy parties upstairs." He continued to look for information. "Here it is, they didn't list the entire name here, but it has the initials, J.M."

Faye wished that she knew the names of her neighbors. She never paid attention to anyone in the building before now.

"Do you know a downstairs neighbor with those initials?"

Faye shook her head. "Did they have anything else on me? That hardly seems enough to arrest someone."

"Well, they also have notes from an FBI report here."

FBI? The night replayed in her mind. *So much for keeping it quiet.* "How did you convince a judge to let me go?"

Al closed the file. "I've been doing this for some time, now, Faye. I saw inconsistencies in the FBI reports that brought about questions in the police investigations."

Faye didn't understand that statement, but maybe she didn't need to understand it. This man did an excellent job helping her receive fair treatment. She paused before she asked the next questions.

"Can I ask who called you?"

Al returned her smile like they both held onto a secret but didn't want to share it with anyone out loud. "Faye, I've been your family attorney for years. Your sister called me."

Forty-Eight

Don spent his break in the Media Center office. He pulled the 2003 yearbook in hopes to eliminate people as suspects. He located Elaine, but didn't recognize the other names listed. If the murderer had been an adult, he would have graduated before 2003. He scanned the book from 2002 also. He located Gina. The grim smirk gave her away. *Some people really don't change after high school.* He hoped to find Trish, but she must have graduated later. Albert stood among the underclassmen. He gave a confident countenance. The irony wasn't lost on him.

"Can I help you on your trip down memory lane?" Susan joined him at the table.

Don looked up and closed the book. "I had some time and thought I would look up our current faculty. See what they were like back in the day. I found Gina Mazzi."

"Ooo, this sounds like fun." Susan ran to a stack of books. "Check out this one."

She handed him the class of 2001. Don flipped to the senior class. The full color photos popped off the page with Trish Schmidt front and center.

"Someone, enjoyed attention." Susan rolled her eyes.

Trish's photo didn't surprise Don as much as the person right above her, Chloe Daschle. *I guess her name's Chloe after all.* Faye told him that she met Jodi in Chicago. *Does Faye know about this?*

"This one is probably my favorite." Susan opened the class of 1995.

The older book didn't have full-color photos. Instead, it used smaller photos with the names in a a list on the side. Don scanned the list for names he recognized.

> Morgan, Stacy
> Mason, James "Jesse"
> Mazzi, Joseph

Don shrugged, and Susan pointed to a photo of a young man with a giant afro. Don didn't know what she meant by it.

"That's Mr. Mason." She kept looking at Don for a reaction, "J.J.!"

"What?" J.J.'s photo had surprised Don, but he had responded to the name below. "Who is this?"

"Joseph Mazzi?" Susan looked around the room and into the media center. "I'm not at liberty to say."

"Oh?" Don spoke through his closed lips. "Why is that?"

Susan put a cup to her mouth and smiled with her eyes as she responded, "Dangerous family."

She mumbled the last word, but Don got the picture. He had looked into John Mazzi, but not enough to reveal any real information about the family.

"Related to our friend, John?"

Susan responded with a, "mm, hmm."

"Have they been in Arlington all along?"

Susan closed the books with intentional noise. "I just can't say."

"Now, I gotta know, Susan," Don smiled to relieve the tension.

"Do you know Jack and Judy. Faye's parents?"

Don stood to leave. "I do."

"They're good people." Susan left it at that.

Forty-Nine

Faye stepped outside toward her car. The cold, February air smacked her in the face. She stopped to let it whip through her hair. Free. The word itself lifted her shoulders. She stood taller and stretched out her arms. The sun came out from the clouds to shine on her face. She closed her eyes in the heat of it.

Her phone buzzed and disrupted the moment. Faye pulled the phone from her pocket to check the message. Unknown caller. She shrugged her shoulders and continued her walk toward her car. Out of the corner of her eye, she spied a black town car approaching. *Not today. I'm done with Elaine and the family business, whatever that entails. I'm done with police and jail and lawyers. They can pick up someone else. Anyone else.*

Her phone buzzed again. Faye kept walking toward her car.

Buzz.

Nope. She increased her pace.

The town car pulled into the school lot and headed toward her. Faye got into her car and locked the doors before she pulled out the phone.

Unknown: Faye, this is Jeffrey. New phone. Can you meet me at the Auction House?

Faye: Jeffrey? What happened to your phone?

Unknown: Dropped it in paint thinner. Ugh. Can you meet me?

Faye: When?

Unknown: Are you out of work yet? I'm here now.

Faye: Yes, I'm out. I'll see you there.

The moment she sent the message, Faye had a sick feeling in her stomach. She pushed the feeling aside and started the car. She passed the town car on her way out, but couldn't see who might be inside. The sick feeling returned, but Faye dismissed it as something to do with the town car. She decided to stop at her apartment and freshen up before she met with Jeffrey.

The apartment looked just as she'd left it, but it felt like home. Faye walked in and breathed a sigh of freedom and excitement. She remembered the feeling of moving into this unit for the first time, that feeling of freedom and success. *Thank you.* Her small prayer brought tears to her eyes.

For the first time in weeks, Faye had hope. She had new images in her mind to paint. She wanted to put the ravine and murder and the attacks all behind her. The drugs and the person framing her could answer to her lawyers. She was done with it all. Jeffrey wanted to meet with her. Maybe, she could focus on relationships. It had been a while since she had seen Jeffrey. She decided to put on something nice.

***

The sun had gone down before she left her apartment, but Faye didn't mind going to the Auction House after hours. She messaged Jeffrey to let him know she would be a little later. Faye pulled on the front door of the Auction House, but it wouldn't budge. She put her face to the glass. The window displays would not allow anyone to see into the back. She did see a tiny light behind the curtain. So, she walked along the back of the building.

A streetlight provided dim lighting in the ally between the buildings. The cobblestones made it difficult to walk in heels, but not impossible. Faye remembered coming this way with Jeffrey on her first visit to the Auction House. It seemed natural that he would expect her to come this way again.

"Jeffrey. Jeffrey. It's me, Faye."

Faye located the door and tried the handle. It moved easily, but the door wouldn't open. She tried again, but it wouldn't budge.

Something blocked it. So she ran her hand along the door jam to feel for the blockage.

"Jeffrey! Something's blocking the door. I think something fell onto it from the warehouse. I need your help."

Faye heard footsteps moving quickly toward her from the other side of the door. She stepped back, but not fast enough. The door swung open and something fell on her. The weight of it combined with the uneven cobblestones caused Faye to stumble to the ground. Someone had fallen on top of her.

"Hey!" Faye called out, but the person didn't move or speak.

The footsteps from the other side of the door moved closer.

"Hey!" Faye cried out again.

The person stepped over her and continued walking down the ally.

Faye gathered her strength and shoved this person off of her. The lifeless body moved off of her and rolled onto its back. Faye scrambled to her feet and pulled out her phone for the flash light.

"Are you ok? Should I call for help?" Faye couldn't seem to hold onto her phone. The face ID wouldn't work when the phone lit up. Her hands were wet. She wiped them on her pants and turned on the flashlight.

Blood.

She shined the light onto the person in the ally. "Hello? Are you ok?"

Faye looked down at the dead body. She couldn't see the injury just the blood. The image of Albert Schmidt laying in the ravine covered in blood come into her mind and stole her breath.

"Is that?" Faye shook her head in disbelief. Her legs gave up and collapsed on the wet cobbles.

"Gina?" Faye called out toward the body. "Gina!" She called again with no response.

Gina Mazzi didn't make a noise at all.

"What do we do, Gina?" Faye started shaking and tears streamed down her face.

She sat in the alley unable to move. She needed to call for help. She willed her arms to move, but only her fingers obeyed. The phone came to life, and her fingers made the call.

"Hey Faye, what's up?" Don responded from the other end.

Tell him. Faye's mind commanded her mouth to speak.

"Faye?"

Tell him! Another command disobeyed.

"Faye, are you ok?"

Say something! Anything!

Someone started walking toward her. She saw a tall, dark shadow.

Who is that? It's not Jeffrey. Faye pleaded with her head to look at the man approaching her, but she couldn't take her eyes off of Gina.

"Faye!" Don's voice echoed from her phone.

Faye groaned and managed the words "Auction House." Her vision blurred as the stranger walked toward her. She felt a pair of strong hands pick her up before everything blacked out.

Fifty

Don arrived at the Auction House along with the police. He parked a distance away and walked toward the crowd to get a look at the scene. The familiar scene caused concern, but he could handle Detective George. He dialed Brandon. No response.

As he walked closer, Don felt his stomach drop. A body. *Please, not Faye.*

"Sir, you can't be here." An officer stepped in front of him to stop him.

Don shoved the officer out of the way and kept moving forward.

"Sir!" Another officer called after him.

Immediately, Don could tell it wasn't Faye. A woman, yes, but not Faye.

Several officers came to him and pushed him away from the scene.

"Who is it?"

"I'm not at liberty to disclose that information," the officer responded.

On his way back to his car, Don saw Detective George. He seemed visibly upset by the scene. Don approached him.

"Detective."

The detective wiped his eyes and pulled himself together. "Mr. Ambrose."

"What's going on here?"

Detective George stood taller and spoke with a deeper voice. "You know this is under investigation."

"It'll be in the papers tomorrow, George," Don continued. "Who died?"

Detective George looked away. "Gina."

"Oh no, George. I'm sorry." Don patted him on the shoulder.

The detective looked away.

"Hey, is there anything I can do for you?"

"No, thank you. I appreciate it."

"I'll leave you to it, then."

Don tried to call Brandon again with no response. So, he drove to Faye's apartment to try her there.

"No, sir." Jay checked his ledger. "She left earlier. I assumed she was meeting with her boyfriend. You know." Jay gave him a look like Don knew the secret. Then, he cleared his throat. "But I haven't seen her return."

"Thank you, Jay."

Don tried Faye again on the phone hoping she would answer. The not knowing was killing him. No answer.

Did Faye watch Gina's murder? Does the murderer have Faye?

Don needed help with this one, but Brandon had gone off the grid. He called Jack Unger to see if Faye had gone there.

"Hey there, Don, good to hear from you."

"Jack, how are you doing tonight?"

"Very well, my friend. What's on your mind?" Jack never engaged in a lot of small talk. Don appreciated that about him.

"I'm calling to see if Faye might be at your house. A bunch of us were going to get together tonight, and she's not answering her phone."

"She does that a lot, Don, I don't know why. Hang on a minute. Let me ask Judy."

The last thing Don wanted to do was to worry them. They do seem to know a lot of things, though.

"Hey, Don, Judy hasn't heard from her either. You might try that boyfriend of hers."

"Thanks, Jack. I'll do that. Y'all have a good night."

Don didn't have Jeffrey's number, and without Brandon's help probably couldn't contact Jodi either. He decided to head to Mazzi's house. Maybe Faye went to tell him what happened.

***

Don could see the lights from the police cars down the street. This would not be a good time to visit with John. Like any decent neighbor, he drove past the house slowly to see what he could find out. Mazzi's house sat on the edge of the creek that formed the ravine. Don hadn't driven this route since his attack in the summer.

Tonight, however, the mission was to find Faye. With her at the front of his mind, Don inched down the street toward the ravine. His eyes darted across both sides of the street so he wouldn't miss any clues. That's when he saw it. Movement at the edge of the trees.

He pulled over and parked the car. The closer Don got to the ravine the better he could see it. Someone writhing on the ground. Don ran over to help the person crawling out of the ravine.

Fifty-One

A tear made its way down Faye's cheek as the water in the sink turned pink. She closed her eyes. The sensation of the wash cloth on her face soothed her. She sat on the edge of the bathtub trying not to pass out. The images of dead bodies slowly made their way to the back of her mind as the warm cloth caressed her skin.

"It's going to be ok, Faye." Stephanie Brown spoke in soft, calming tones as she rinsed the cloth. "Take a deep breath, you're safe here."

Another tear made its way out of her eye and down her face. The wash cloth met it and whisked it away.

"I have more clothes here." Anna Gardner stepped into the bathroom arms full of folded clothing.

"You can take these." Stephanie nodded toward a paper bag in the floor.

Faye opened her eyes and looked down at her arms. Clean. Stephanie grabbed an arm and began to massage lotion onto her hand. Faye moved her fingers. Their movements, heavy at first, became lighter. Her arms followed and slid themselves into the clean shirt.

"Take your time," Stephanie whispered, "you're safe."

Faye didn't answer, even though she wanted to. Something shifted in her mind when she saw Gina. Memories returned with an influx of information. Her mind needed time to sort it all out. She paused to listen to the conversation in the next room.

"Is she injured?" Don's voice sounded concerned.

Faye looked at her arms and legs. Red marks on her arms resembled early bruising, but she couldn't be sure.

"She has a pretty good concussion," Steve Gardner spoke softly, "and a nasty lump on her head."

Faye reached back to feel the lump on the back of her head. That explained the headache. She followed the voices into a sitting room. The fire drew her attention and she took a seat next to it. The flames calmed her, so she watched them dance around. Anna walked over and tossed Fayes's shirt into the flames. The fire cracked and spit with the fuel.

"Faye needs us to remain calm for now," Steve whispered to Don, but everyone in the room heard him.

"It was the same." Faye spoke and her words surprised her.

Don came to her side. "What was that?"

"It was the same." Faye repeated, and looked around the room. Confusion spread across their faces. "It was the same guy from twenty years ago."

"Are you sure?" Don moved closer to her and placed his hand on hers.

Faye shuddered. "Where did you find me?"

Don looked up at Steve for permission to speak. He shrugged his shoulders and Don proceeded, "In the ravine."

"The man knew I would come, and he waited for me." She closed her eyes tight. "Did he try to kill me?"

Stephanie brought her a hot cup of tea.

Steve answered, "You don't have any injuries to suggest that anyone tried to kill you."

Faye looked into Stephanie's red eyes. *Has she been crying? Was it about me?* These people carried her out of the ravine and took care of her. More tears formed, but she tried to call them back.

"Do you think you know who did this?"

"Don," Steve interrupted, "let's give her some space. I'm sure it will all become clear in time."

Faye sipped the tea while Steve scribbled a note. "Here is my medical opinion on her ability to work or take part in any investigation." He turned to Faye. "You need rest. Don't push it. Concussions take time to heal. Let the police sort this one out."

Faye managed a grin then turned her attention back to the fire. A wave of exhaustion came over her, and she closed her eyes. The men went into the next room, but Faye could hear them through the wall. Their mumbled voices lulled her into a deep sleep.

Fifty-Two

Don and Jason helped Faye into the spare bedroom before heading into the kitchen with the others.

"How are you doing?" Anna spoke softly to her friend.

Stephanie looked up at her and shook her head. "Who would do this?"

"Did anybody grab Faye's phone?" Don looked around the room for Faye's belongings. "She said someone knew she would be there. I'm thinking she may have gotten a text message."

They located Faye's phone, but couldn't unlock it to get inside. Don knew a few ways to get around the lock screen, but he decided not to blow his cover yet.

"I have an idea." Anna grabbed the phone and headed toward the spare bedroom.

She emerged triumphantly. "I'm in."

"Great." Don didn't ask how she did it, and he knew Faye would not remember granting them access. "Check her messages. Let's see who she was meeting."

"Her last message just has a phone number with no name." Anna focused on the phone. "Ok, it says she was meeting Jeffrey."

"No way!" Stephanie shouted prompting a collective shhhh from the rest of the group. "It's just that I don't see Jeffrey asking to meet Faye at the ravine."

"They weren't meeting at the ravine. He wanted her to meet him at the Auction House."

"That makes more sense." Stephanie whispered.

"No it doesn't," Jason spoke up. "I mean we pulled her out of the ravine. How did she get from the Auction House to the ravine?"

Don put out his hand for the phone. "It has to be someone posing as Jeffrey. Let's call him and see what he has to say."

Anna handed Don the phone. He located Jeffrey's contact and placed the call on speaker so the room could all hear.

Jeffrey answered, "Faye, darling, it's so good to hear from you. Where have you been hiding these days?"

"Jeffrey, this is Don Ambrose, Faye's friend. I think we met at her party."

"Oh? Hello there."

"Faye's been in an accident."

"What? What happened?" Jeffrey practically screamed the last line.

A collective gasp came from the room. Don put up his hand to quiet them all and continued. "Someone attacked her tonight."

"Oh my! No!" Rustling sounded in the background. "I should come. Where is she? Who did this?"

"I was hoping you could help us figure that out. She has a message in her phone to meet you at the Auction House.

"Me? No, that can't be me. I'm in Chicago all week. I knew she would be busy with the tournament at work, so I made the trip for acquisitions this week instead of next. I should come help. I can leave tonight."

"I don't think that's necessary, Jeffrey. Do you know anyone that might want to hurt her?

"No more than usual. Elaine gave her a security detail. I can't believe anyone could get to her." More rustling sounded in the background. Then, he spoke away from the phone, "Oh. This is not good. Not good."

"Jeffrey, stay with me, man. Faye's going to be ok. We have a doctor checking her out. Don't worry. I'll have Faye call you later." Don ended the call before Jeffrey could respond.

"I guess we can rule out Jeffrey." Jason stated the obvious.

"No surprises there." Stephanie went into the kitchen and brought out chips.

"We could call Jodi next." Anna grabbed a few chips too.

"Speaking of Jodi, does anybody heard from Brandon?"

Don looked down at his phone. No messages. He messaged Brandon hours ago, and it wasn't like him to not answer. Don walked into the other room and called him.

A recording picked up, "Sorry, I can't talk right now. Please leave a message."

"New developments. Come over ASAP."

Don walked into the living room and the front door opened.

"Brandon!" The room exploded in cheer.

"That was fast." Don shook his hand. "We were starting to get a little worried."

"What can I say? I'm a busy man."

"Well, in light of other events tonight, we're glad to see you're ok." The team gathered over chips and salsa to recap the new developments with Brandon.

"Do you think Jodi had something to do with this?" Brandon sounded surprised.

"That's what we're asking? You know her better than any of us. Did she have any problems with Faye? Maybe arguments?"

"No," Brandon chuckled and grabbed a handful of chips. "You ask me, I think it's Elaine. She's been a little controlling with Faye… sending the security guy."

"I'm sure the police are looking into everything. We probably don't need to waste our time talking about all of this." Stephanie left the crew to sit by the fire.

Jason joined her followed by the rest of them. Anna grabbed the paper bag that had held Faye's clothing and tossed it into the fire. A piece of denim fabric fell to the floor.

"What's that?" Stephanie pointed it out.

Anna picked it up. "Looks like blue jeans."

"Faye wasn't wearing jeans."

Don stepped forward and took the fabric. "This matches Brandon's jacket."

Brandon grabbed the fabric for a closer look. "It could be from anywhere." He put the fabric in his pocket. "So, are we meeting back up tomorrow? I'd like to hear what Faye has to say about things."

"Not so fast." Steve stood up. "Faye has been through a lot. We don't need to pressure her to talk."

"I agree. You didn't see her earlier, Brandon." Don shook his head. "Someone roughed her up pretty good tonight."

"Don, I can stay with her tonight." Stephanie offered.

"Yeah, we have a guest room with your name on it." Jason grabbed his coat.

"Good idea. Let's meet back here in the morning." Don excused himself to grab a bag and his coat.

Fifty-Three

Faye woke to the smell of fresh coffee the next morning. She made her way into the kitchen feeling surprisingly refreshed.

"Good morning." Anna greeted her with a smile.

"Good morning." Faye's voice sounded groggy from the long sleep, but she delighted in the ability to command her body again.

"Did you sleep well?" Stephanie offered her a pastry.

"Oh, yeah. The best I've slept in a long time."

"Steve added a sedative to the tea last night." Stephanie smiled. "He said you might need help sleeping."

"I feel amazing today."

"That's good news." Don walked in with a newspaper and tossed it on the counter.

The Auction House of Murder?

A woman found dead near the Auction

House has local police stunned. The

unidentified woman had been shot and

was left for dead Friday evening.

Auction House employees discovered

the body this morning. Local police

have secured the scene. Police

reported two different sets of footprints

leaving the scene. They are looking for

witnesses in connection with the

shooting. If you have any information,

please contact Detective George

Schmidt immediately.

Faye looked at Don with eyes wide open.

"Faye, were you at the Auction House last night?" Don spoke calmly, but Faye could tell some other emotion lurked behind the quiet question.

"Yes. I got a text from Jeffrey asking me to meet him at the Auction House." As she spoke the words, panic rose within her. This was worse than the drugs. *Murder?* "Don, what do we do?"

"We start by having you tell us what happened." Don pulled out a chair. "Faye, do you know something about this murder?"

She nodded. "I got to the Auction House, but no one was there. I mean the doors were locked. So, I went around the back." Faye paused to sip her coffee. "Jeffrey had taken me there before, I thought he might be there again."

"Did you see this dead person?"

"Not at that time. I tried the door but couldn't get it open. The handle turned like it was unlocked, but it wouldn't budge."

"Did you see anyone else there?" Don sounded impatient.

"I heard footsteps on the other side of the door. So, I asked Jeffrey to help me open it. At least, I thought it was Jeffrey." Faye tried to take another sip of coffee, but her hands shook too much to hold the cup.

She looked around the room. Everyone's eyes were on hers. Faye appreciated the small audience. Then, someone knocked at the door. *Trust no one.* Al's words echoed in her mind. *But Don's safe, right?*

Faye looked over at the door determined to finish before someone new entered. "The door gave way, and she fell on top me. A man stepped over us and walked away. I tried to call for help. Then, someone else came, and I woke up in a ravine."

Jason walked through the door with a box of donut. "Did I miss something?"

"Faye." Don sounded more sincere this time. "Did the man speak to you?"

She put her hand on her forehead and closed her eyes. "I think so. He said something about tattletales."

Jason chuckled. "That's what Jo Mazzi used to call Gina and Trish, remember?"

Stephanie smiled at him and nodded.

"I didn't kill Gina, Don. I didn't do it. Somebody else killed her before I got there."

"Gina?" Stephanie cried. "Gina?" She didn't get out any other words but started pointing at the newspaper.

Jason ran over to his wife. "I'm sorry. I knew you two would work things out."

"Faye." Don stepped around the table and sat next to her. "Did you see who it was?"

Faye shook her head. "Gina fell on top of me when the door opened. I couldn't see anything, but I would recognize his voice. Don, I think it was the same person who killed Albert years ago."

Another knock on the door made them all jump. Brandon stepped through with a newspaper in his hand. "Did you all see this?'

Faye looked around the room. No one responded to Brandon. Jason had his arm around Stephanie who dabbed her eyes with a tissue. Don scribbled in his notepad. Anna started cleaning the kitchen with tears streaming down her cheeks.

"What's going on?" Brandon walked over to the table and put his paper on top of the other one.

"We're talking about the article in the paper." Don pointed to the newspaper. "Faye seems to think that the unidentified woman was Gina Mazzi."

"Really? How would she know?"

"You need to show up on time, Brandon." Anna handed him a cup of coffee. "We already knew that Faye got a message to meet someone at the Auction House last night. Maybe, Gina got the same message."

"Has anyone talked to John?" Jason pulled out his phone.

"I saw the police there last night." Don shook his head.

Stephanie spoke through tears, "Gina had her issues, but she didn't deserve this."

"Do you know where they went last week?" Don got up and poured himself a cup of coffee. "She and John missed the first day of the tournament. I think they were out of work a few days before too."

"They were at the jail on the first day of the tournament." Faye spoke through the steam of her coffee cup. She took a deep breath to steady her hands for a sip. "I don't know why."

"She came by to see me Sunday afternoon." Stephanie pulled out a tissue and wiped her nose. "She said she wanted to make things right. It was good to have my friend back."

"I texted John." Jason put his phone back into his pocket. "I guess we'll see if he responds."

"I can go by and see him later today." Brandon grabbed a donut. "I'd like to take a look at the ravine in the daylight."

"We really should leave this to the police," Stephanie spoke in desperation, "Faye, you should tell them what you saw."

"I can't go there." Faye's hands started to shake again. "But you're right. Let me call the lawyers first." She left to retrieve her phone.

Faye appreciated the quiet of the spare room. She realized that she didn't have the number for her lawyer. She could call her parents, but the thought of reliving the story made her nauseous. Elaine called them the first time. S he would know the number, except Faye didn't know how to contact her. She sat on the bed in defeat. She needed courage.

The phone lit up in her hand.

Unknown caller. *Do I answer?* The last time had been disaster. However, it could be Elaine.

"Hello?"

"Faye, thank God. They got Frank. I'm so glad you're safe."

As much as Faye hated to admit it, she was glad to hear Elaine's voice, "What happened to Frank?"

"They shot him, but I think he'll pull through. I'm sending a car to come get you. The lawyers are already here. Can you get away?"

"I'll try." Faye looked out the window at the town car sitting outside.

"Good." There was an uneasy silence followed by Elaine clearing her throat. "I'll see you soon."

Fifty-Four

Don volunteered to go with Brandon to check out the ravine. He needed to find out why Brandon kept showing up late. It put him in a terrible position. Brandon had shown him the ropes, which made this all the more important. *Is it Jodi?* Don never agreed with his choices in relationships.

"So, what has been going on with you?"

"I'm not sure what you mean?"

"Brandon, you just don't seem to be with it lately."

Brandon shrugged it off. "Don't worry, Don, I still got your back."

"That's not what I'm talking about."

"They got me working another thing on the side. It's nothing. I'm still on this case."

"Are you sure?" Don couldn't help raising his voice. "They got to Faye last night and you had eyes on her apartment. How did you not know she left?"

"Thanks for your concern, Don, but I can't talk about it. Let's just do what we came to do." Brandon got out of the car and made his way to the ravine.

This wasn't like Brandon. For the first time, Don didn't trust him. He got out of the car and joined Brandon at the ravine. As he walked up to it, Don understood why the kids loved to play here. The drop wasn't too far that you would get hurt jumping into it. Just far enough that you would be hidden from looming parents.

Last night, Faye had trouble crawling up the side. This morning, the ravine didn't appear too difficult to climb. He shook his head at the realization that someone had hurt her that bad.

The ravine spanned two streets. Drains emptied into it from both directions which helped during heavy rainfall or melting snow. The area between the two streets opened to the park and covered about 200 yards. Faye could have been anywhere within that area, but Don found her right away. He marveled at the providence of God looking out for her.

Brandon had no trouble locating the spot of Faye's attack.

"Do you see anything?" Don approached carefully..

"Not off hand." Brandon squatted close to the ground. He picked up something and put it in his pocket.

Don walked down a few yards. "I'm not exactly sure where we found her. It was dark last night."

Don looked over the side of the ravine in Brandon's direction. Footprints. He looked to see if he could get a better look, but mud coated the sides of ravine. He pulled out his phone and zoomed in for a photo. Then he moved closer to Brandon. With the phone in front of his face, Don nearly fell on top of him.

"Oh man, I'm sorry." Don's phone snapped several photos before he got control of it again.

"Watch it!" Brandon wiped the mud from his hands onto his pants.

"My bad." Don reached out a hand to help him up.

"Thanks." Brandon stood to his feet. "Did you see something?"

Don shook his head, "You?"

"I found this." Brandon pulled out the locket Faye had gotten as a Secret Santa gift.

"Huh." Don took the chain in his hand. He had never seen Faye wear it. In fact, it repulsed her when she open the gift. *Why keep it around?*

Brandon held out a plastic bag, and Don dropped the necklace into the bag.

"Let's go talk with Mazzi." Don said walking across the street.

Mazzi opened the door and stepped aside for them to enter. Don walked in and embraced him.

"I'm so sorry, John." Memories of Julie's murder rose the to surface of his mind.

Mazzi pulled back and wiped his face, "Thank you. Please come in."

"I saw the police here last night when I drove past. I should've come on over."

"Yes, they came by last night and told me."

"Do you know why she was at the Auction House?" Brandon took a seat on the couch.

Mazzi shook his head. "Probably, Looking for me." He turned his head and walked toward a box of tissues.

"Were you there?" Don handed him the box.

Mazzi shook his head. "I am most nights, though. She had good reason to look for me there."

"Were you seeing Elaine?"

Don shot Brandon a look of shock. In most investigations, that would be a routine question. However, undercover operations required discretion and finesse. *Is Brandon losing his edge?*

"No. I loved my wife, Brandon. I enjoyed working at the Auction House. Elaine and I knew long ago that we could never be together. We accepted it."

"What do you mean by that?" Don allowed curiosity to get the better of him.

"Haven't heard of the rivalry between our families?" Mazzi looked at Brandon for a moment before he spoke. "We dated in high school, but they forbid us to see any more of each other. We understood and got over it."

Don made a mental note to look into the history of the families.

"Is that a thing here in Arlington? I didn't realize families were so involved in matchmaking."

Mazzi smiled, "I love your simple mind, Don. I don't know if all families do this, but my family is old fashioned in that way." Mazzi gave Brandon another stare. "In fact, they introduced me to Gina and encouraged our marriage."

"It is a good thing when families approve," Brandon added.

"You bring Jodi over to meet your family yet?" Don asked.

"Very funny," Brandon stood from the couch, "Let us know if there is anything we can do for you, John."

Fifty-Five

Faye waited until Don and Brandon left to exit the house. Jason left shortly after, and Stephanie, preoccupied with Gina's death, waved her off. Faye made sure to pack her phone and keys so she could stop at the apartment.

The first time Faye got into a town car, she had little knowledge of her surroundings. She enjoyed riding with Frank, and it pained her to know that she was responsible for his injury. The new driver said nothing as she entered the car. He didn't even step out to open to the door for her. She rolled her eyes as she climbed into the back.

"Faye."

Faye recognized the voice and sat up as the cold sweat of terror filled her skin. Clearly, she'd had too many surprises.

"Elaine, what are you doing here?"

Elaine pulled off her sunglasses. "There are things I need to tell you. I should have told you a long time ago. It's just… I thought you knew."

"About the family business?" Faye kept her comments short, "I know. Mom and Dad told me." At least they had started to tell her until her dad stormed off.

"Do you remember the night I left?"

Faye had vague memories of waving good bye. She recently put it all together that she waved to Elaine. The question remained whether she could trust Elaine with this information.

"Did you call the lawyers for me?"

Elaine nodded. "About the night I left." She paused to look out the window. "I didn't want to leave, you know."

"I don't remember. Honestly, I forgot that I had a sister until recently." Faye failed to consider the impact of those words.

Elaine pulled out an embroidered handkerchief to dab her eyes, "You went to the ravine to find me. I never told you where I had gone or why. I found you there unconscious, Faye."

That's why I went to the ravine. She almost remembered who murdered Albert. Almost. She couldn't get the image of Albert lying there out of her mind. With Elaine talking, she might as well get as much information out of her as she could.

"So, where had you gone?"

"I met with John Mazzi." Elaine folded the handkerchief. "We had been meeting together secretly for some time."

"Why secretly? Who would care?"

Elaine looked at Faye in surprise. "I thought Mom and Dad told you about the business."

"They did, but what does this have to do with Mazzi?"

"The Mazzis have rivaled us for as long as I can recall. Don't you remember the war when we were kids?"

Faye shook her head.

"So many people died." Elaine shuddered. "When we all made peace, we had a party with both families and the police."

The garden party that I painted with young Mazzi. A smile crossed her face. "I remember the party, but how did you get connected with John Mazzi?"

"We met at the party and became friends. Then, he invited me to homecoming." Elaine signaled with her hands that things rolled on from there.

"We had peace, so why couldn't you two date?"

"Some people had issues with it. Dad told me to break it off and keep the peace, but I didn't. I messed up, Faye, and you got hurt."

Faye brushed it off. "I'm fine, Elaine, really."

Elaine leaned forward and placed her hand on Faye's, "but you're in trouble."

Faye looked down at her hand. Elaine squeezed until Faye looked her in the eye.

"You saw the man who killed Albert, and he is coming after you."

"I don't remember who did it, Elaine. I can't ID anyone."

"Faye, you don't get it. They don't know that. This family is ruthless. I had to go to Chicago to get away from them. Why do you think I walk around here with security?"

Faye looked at the driver and remembered the men that followed Elaine everywhere she went.

"Did they plant the drugs?"

"I don't think so, but I don't know. If they can discredit you, they will."

"Do you know about what happened to Gina?"

Elaine gave a slight nod.

"Oh my…" Faye gasped. "Did you have something to do with that?"

"None of my people were anywhere near the Auction House last night." Elaine fumbled through her purse and for her cigarette case. "My sources tell me that you received a message to go to the Auction House."

Faye watched Elaine pull out a cigarette and try to light it. Her hands shook with the lighter until she gave up. Then, she stared at Faye.

"I did, but, for all I know, so did Gina."

"I don't think Gina was supposed to be there last night."

"How do you know all of this about Gina?" Faye reached over and grabbed the lighter for Elaine.

"I know that she and John gave statements to the police about the person they know to be after you."

"So, that's why they were at the station. Do you think the killer mistook Gina for me?"

Elaine sat back. "Perhaps. At least, now, you see the danger ahead of you."

"Who is behind all of this?"

"You already know." Elaine took a long draw off the cigarette. "I can only guess that it is either a Mazzi or a Schmidt."

"Why would a Mazzi kill another Mazzi?"

Elaine shook her head. "Gina could never really be a Mazzi. That marriage served as a front for other purposes. Uncle Marcus sent me here for a reason, Faye. Gina will always be a Schmidt."

"So, what do we do?"

"The lawyers are waiting for us at the restaurant. They'll take care of that for us. You need to give the name of the murderer to your FBI friend."

"FBI friend? I didn't call those guys."

Elaine ignored Faye and continued to smoke.

"Should we call Mom and Dad?"

Elaine shook her head. "They called me. Let me deal with the FBI. You can talk with the lawyers."

Fifty-Six

Judy Unger answered the door. "Please come in Mr. Ambrose.
I'm sorry we didn't invite you over sooner. You've been a big help
to our Faye."

"Thank you, Ms. Unger. Please call me Don."

Judy ushered him to a sitting room where he met Faye's father,
Jack.

"Thank you for having me," Don said as he took a seat.

Judy passed around coffee and cake until she was satisfied that
the men had enough to eat.

"How are you holding up there?" Jack asked.

Don moved his arm around to demonstrate the healing.

"We heard about what happened with Faye the other night," Judy
began, "we appreciate the way you stepped in to help our daughter."

"I can't imagine what it must have been like for you to hear,"
Don sipped his coffee and tried to figure out how to ask them about
Elaine.

They could give him all the information he desires to close the case. However, if they are who thinks them to be, they could end it for him too. Should he dare to accuse them of involvement in organized crime?

Jack interrupted his thoughts, "We want to be up front with you, Don."

Don sat up straighter and leaned in closer.

"We know about you, Agent Ambrose, if that even is your real name."

"Please?" Don nearly choked on the coffee.

"Yes, we know you're here under cover. It's ok. We've known for some time."

"We learned about it when they ordered the hit on your wife," Judy said to clarify.

"Who ordered a hit on my wife?" Don could feel the heat in his cheeks. *Did they order a hit? Was it the Andrews family?*

"I think you already know the answer to that question," Jack said. "When we spoke over the phone, you said that you had some questions for us."

These people were professional. They knew how to get into his head. Don needed to regain his composure and keep up his guard. He took a deep breath and readied himself.

"I'm afraid we may have gotten off on the wrong foot," Judy looked at them both. "Don, we have connections that we're not proud of, but through those connections we heard about the plans concerning your wife. We immediately set people in motion to stop it. I'm sorry, we were too late."

Don needed to refocus. *Remember the task at hand. Focus.* While he ordered his thoughts, Don attempted to separate himself from the situation. *Remove the personal names. Concentrate on the evidence. Faye's life was at stake. Her parents could prove valuable allies.*

Don jumped back into the conversation, "I apologize for the outburst. Faye said something about having a sister."

Both of them nodded and waited for the question.

"Can you tell me about her? Is she sill alive?"

"Sort of." Judy looked over at her husband.

"Her sister's name is Elaine Andrews," Jack started, "we all had a falling out years ago. Elaine didn't agree with us and went to live with some relatives in Chicago."

"You see, " Judy explained, "we wanted a different way of life."

"So, we changed our name to Unger." Jack grabbed a piece of coffee cake. "Elaine disagreed with us. She kept the last name and moved."

"Where did Faye fall into this?"

Judy looked down and shook her head.

"Faye got lost in the middle of it." Jack answered for the two of them. "She stopped talking altogether. We weren't really sure what to do. Doctors said she'd come around."

"And she did. It's just that her mind blocked it all out," Judy trailed off in her explanation. She pulled out a handkerchief and touched her nose.

I need to be gentle in my questions. "What do you know about the relationship between Elaine and Faye?"

Jack responded, "We called Elaine last night after we heard of the attack. We needed the safe house ready." Jack looked at his watch. "The lawyers should be there now."

A safe house? What kind of parents throw their daughter into the ring with a crime boss like Elaine Andrews? "So, you knew that Elaine had contacted Faye." Don spoke with caution.

"Of course, dear." Judy poured herself some coffee.

"Where do you think the security detail came from?" Jack raised his voice slightly.

Judy placed her hand on his knee.

"Did you know that Elaine offered her a position in the art community? Something about commissioning her paintings so she wouldn't have to teach again."

"No," Judy placed her cup on the table. "She is called to teach. We'll have to talk to Faye about that one."

Don's phone started buzzing. He held up a finger. "Please excuse me." Then, he left the room to take the call in the hallway. As soon as he left, he could hear Jack and Judy bickering in whispered tones.

"Hello?" Don addressed the unknown caller.

"Mr. Ambrose, we need to meet," came a woman's voice from the other end of the line.

"Who is this?"

"Our friend, Faye, needs attention."

This had to be Elaine, especially since she refused to reveal her identity over the phone.

"I'm listening."

"Luca Bistro, 3:00." The voice didn't wait for a response before it ended the call.

Don returned to the Ungers. "Thank you for your hospitality." He reached out to shake Judy's hand. "I'm afraid I must go."

Judy and Jack stood together.

"I appreciate your confidence." Don reached for Jack's hand.

"Of course." Jack shook his hand. "We're in the business of confidence, Don. I hope we can call on you in the future."

Don smiled. He felt uneasy about the implications of that agreement, but one battle at a time here. They had assured him they wanted out of that life. This could prove to be a valuable connection.

***

Don pulled into the empty lot at the Bistro and adjusted his ear piece. "Brandon, sound check. Can you hear me?"

"Copy. That lot looks like a ghost town, but I'm good across the street. Over."

As he approached the door, a man opened it for him. "Good afternoon, Mr. Ambrose. We're expecting you."

He nodded to the doorman and stepped inside. A waiter stood next to a single table in the back. The table had already been set with crisp linens and fine china. The waiter pulled out the seat for him.

"Your host will join you shortly. Would you care for a glass of wine?"

Don placed his hand over the glass. "No, thank you. Water will be just fine."

"I don't blame you, Don." Brandon's voice echoed in his ear.

Don waited patiently for quite some time. "Perimeter check. Is everything clear?"

"I've still got eyes on the building, Don. There's no additional movement out here. If she's coming, she's already there."

At that moment, Elaine walked out of a dark hallway and appeared at his table. "Sorry to keep you waiting. I hope you were able to enjoy some wine and bread?"

Don stood to greet her. "Glad you could make it."

"This is probably the best restaurant in the city." Elaine stepped around the table to take a seat.

"I don't think I've ever been here before." Don waited for her to sit before he joined her, "It's nice, though."

"I appreciate you coming. I've been meaning to get in touch with you."

Don looked at her rather than answering. Brandon didn't hide his feelings. "Really, lady? Didn't you already get in 'touch' with my face and ribs?" Don coughed a little before taking a drink.

"It's a shame about Julie." Elaine paused for effect and looked Don in the eye. "She was really good at her job. I had only started working with her."

"WHAT? How dare she bring up Julie!" Don wished Brandon weren't in his head.

"I'm sure I don't know what you mean." He responded to Elaine, "She didn't talk about you." He wasn't ready to divulge his conversation with her parents on the subject. Elaine clearly possessed the same skills for getting into someone's head, but Don had control of his emotions. He wouldn't let her rattle him.

"I know. Like I said, masterfully professional at her job." Elaine looked around the room as if someone were listening.

Don took a deep breath before continuing. *I should've known she'd bring up Julie. Help me focus. Give me the words I need here, Lord.*

It would seem, Brandon had some to offer. "I wouldn't trust her. We don't know enough about her."

"Mr. Ambrose, I want to help you." Elaine continued to speak in a quiet tone as to not draw attention from the waiter.

"I'm not sure how you can. Did you try to help Julie?"

"I'm afraid her contact with me may have been what put her in danger."

"Do you know who killed her?"

Elaine gave a nod and nothing more.

"Well? Is she going to tell you or not?" Brandon sounded as though he were ready to bust through the door.

"I have information to offer you, but I will need something from you first."

In this line of work, Don had been in numerous negotiations with criminals. Elaine had done her homework. He took his time before answering, "I'm listening."

Elaine continued unconcerned by Don's hesitations. "I believe you know my sister."

"I do." Don pulled off a piece of bread in order to give his hands something to do. "It's a shame what happened."

"I agree."

"I thought you offered her protection." Don tried not to raise his voice, but he could not control the change of tone. "What happened to Frank?"

Elaine looked out the front door and back at Don. "He's recovering."

Brandon remained quiet on the other end.

Elaine slid a note across the table to Don.

"What's this?"

Elaine put a finger to her lips and shook her head.

"Did she give you something? Don, come in. Say something," Brandon sounded edgy on the other end.

Don could only imagine what it must be like to get the information second hand. He looked down to read the message.

Don't trust anyone

Don looked up at Elaine. "You're right, this bread is good. What do you suggest from the menu?"

She placed her hand to her ear and tapped it twice. "Stay away from the onion soup. It has a thick cheese covering it, and onion can be bitter."

She must know that Brandon is listening in, but I gotta know for sure. "The recipe has been around long time, though. Surely, they've made improvements."

"That recipe has been around since the early 90's, but it's still as stale today as it was then." She took a sip of wine. "I think they may have tried to rename it at one point." Elaine gave Don a sinister look with the last phrase.

He called the waiter over and ordered the Salmon. Elaine ordered some other kind of soup that Don couldn't pronounce.

"You guys really ordering lunch? I thought you were using some kind of code. Get to the point, Ambrose." Brandon's voice rose, and he nearly shouted, "We need to get out of here."

Elaine reached across the table to grab the note. She scribbled something else onto it, and showed it to Don.

Jo Mazzi

"I think you'll enjoy the meal, but about my sister." Elaine seemed to be waiting on Don.

"Yes?"

"She needs protection until the murderer can be apprehended. Our lawyers are working on a motion to allow her to join our family in Chicago."

"You don't think she will be safe in her apartment? We have a friend living next door. I'm sure he can keep a good watch on her."

Elaine pointed to the name on the card and shook her head.

Wait. Brandon? No way Brandon is Jo Mazzi. Don needed to keep his thoughts in his head and not let any come out of his mouth. Until he knew for sure, he couldn't divulge any of this to Brandon. So, Don devised a ruse.

"There is a hotel in the city with good security. No one from Arlington frequents it. We can set her up under a false identity." Don nodded to Elaine to alert her that he understood the situation.

Elaine motioned for the waiter. "Thank you." She pulled out a lighter from her handbag and lit the card with Jo Mazzi's name on it. The waiter stepped forward, and she placed the burning card onto his tray. Elaine returned the lighter to her handbag, and pulled out a business card. She slid the card toward Don.

Don picked up the card. The artwork looked familiar. For someone who wished to appear anonymous and discreet, Elaine had distinct business cards. This card contained no contact information except that of the Auction House. He turned it over to find a series of numbers. Coordinates. This must be a real safe house for Faye.

"I will be in touch in a few days." Elaine stood. "That should give the lawyers enough time."

Fifty-Seven

Faye's meeting with the lawyers went smoothly. As expected, they asked questions about what she saw. She talked while associates typed. They talked to each other in words that made no sense to Faye, so her mind began to wander. Elaine had beautiful artwork all over the room. She focused on a painting across from her. The deep autumn colors invited memories of hot chocolate and bon fires.

In her mind, she stepped into the painting and imagined the conversations among the people there. Smartly dressed, their conversations revolved around wine and recent trips to the vineyards of Italy. Faye felt like one of them mingling through the crowd until she saw him. A sense of dread stole her confidence.

The young man appeared tall and handsome. He laughed with the others in the crowd until he looked at Faye. Her imaginations carried her away into fictitious endings. He didn't know her, really.

He started toward her and his smile faded. Faye noticed something familiar in his gait. He maneuvered through the crowd like the tall stranger that followed her to the coffee shop some months ago.

"Thank you for your time, Ms. Unger."

Faye looked away from the painting at the mention of her name.

"You've been through a lot." Al stood giving her the cue to do the same. "I hope you're able to get a good night's sleep."

Faye smiled and shook his hand. She walked into the corridor unsure how she would get home. Then, the door to the dining room opened for her. She looked around the room and noticed Don seated at a table with Elaine.

Elaine stood and Don looked in her direction.

"Faye, this is certainly a surprise." Don walked over to her.

"I didn't expect to see you here either. I didn't know you liked French food." Faye reached out to shake his hand, but he pulled her in for a friendly hug.

"Can I give you a ride?"

Faye looked at Elaine.

"Your friend here is making some arrangements for you to stay in a hotel downtown." Elaine patted Faye's shoulder. "It would serve you well to be discreet about the arrangements until this is sorted out."

"Can I stop by my apartment for a few things?"

"Of course." Don started walking toward the entrance.

"I have security in place as we speak." Elaine gave Faye a hug, "Call me if you need help." She slipped a phone into Faye's pocket.

Faye whispered, "Thank you."

Don opened the car door for Faye. He got in the car and held up his finger to his mouth, signaling her to remain silent. Then, he pulled a device from his ear and placed it into a tiny box. He removed his phone from his pocket and turned it off. All of the devices ended up in the trunk. Faye didn't know what to think of this. She patiently waited for him to do the talking.

"How are you doing?" Don spoke to Faye, but he pulled out paper map of Arlington and unfolded it in front of her.

"What is going on here?"

Don stopped to answer her. "We can't trust anyone." He closed his eyes and shook his head.

"Are you talking about Brandon?"

"Anyone. Faye, I don't know how far this goes. I talked to your parents this morning." Don took a deep breath and blew it out slowly.

Faye knew that feeling. "They're not that bad."

"I'm glad you don't know the extent of it, Faye." Don pointed to a spot on the map and refolded it.

Faye didn't notice anything unusual in her apartment building. Jay welcomed her warmly.

Don had warned her, "Your apartment is probably bugged. Don't look into anything or say anything. Pack some clothes in handbags or a backpack. No luggage."

Faye followed directions and found herself in Don's car heading away from the city.

"I thought I would be staying in a hotel downtown." Faye envisioned a posh, boutique hotel with a salon and spa.

"Change of plans." Don turned off the headlights before he made a series of turns.

They pulled off the road into the woods behind the school. The gravel drive meandered through the woods until it reached a small cottage. It was no wonder Faye had never noticed it before. She could hardly see it now.

"Stay here." Don exited the vehicle and turned on his flash light.

Faye could see the outline of a stone path leading to a door. Don reached behind something, maybe a loose board. He unlocked the door and went inside. Faye heard the clang of the screen door, but lost visual. She waited in the silence of the winter woods. She closed her eyes. *Sitting in the dark isn't as scary with your eyes closed.*

Your are my hiding place; you will protect me from trouble and surround me with songs of deliverance. Psalms 37:5

Faye learned the psalm in her quiet years. With her eyes closed, she remembered scary moments as a child. Her parents did a great job keeping things from her, but they couldn't keep everyone from her. Faye encountered more than one scary person in her lifetime. In the quiet years, Faye learned peace by meditating on the scriptures.

Don tapped on the window and Faye jumped. She rolled down the window.

"All clear."

Faye appreciated that Don had turned on the lights in the cottage. Though cozy on the outside, the cottage appeared luxurious on the inside.

"What is this place?" The last thing Faye wanted was to break into someone else's house.

"I think it's an old custodial cottage for the school. That's the only way I can explain the access road and the lack of address." Don started going through the cabinets in the kitchen.

"How did you hear about it?"

"Your sister."

Faye shook her head and set out to explore the cottage. The living room had two large sofas that looked antique. The wooden side tables were hand-crafted with engraved legs. The simple mantle over the fireplace looked like reclaimed lumber from a barn. The photos sitting on top of it captured her attention. Faye picked up one of the photos and pulled it out of the frame. An inscription on the back read, "Andrews Family Christmas 2002: Ron, Jackie, and Judy."

Faye smiled. Her mom looked so happy. "Ron must be into antiques. This furniture is amazing."

"Ron?"

Faye held up the photo. "It says on the back. I think he's my uncle?"

"Makes sense. I guess your family needed a safe house from time to time."

"I think we used to do Christmas here." Faye looked around, "it feels familiar."

Don went into the back rooms while Faye reminisced.

"Do you want me to stay with you?"

Faye looked at him in surprise. "Why?"

"Do you feel safe here?"

"I'm sure Elaine will have someone watching the property. They probably have cameras."

"Ok." Don made his way to the door. "Call me if you need anything."

Don left Faye to the silence of the woods. She found a stereo in the living room and put on some smooth jazz. This wasn't her apartment, but the familiarity of the room provided comfort. Faye danced her way to the bedrooms in the back. She chose the spare room on the right. It suited her.

The linens were warm as though someone had just put them on the bed. Pillows had been fluffed and the room had been dusted and cleaned. Elaine thought of everything. Faye opened the closet and unpacked her clothes. They needed to hang for the wrinkles to release. She pulled back the winter coats and noticed an old shoe box in the bottom of the closet.

Treasure? Faye used to play hidden treasure as a child. The box had been covered in construction paper with drawings on the sides. Curious of the contents, Faye pulled it out and opened it. Suddenly, she dropped the box.

Fifty-Eight

Don checked his phone before he left the cabin. No messages. He sighed relief. Usually, Don did things by the book. That meant relying on a partner to have your back and keep your secrets. He didn't feel right hiding things from Brandon, but he needed to keep the information to himself until he got to the bottom of it.

When he got into his car, he felt the stab from the hotel key in his pocket. He pulled it out and tossed it into the glove box. He needed to focus. There might be clues in Julie's notes. Perhaps, he could find something on Jo Mazzi. Brandon read out the files earlier. He didn't mention anything about it.

The drive home gave Don time to comb through the facts in his mind. What did he really know about Brandon? Well, he enjoyed entertaining women. Don had never known him to settle down with anyone for a long period of time. This relationship with Jodi lasted longer than most, and she was young compared to him.

Brandon served with him in Afghanistan, but Don didn't know anything about his life before. Their time together made up the bulk of his trust in Brandon. Don had never met any of his family members. He recently learned that Brandon graduated from Arlington. He needed that graduation date. Don didn't even know how old Brandon was, only that he had been Don's senior officer.

Don entered the house and went straight to the files in the dining room. At one time, the files had been organized. Now, things piled on top of others and photos had been stashed into folders. He shook his head in frustration as he sorted the paperwork. His phone rang causing him to to drop a stack of photos.

"Hello?"

"Hey, where are you?" Brandon chewed something on the other end.

"Was I supposed to meet up?"

"Don, we were just on a stakeout. We always meet up after."

Don winced. "Yeah, sorry. I got Faye settled and came straight home. Can we wait until tomorrow?"

"Yeah, sure." Brandon swallowed. "That'll give me time to sort through the audio files. There are quite a few pauses. That might be the first time I ever heard of anybody eating a meal with an informant."

They both laughed.

"Well, she was right. It really is good food." Don got off the phone relieved. He needed to find answers fast, because this was killing him.

He gathered the files for Mazzi and started there. It would have been nice to have a family tree or written genealogy, but Don had no such luck. He knew to look for Joseph Mazzi. He found a lot about the Mazzi family. Evidently, they feuded with the Andrews for years. He couldn't locate the beginning of it. So many people died in the last war.

Jack Unger probably knows all about this. *I bet this was what they expected me to ask about.* Getting him to talk would be a different story. He checked his watch, only 7:30. So, Don gave him a call.

"Hey, Jack, it's Don Ambrose, here."

"Hey there, Don. I hear you been taking care of my daughter."

Don cleared his throat. "Yes sir. She's safe. I also had some delicious French food."

"My favorite restaurant." Jack paused. "So what can I do for you?"

"I was hoping you could tell me something about Joe Mazzi."

The phone went silent. Don checked his connection to make sure the call was still live.

"That boy." Another long pause. "Don, it's like I told your wife, I made peace with that family, but that boy threw it in my face. I want nothing to do with him."

Don really needed to check Julie's notes. He didn't want to cause Jack any more pain or anguish he might be feeling. "Alright then, sir. I'm gonna let you go. I just wanted you to know that your daughter is safe and in good hands. We're going to get this whole thing sorted out."

"I'm sure you'll do your best, and this will get sorted one way or another, Don. Mark my word."

Don shook his head and went to get Julie's notes. He hadn't changed anything in her desk since she passed. A maple, roll-top desk sat near the window of the bedroom. Don opened it to the top and glanced at her workspace. He could still see her typing away.

Typing.

Julie wouldn't have written anything down into a notebook. He needed to find her laptop or a thumb drive. He opened the tiny drawers and found paper clips, post-it notes, and envelopes. Then, he moved to the side drawers. He found notepads and file folders. In his frustration, he slammed the drawer. Then, he heard a slap of wood.

He thought he had broken something and his heart dropped. He peered closer at the tiny split near the top of the desktop. The board moved with his finger, but it had not split. *A secret compartment. Beautiful.* He reached into the space and found the flash drive.

Don looked for her computer. It must still be in evidence. He grabbed his own laptop and inserted the drive. He saw one marked "Don." It was probably nothing, but he needed to open it anyway. The file contained a lot of photos and videos. He started opening them, and found himself spiraling down into despair.

"I can't do this!" He pushed his chair away from the desk and closed his eyes. He whispered a prayer. "I can't do this without her. I've been avoiding this desk and these files, because I don't have the strength to do this. Help me."

Tears rolled down his cheeks. She'd been gone over a year now, but it felt like it just happened. Don sat in the silence waiting for a response from God.

His phone rang. He was in no condition to talk to anyone, so he dismissed the call.

"Don? Don? Are you there? It's me, Faye."

He must have accidentally accepted the call. He took a deep breath, "Is everything ok?"

"I was about to ask you the same question. You never take this long to pick up."

"I'm ok. Just looking through some old files." Don closed the video and scrolled to the most recent.

"Well, I found something in this cabin that you need to see." Faye sounded excited.

"What is it?" Don clicked open the file time stamped the same day as her murder. It was a video.

"I drew him."

"Who?" Don wanted to play the video and almost missed what Faye told him.

"The murderer." Faye paused for effect. "I must have done it years ago."

"Oh, I see."

"What are you doing, Don? You seem distracted. I thought you would be interested to know that we have a sketch of the the killer."

"I am. I need to see it, but I just found a video that Julie recorded the day of her murder."

"Ooo, put me on speaker, I want to hear it too." Faye's voice rose with excitement.

"Ok," Don smiled. The despair faded as he opened the video.

Julie sat in front of the camera, "Hey there, Don. If you're watching this, I didn't make it. I'm sorry, love. I love you."

Julie looked out the window before she continued, "Long story short, the Andrews and Mazzis have been feuding for years. They pretty much hate each other.

The Schmidts run the police department and they wanted peace. So, they had a party for both families to sign the peace document. Elaine and John only knew peace between the families, when they started dating. John's older brother, Joseph or Joe, couldn't handle it. He's the guy."

Julie paused to look around her. She looks more than once, and seems spooked.

"The documents don't add up. I can't find a Jo Mazzi. It's like he didn't exist. Nobody talks about him either. After the murder, he's shunned from the family. But I think he's back in Arlington under a different name." The recording stops suddenly.

Don sat for a moment in silence. He wanted to replay the video just to see Julie again.

"Don," Faye's voice broke the trance, "we have a name and face."

Fifty-Nine

Faye walked into the school Friday morning and knew that she would need to change her plans. Susan met her at the office with a stack of paperwork. Don nodded her direction and headed down the hallway.

"Faye, I need your help with the Spring Formal tonight." Her arms frantically reorganized to prevent the stack from toppling. "Did you get a chance to look through the samples I sent you over the break?"

Faye reached forward to help Susan carry the load. With all of the things on her mind, she had completely forgotten about Spring formal. "I would be happy to help you with this. Now, that the tournament is over, I can focus." Faye attempted to calm the frustrated friend.

She never understood why they called it the Spring formal. It usually occurred at the end of February. Either way, this distraction took time away from their research of the killer. Faye knew that sketch to be that of the young Joe Mazzi, but she didn't recognize him as anyone that she had seen recently. She and Don planned to go through the old yearbooks for clues. As Faye neared the Media Center, she realized that their research might not happen today.

The Media Center looked like someone set up for a yard sale. Faye tried to remain calm as she approached the room.

"What time do we need to begin decorating?"

"Now!"

Faye chuckled. "Susan, it's going to be ok. I have classes to teach. I will come on my free hour to help you. Start with the color scheme."

Susan's eyes grew large.

"Breathe, you can do this. Two colors." Faye looked around the room for patterns. She noticed a lot of yellows and greens, "Yellows and greens."

"What?"" Susan sounded irritated.

"You already have a lot of yellows and greens. Let's focus on those two. The kids won't care what it looks like. They need photo ops."

"You're right, Faye." Susan set the stack of things on a table. "As long as nobody asks for books, I'll be fine. See you later."

Faye ran into Don on her way to class. "We can't research today."

"Oh?" Don stopped in surprise.

"Susan's a mess with the Spring Formal." Faye looked around before she added, "I'll clean up, so we can look during the dance."

Don had a pensive look on his face.

"You weren't planning on going to the dance were you? Better get out that suit."

***

Faye viewed the dance as she would any cocktail party. She enjoyed dressing up for the occasion. For the Spring Formal, she opted for a modest, A-line in a champagne lace. She even added comfortable shoes for an elegant look that allowed her to move quickly. She spent the afternoon helping Susan with decorations. The room was gorgeous, and Faye offered to clean up the bits they didn't use. Susan went home early, and Faye combed through yearbooks to set out the years they might want to look through.

Don waited outside her apartment while she prepped for the dance.

"Wow! You look great."

"Thank you." Faye stood taller as she locked the door.

They walked to the car before discussing any part of the plan.

"I organized them by year, but I set them out of the way."

"Thank you, Faye. I'm sure I'll be able to find what I need." Don pulled out into traffic.

Faye grabbed his elbow. "I'm looking too."

"One of us needs to enjoy the dance."

"Neither of us are actually going to 'enjoy' the dance. Don, I need to know who this is today. He attacked me once. He'll do it again."

"He attacked me too, Faye." Don slowed for the turn. "You can keep an eye out."

Faye shook her head. "So, you're going in alone? What about Brandon?"

"Hmm." Don grunted, "He's been preoccupied lately."

"I totally understand."

When they arrived, the media center looked as beautiful as ever. Balloons and streamers covered all of the bookshelves. The dim lights and disco-strobe made it difficult to spot the DJ in the corner playing all the teen hits.

"The kids are going to love this, aren't they?" Stephanie handed Faye some punch.

Faye agreed. "There are a lot of parents here too."

"Well." Stephanie sipped her punch. "You know Arlington."

Faye took the moment to survey the crowd. She noticed teens gathered in groups throughout the room. No one paid attention to the music. Instead of dancing, they posed for photos and typed into their phones. Faye started to walk to the other side of the room, but stopped when a person stood closely behind her.

"Don't turn around." The voice sent shivers down her spine.

Faye wanted nothing more than to turn around and see the face that matched that terrifying voice. Instead, she stood frozen with fear.

"You won't win." He spoke again and her stomach dropped, "tattle tales never win."

Faye felt light-headed but prevented herself from crumbling to the ground. No. This time, she stayed together, or so she thought.

"Faye."

Faye looked for the friendly voice, but her vision blurred. The people in the room moved in slow motion, and the sounds of the music made little sense.

"Faye." Don grabbed her arm. "What happened?"

She turned her head toward him, but the words didn't come out.

"He's here, isn't he?"

She nodded.

Sixty

Faye arrived at school Monday morning unsure how to carry on as usual. There had been nothing usual about this school year. She entered the Math office relieved to be alone and took in the quiet moment. Organizing her desk usually brought a sense of calm. She placed post-it notes in their holder and gathered loose notebook paper. The graph paper went into a binder on her shelf. The bits and scraps found their way into the trash along with used pencils and empty ink pens. She slid open the bottom drawer of her desk and pulled out sanitary wipes for the surfaces.

Clearing the clutter helped Faye clear her mind. She needed to be alert. This man, whoever he might be, knew about her. He knew that she could recognize him. He would be back. *Hide me in the shadow of your wings*, the prayer sent from her mind calmed her spirit. Faye continued preparing for the day. She organized handouts and geometry supplies, and became oblivious to the room around her.

Trish Schmidt slinked into the room, and stood over Faye.

"Can I help you?" Faye stood confidently. Trish certainly hated her, but the man trying to kill her posed the larger threat.

"Probably not." Trish's sharp tone took on new meaning.

"Can I help you find another teacher?"

"It's you, I need to talk to."

Faye took a deep breath before she spoke. "Your daughter isn't in my class this year, Ms. Schmidt."

"I know, Ms. Unger," Trish spat out her name. "There's something I need to talk to you about, but not here."

Faye returned the icy glare. She had no intention of leaving the office.

With one swoop of her hand, Trish launched Faye's copies across the desk and into the floor. Some of them landed in the trash along with her desk calendar and coffee cup.

Despite the undoing of her calm state, Faye remained steadfast. She made no efforts to follow Trish anywhere.

Trish pulled back her sweater to reveal a gun tucked into her waist band. She grasped the handle and pulled it out. "Now, you're comin' with me." She gritted her teeth and pointed the gun toward the exit.

Faye straightened and looked to the door. No one there. She went around the side of the desk toward the door and stopped.

"Courtyard. Move it."

The courtyard consisted of gravel pathways and concrete benches just off the cafeteria. Windows surrounded the courtyard, however, the walkway from the cafeteria to the dumpsters would be dark and empty. No students would be out there at this time of day.

Faye walked toward the cafeteria with Trish holding a gun in her back. *Is no one in the hallway? No one?* Faye knew the locations of the cameras. At each approach, she made efforts to alert someone by staring directly into the cameras. Before entering the cafeteria hall, Faye gazed at the main office in desperation.

"Keep goin'!" Trish shoved Faye in the back with the gun.

Faye waved her arm wildly as she made the turn. *Surely, someone saw that!*

They entered the open area of the cafeteria. Trish made her move along the wall toward the courtyard. They could move from the cafeteria to the dumpsters and away from the windows. Once there, Trish turned Faye around and shoved her into the side of the dumpster.

"What do you want from me?" Faye cowered.

"I want your sister. Dead."

"Then, why point your gun at me?" Faye closed her eyes tight and covered her face with her arms. "You want her, go get her."

"Killing you will bring justice. Then, she can know how the rest of…" Trish's voice stopped and Faye heard a thump.

She peered through her arms for a glimpse of Trish, but couldn't see anyone. She lowered her arms to find Don kneeling over Trish's body.

"She's fine." Don rolled her over on her side and fastened a zip tie around her wrists. "She'll have a nasty lump on her head when she comes to." He picked up her gun with a cloth from his pocket. After emptying the bullets, he wrapped it in the cloth and tucked it into his belt.

"Breathe."

"It's just…um…how did you…?"

"I saw you on the camera and got here as fast as I could."

"You have access to the camera feeds?" Faye looked up and secretly thanked God for answering that prayer.

Don shrugged, "Don't be so surprised."

"What do we do about her?" Faye asked as Trish started to wake up.

"Leave her. I already called for backup."

Don motioned for Faye to follow him along the periphery of the building. They edged along the brick wall before coming to a metal door.

"What's this?" Faye couldn't remember ever seeing this part of the building before.

"It's a utility room." Don opened the door and reached for the string to turn on the light. "Come on."

They walked into the tiny room and squeezed between metal shelving racks that held lawn tools and garbage bags. Just past the shelves, they came to a table with two chairs. Don motioned to a chair for Faye, then he walked up to a counter behind the table. He pulled two bottles of water from a small refrigerator on the counter and handed her one.

"Are you ok?" Don asked.

Faye took a sip of water with little expression on her face.

Don reached over and placed his hand on hers. "Faye, what happened?"

Faye's mind shifted into a different gear. Peace rested on her. As she sipped the water, strength returned to her bones. "What do you mean?"

"With Trish in the courtyard. Why were you there?"

"She came to see me in the math office." Faye paused and looked around. "How did you know about this place? I've lived here my whole life and never knew it was here."

Don answered in frustration, "This is a supply shed for the janitor. I helped him last year with a couple of projects around the school. We took breaks here. It's a safe place to take a break for now."

Faye sipped the water and felt the feeling coming back into her legs.

"What did she say to you?" Don's voice calmed Faye and her hands didn't shake so much.

"She said that she wants Elaine dead. Something about killing me would be justice. Does she know that I saw Gina dead?"

"Maybe." Don pulled out his phone and checked the cameras. "Time to go." He handed his phone to Faye. The cameras near the media center showed a crowd of people and paramedics wheeling a stretcher.

"Oh no!" Faye gasped.

"Come on." Don stood and waited for Faye. "This distraction will help us."

He moved through the room to another door to the right of the counter. It opened into the hallway between the cafeteria and Media Center. Don and Faye inched past the medics toward the math hallway. By now, a large crowd gathered near the courtyard. Rumors floated toward the math office about the attack.

"She was mugged," a voice called over Faye's shoulder.

"No, she wasn't. She just fell," came another from inside a classroom.

Faye ignored the rumors as she and Don headed to the emergency exit in the back of the office.

"The alarm!" Faye whispered and pointed to the red sign on the door.

"Don't worry." Don pulled out a small key. He placed it into the alarm mechanism, disabling the alarm. "Don't look back. Just keep walking."

Faye spotted a black town car parked in the back lot. "My ride."

They walked quickly toward it. Don opened the back door for her, and Faye climbed into the back seat. Don closed the door and patted the roof of the car.

The car lurched in reverse and flung Faye into the floorboard.

"I knew he would take you out the back," the sinister voice sounded from the driver's seat.

Sixty-One

The tires squealed as the car exited the back side of the parking lot. *Who's driving today? That's not like Frank.* Don's stomach dropped with the new realization. Memories of a man escaping out the back door while his wife clung to life in his arms flooded his mind. *Not again.* Don closed his eyes and Julie's face appeared.

He's got her.

He needed to push the memories aside and respond as an agent. He didn't want to alarm the other teachers. Emergency vehicles remained at the entrance, and he couldn't be sure who he could trust at this point.

Who was the driver?

Don felt for his keys and hurried toward his car. *Focus on the case. Who else knew about that exit?* Don scrolled through the Math teachers present and past. The school hadn't changed its layout. People that graduated from Arlington High School might have used that exit while they were students. This didn't narrow the list of suspects, but Don needed more information to know how to proceed. He drove off through the back exit of the parking lot in the direction of the town car.

Time moved slowly as his vehicle sped through town. *Is it someone connected to Trish?* Crimes rarely involve coincidence. Someone put Trish up to it. Handed her a gun. Don felt the gun pressed against the small of his back. He pulled onto a side street to examine it.

Standard issue for law enforcement. No surprise there. Trish Schmidt married the police. Of course, she would have access to a gun. Don turned the gun over and noticed an inscription on the bottom. The engraving, worn with time, didn't reveal anything. *Had it been scratched off on purpose?*

Don slammed his fist on the steering wheel. "Ahhhh! I can't do this!" He lifted his head and pointed to the sky. "I need your help here!"

He took a deep breath and let it out slowly. He kept thinking about Faye cowered under Trish's threats.

"Think! Think! Who has he?"

Someone who can best Elaine's security detail. *The Mazzis probably have their own hired guns.* Someone who knows where the teachers park. Someone who knows Trish.

"Who knows Trish?" He pictured her file in his mind. The file contained Trish's profile with her personality quirks and history of aggression. This person not only had to know Trish, they had to know how much Trish hated Faye. Everyone knew how much Trish hated Faye. That wasn't a secret.

"Who saw their interaction at the beginning of the year?" Faces of people came to mind. He chose not to rule out any of them. He pulled out his notebook and wrote names.

"Who saw them at Faye's party?" Don pictured the party and the people surrounding Faye and Trish. He made a separate list.

He stared at the lists for patterns. Then, it hit him. "Of course!" He started the car. "Why didn't I see it before?"

Don turned the car around and headed in the direction of the coffee shop.

"You're right!" He pointed to the sky again. "He graduated from Arlington and left after the shooting. He made a new name for himself before he returned."

Don shook his head as he drove a little faster. "He planned this a long time ago. He knew Faye would draw Elaine back to Arlington." The more he thought about it, the more enraged he became.

"He lied to me this whole time. Recruited me to join him. I helped him get to her." Don stopped at the light and tightened his grip on the steering wheel. "I led her right to him."

He took a deep breath and continued. "He knew how I fought, because he trained me. Of course, he could take me down in the ravine. He wanted me to avoid that place."

Don drove down a different side street, so he could come around the back side of the ravine. He needed to drive through the trees where they wouldn't see him.

"He had access to the cameras in the building, so he knew where we would go and how to get to her." Don parked a distance away and pulled his own gun from its holster.

"But I moved him next door and gave him access to her apartment!" Don shivered at that thought as he exited his vehicle.

He checked his phone and texted Rogers for back-up. "Ok, Joe, it's time to take you down."

Don located a shed at the edge of the ravine. He had seen part of it in one of the crime scene photos, but he couldn't tell what it was until today. Faye didn't seem to remember it either, but Don had seen it in her painting.

"I'll give it to you, Joe, you did a great job changing your appearance." Don whispered to himself as he edged toward a large pine tree.

He moved slowly to reduce the noise caused by his feet. Then, he noticed someone just over the edge of the ravine. He crouched into position to get a clean shot. Joe's movements popped in and out of view. *He's digging.* Don measured the cadence of Joe's movements and fired.

"UGHHH!" Came the injured Joe.

Don waited to see if he could get another shot.

"Don? Is that you?" Brandon's voice echoed through the ravine.

Don controlled his breathing to keep focus. Then, he shouted, "Brandon?"

"Over here."

"Where's Faye?"

"Hmm." Brandon groaned and dropped to his knee. "I haven't seen her."

Don shook his head, the scowl on his face deepening. He snaked behind trees for a better view of the ravine. As he passed the shed, he heard a thumping inside. *She's still alive.* A surge of relief pushed him forward toward the ravine.

"That's close enough." Brandon emerged from shrubs, his right arm held close to stomach. His left pointing a gun at Don. "I don't want to kill you, Don."

"Where is she?" Don returned the gaze pointing his gun toward Brandon.

Brandon's face twitched as he shook his head. "I can't say."

Don didn't think about what to do next. The gun went off in his hand. Brandon managed to get off one shot before he collapsed on the ground. The bullet grazed Don's shoulder, but he charged ahead disarming his former friend.

"Units are on the way." Don collected the weapon.

Brandon lost consciousness.

Sixty-Two

Faye woke up in a hospital room. She moved forward to sit up, and pain surged through every part of her body.

"Don't try to move." Elaine's voice startled her, but she grabbed Faye's hand and held it gently.

Faye groaned. She remembered the car ride to the ravine and the wooden floor of the shed. The parts in between blurred. She tried to focus and remember.

Elaine interrupted her thought. "It's a miracle you're still alive, Faye. An inch to the right and we would have lost you."

Gunshot. She remembered Trish holding her at gunpoint. "Where's Don?"

Elaine looked over her shoulder and nodded to someone across the room. Faye turned to see Frank pulling aside a curtain. It made her happy to see Frank doing well.

Faye gasped when she saw him laying there. "Is he ok?"

"Yes. He took a gunshot to the shoulder and needed surgery, but he'll pull through."

So, Don had come for her. She remembered hearing something outside the shed. She had tried to get his attention before she blacked out. She remembered the tall stranger pulling her out of the car and into the woods.

"Brandon?" Faye's breath quieted.

A tear rolled down Elaine's cheek. "Don said that he was digging a grave for you."

Digging. That must have been the sound she heard. "Did they catch him?"

Before Elaine could answer colleagues and friends flooded her room with flowers and candies.

"Faye!" Stephanie pushed through to be the first at her bed, "I'm so glad you're ok. My heart dropped when they told me."

"Me too." Donna smiled.

"What are you all doing here?"

Anna set a vase of flowers on a table across the room. "We're your friends, Faye. We show up for you."

"Don't worry about your students. I'm taking care of your classes for a while." Mazzi stood by Elaine and placed his hand on her shoulder.

"Yeah, I don't know what to do about the Math department for the rest of the year." J.J. rubbed his chin. "We lost three people in just a few days."

"So, they caught him?"

"That's what I hear." Susan chimed in.

"But we want to know the real story." Richard glared at Susan.

"Well, I only know half of it." Faye looked over in Don's direction. "I'm sure he could fill in the parts I don't remember."

Susan pulled up a chair.

"It started with Trish in the Math office. She pulled out a gun and forced me through the cafeteria to the dumpster. She said she wanted you dead." Faye squeezed Elaine's hand.

"And then?" Susan leaned in.

"The next thing I knew, Trish was on the ground and Don walked me back through the office. I was going to go home for a bit." Faye looked at the crowd. "She held me at gunpoint."

"We totally get it," Susan encouraged her, "but how did you get to the ravine."

"I got in my car. Well, I thought it was my car."

"Brandon Foster stole your car?" Richard spoke up in disbelief.

"He wasn't Brandon Foster," Don spoke from across the room. "He was Joe Mazzi. A trained soldier. He changed his name in the army. We served together, and I only knew him as Brandon. Never talked about his past. No details anyway. He loved his family, but always kept to the basics."

"So, he kidnapped you and carried you to the ravine. When did you get shot?" Susan wanted details.

"All right, everybody." Steve Gardner walked into the room. "Visiting hours are over for the day. You'll have to come back tomorrow."

"Agreed." Elaine patted her hand. Frank moved to escort the people from the room.

"No problem. We're just glad you both are doing ok." J.J. called out over them as they left.

Elaine spoke softly, "He won't come after you any more, Faye."

"So, you caught him?"

Elaine nodded.

"It's taken care of," Mazzi answered for her.

"Don't worry about mom and dad. I'll give them a full report."

"Thanks." Faye grabbed Elaine's hand between both of hers. "I'm sorry I forgot you. You have helped me so much." Tears filled her eyes. "I remember now. I remember it all. Twenty years ago. I was looking for you." Tears flowed easily now.

"I know."

"I love you, sister."

Elaine pulled an embroidered handkerchief out of her pocket and dabbed Faye's tears. "I love you, too." Elaine stood to leave. "Get some rest."

"I'll walk you out." John Mazzi placed his hand on the small of her back and escorted her out of the room.

After they left, Faye tried again to sit up, but winced.

"There's a button on the side that will raise the bed for you." Don pointed to a section of the bed. "I learned that one the over the summer."

Faye pressed the button. "I need to know. Why did he do it?"

Don shook his head. "You were the last witness. He needed to get rid of you before you spilled your guts."

"But why kill Albert so many years ago?"

"Same reason." Don took a drink of water. "Albert uncovered the illegal drugs and confronted Joe. So, Joe killed him. He didn't know Albert's involvement with Elaine or that you had followed him there."

Faye thought about it all. The paintings revealed the murderer. She had elements of Brandon's face in each painting. The ravine held footprints and blood spatters. Shadows of the tall stranger. Brandon couldn't remove them all.

"Was he behind the drugs in my apartment, too?"

Don shrugged. "Probably. The family has a history of drug trafficking. I'm sure he's the one who sent Trish after you the first time."

"What'll happen to Trish?"

"She's a Schmidt, so she'll probably get off."

"Not if my dad has anything to say about it."

Don laughed and then winced.

"What do we do now?"

Don smiled. "Maybe, when we get out of here, we get a cup of coffee?"

ABOUT THE AUTHOR

Dr. Kathy Hendley is a teacher, author, and speaker. She is a member of Word Weavers International and Advanced Writers and Speakers Association. Kathy's mission is to encourage others to overcome obstacles, achieve their goals, and commit to their calling.

Kathy hosts virtual writing retreats several times a year called Write on Purpose. She's also hosting a Mysterious Book Club for people who love to read a good mystery. When she's not working, Kathy serves on the worship team and the prayer team at her church. She's also a self-proclaimed Bible study junky traveling the globe for a good women's Bible study.

Kathy believes that stories can bring healing. Children read stories to help them deal with difficult things in life. Adults should do the same. Reading helped her overcome difficult personal trauma, and Kathy hopes that her stories can do the same for others. You can connect with Kathy through her website kathyhendley.com.

www.ingramcontent.com/pod-product-compliance
Lightning Source LLC
Chambersburg PA
CBHW060818120726
47909CB00006B/1975